Mr. Jones

By Jamie Stewart

Contents Page

Dedicated to Claire without whom this would never have been finished.

Act 1

Murder Of Shadows

2005

April – June

1

Eli preferred the secluded lane as his route home.
Tall giants, oak, ash, and pine, stretched and arched
above. Secluded: his mother would have been pleased
with him using such a word. Though on this occasion
the rarely used lane wasn't so. This time there were
predators, and they were hunting.
'Hey, look who it is, it's old cocksucker,' said a voice.
'Old, fag end,' a second voice added.
'More like nob end,' said a third.
The red muscle in him tightened.
He knew who they were, of course. It was a knowledge
that propelled him until his calves grew taut. The
predators did not like that.
'Hey, where do you think you're going?'
There was a race of feet, and the voice's owner
stepped before Eli. The leader.
He had to crane his neck to meet his gaze. Though that
wasn't what was frightening about Dominic Coyle. He
looked like a troll from a children's story with his
formidable size, his ratty buzz-cut, and beady eyes.
They gleamed at Eli now and whatever they saw
caused Dom to smirk. Yet, that wasn't all there was to
him.
What completed Dom was the fact that he relished his
role. He was the first year bully of Hazel Grammar
School, and he was blocking Eli's way.
As if to signify this, he lightly tapped Eli on the chest.
Each tap emphasized a word.
'What are you doing, huh? Where are you going to go
orphan boy?' he asked.

As each question ended, his voice upturned and became barbed.

Eli shuffled back beyond the reach of his unnerving touch. His eyes never left Dom's shadowed face or the sun glaring above his crown. He huffed a sigh.

'Leave me alone,' he said.

Then he was brushing passed Dom. Then he was walking.

The day's heat, a constricting anaconda, seemed to lessen. He breathed in and out and discovered how severely his school shirt stuck to him.

Something slashed across the nape of his neck.

Pain, brilliant and dazzling, erupted there and he cried out. Surrounding this was a duller throb that forced him to stumble forward. Eli hit the dirt with a dusty clap.

Laughter: not a dead pattering, but riotous, monstrous cackling commenced. Eli could hear interludes of 'what a dick,' 'see how he fell,' and 'orphan,' as blood poured through his clamped fingers.

Like a sponge, his collar was drinking it and darkening to crimson.

'Look at him,' cried the owner of the second voice.

'Look at the little, dump, dodo.'

He was pointing at Eli as he lay in the dirt.

The owner of the second voice was anorexic in comparison to Dom's grotesque size. His features were sharp, his nose was beaky, and his eyes had a feral quality. They darted from Dom to Eli, never resting, behind a pair of glasses that blazed silver when they caught the light.

His name was Michael McBride.

Eli held out his bloody hand as they continued to laugh. He looked to the trees, to the shadowy recesses underneath, and to the stone that had hit him.

Its edge was splashed red.

His face clenched on viewing it. He pushed to his feet, grasping the red stone as he did and hurled it, which was the exact point were his troubles got worse.

Eli threw in anger without any precision or thought. It was no surprise that the rock missed Dom entirely. The surprise was when it hit Michael instead. That much was clear from how their laughter ceased. The rock had struck his lips hard enough to send his glasses rocketing to the sky. They landed some feet away. The lens's beamed a rainbow in the sunlight. Dom's other friend and Michael's sister, Fern was screaming while running to his aid. She was not quick enough to catch him, and he thudded to the ground as Eli had.

Dom had yet to move. He appeared to have frozen, glaring at his two companions, as both became to cry and wail.

They aren't bullies anymore, thought Eli. *They're kids, and kids can be hurt.*

As if he heard, Dom's head rotated onto him.

The face that sneered at Eli wasn't that of a predator. It was the face of someone exposed and having found the person who caused such exposure.

Knowing this, Eli knew his fate before Dom knew what he was going to do with it. He knew as any victim does; experience. He also knew he couldn't escape.

His legs felt rooted, and despite what alarm signals wailed at them, they wouldn't move.

Dom's legs had no problem. They marched at him. His lips pulled back over his teeth in a vicious snarl as he started to speak.

He was, however, intruded at that moment by an explosive boom.

'What the hell is going on here?' it said.

The voice was a tempest.

Every impulse and feeling in him was erased by it. To Eli, he felt scooped empty with only his jangling nerves left. The others seemed to snap to attention.

The adult had materialized out of nowhere. At least that's how it seemed. He stood on the bay of a driveway, tall, dark, and lean.

It's him, the man with the guitar, Eli thought, remembering the day before.

As he walked down this very same path, he had heard the music he couldn't identify. It had come to him through the trees, and perhaps because he was bored, bored of school, of the town, he decided to find out more.

He had crept through the trees, using them as cover as he spied upon this man playing guitar. Only, he didn't have it with him now. Instead, he stood in blue jeans and a white shirt and with a face that seethed contempt. Being under that gaze made him feel tiny.

'He hurt my brother,' wailed Fern.

'Yeah, he did,' said Dom.

'Olok,' croaked Michael, holding his arm aloft.

His chin was coated red from his bleeding mouth. Eli's shoulders sank.

'Olok wahat he did.'

'You deserved it, you little fucker,' said the adult. 'I heard everything. So don't try and pull the wool over my eyes. Now, piss off before I march you back to your parents and tell them what you did, and I wouldn't be so honest about it'.

The trio stared at him. Stunned at having been caught, at being sworn at by an unknown adult and with such ferocity.

Slowly, Dom helped Fern in helping Michael to his feet. The siblings being side by side only highlighted the fact that they were twins. Both shared the same feral and rodent-like appearance.

Neither looked at Eli as they passed, but Dom did.

'There's always school tomorrow,' he whispered.
In the light and with this unknown savior near it was
Eli's turn to smirk. He watched them walk down the lane
and disappear around a bend.
'I have no time for bullies,' said the adult.
*He looks like Clint Eastwood from Ryan's films, except
he's black.*
Eli had to crane his head a great deal to meet his face.
The man peered down from his mountainous height, his
cheek muscles contorted by a raging storm.
A pang of anxiousness electrified Eli. He wondered if
the man knew he had spied on him yesterday.
My turn to get sworn at, he thought, tensing. However,
as he gazed at him, Eli watched his chocolate eyes'
soften and his face relax. The stranger extended out his
hand.
'My name's, Jones,' he said.

The hand was calloused and rough.
He did not shout but spoke in a rusty, grumble. Eli
trusted him immediately, which did nothing but combine
his anxiousness with guilt for the day before.
'You're all right now,' said Jones.
Eli nodded then and gasped as his neck flared. Jones's
fingers opened to reveal Eli's own and gripped his
shoulder. They were long and swift, and the touch
would have been alarming if his eyes hadn't been so
focused on Eli's neck.
The collar of his shirt was soaked. He could feel blood
drying between his greasy shoulder blades.
'I know children have a gift for making their parents
mad with concern,' he said, an amused grin prying at
his lips. 'My own kid sure drove me nuts, but I think I
can save yours from insanity this time. I have a first aid
kit in my house if you want to clean up'.
He had already retreated away, putting a safe distance
between them.

Eli gaped, thinking *this man had helped him. How rare was that?*

This was not Eli's first experience of bullying, and what he had learned was that people would confront bullies if their victims were a loved one or they were being paid to do so. But when the victim is a stranger people tut and complain about why hasn't anyone else stepped in. He was used to the latter.

'Please,' Eli replied.

Jones led him down his drive, maintaining that distance.

'What's your name, kid?'

'Eli Donoghue,' he said.

'Named after a prophet no doubt.'

Jones grinned at him, causing his salt and pepper beard to stretch toward his ears.

'Only pulling your leg, kid.'

Eli's lips performed a meek imitation of a grin. That anxious cocktail was swirling rapidly in his belly.

'Want to tell me what that was all about?' he asked.

'Its nothing,' said Eli.

'Take it from me kid that wasn't nothing.'

'Just some idiots picking on the new kid,' he said, quickly.

Jones gave him a glance over his shoulder. Eli's belly stopped swirling and steeled.

He was about to be asked something else he was sure, adults always tried to pry. He already had his tongue moving to lie when Jones turned away.

Eli's eyebrows drew closer, perplexed.

The drive ended at a squat garage that needed fresh paint. The trees on Eli's left fell away, revealing a neat garden, jeweled by colorful flowerbeds. A stepping stone path provided passage over the green grass to the house's porch steps.

It was a strange home Eli had to admit, even though this was the second time he had seen it, he still felt so. However, he could now see why he did.
The house was a red-bricked one-story. Perfectly normal except it had an overhang. Its roof of navy tiles protruded beyond the home itself to cover a wooden porch. The result was that it had an American feel to it. Like it should exist in the Deep South.
Although twelve Eli had seen enough movies to know this was true.
'I like your flowers,' he said, and he did.
They were alive with insect buzz. In the surrounding woods, birdsong twittered.
'Thank you, my wife's hobby, but I seemed to have inherited by it. I'll just be a second, the kits inside'.
He was left on the porch. He could feel the boards dip slightly under his feet. The aroma from the flowers and old wood sweetened the air.
It was bizarre to be bleeding and yet slightly happy.
There was a loud crash from inside the house. Curses followed.
The porch was bare except for a bench chair and …
Eli's throat hitched. The air, which was delightfully refreshing under the overhang, dropped to icy.
It lay between the bench chair and the railing. The guitar. Its color was fire red; its body rounded, pregnant, and decorated with black knobs. It was mesmerizing.
'Here we go,' said Jones, emerging with a green box in his hands.
His eyes twitched to the guitar on seeing him.
'You can clean your neck with this while I look for a plaster.'
He handed him a wet cloth and sat down directly beside the instrument.

Eli wiped his neck, expecting pain. Instead, the flesh there seemed to sigh upon feeling the cool cloth. He swabbed the wound, looking to see the grit and his own blood in the wet fabric. He sat down.

'Have you made a pig's arse of it … no … here this will cover it. It's still bleeding so that plaster is gonna have to be changed. Can you handle that? Good. I can't do much else for your shirt mind … on that department you're on your own'.

'I have my blazer in my bag,' muttered Eli.

Stop looking.

'Good, you hurt them a lot more than they hurt you. Kids like that can't stand being knocked off their pedestals, hell people can't. Something caught your eye'.

'Huh,' he grunted.

Jones reclined backward, a bemused grin on his lips. In doing so, Eli got a clear view. He chuckled. 'I've seen that look before. I've had it myself. That oh shit look. There's something for everyone in this world, but a lot find it's this thing'.

Jones gripped the guitar by its neck and cradled it in his lap.

'Do you play?' asked Eli before feeling stupid.

The man named Jones smiled, and this time, it was a vast ear-to-ear crescent.

'Kid, I'm the best there is,' he purred.

Eli hadn't laughed in a long time, not in any way that felt genuine. He did so now, and it felt natural and warm and distracting.

He forgot about how he came to be on this bench.

'Would you like to hear a tune?'

'Absolutely.'

Jones plugged a wire into the guitar's body. A sound resonated from the amplifier that sat in the corner.

How didn't I see that before?

Because I had only eyes for the guitar.

Jones's calloused fingers ran delicately over the golden strings. One settled into some claw-like position while the other began to pluck.

The song was a wiry twang that Eli had never heard before. He had never heard a sound like that before. He watched hungrily, sometimes looking to Jones's concentrated expression but mostly he watched his hands. They didn't seem like extensions of his body but as if they were separate beings. The music was their language. They built it, rising from a twang to a dirty growl.

Eli felt pulled along for the ride. The porch had become a pocketed dream where outside didn't exist for the duration that this stranger played. When it ended, Eli released a breath. He had been holding it.

'That was cool, what was it?'

'Just something I've been noodling with ... here, what's the time? You better be going before your parents start getting worried. Do you want a lift? I can drive? Those kids are still out there. I don't think they'll try anything now ... but'.

'It's fine,' said Eli slinging his backpack on his shoulder. His shoes clapped down the porch steps. He paused at the bottom, looking up.

Jones still sat with the guitar in his lap. His face as flushed as his own.

'Thanks for that,' said Eli.

'Welcome, and here next time you want to listen come to my porch. Don't hide in the bushes'.

Eli's jaw became unhinged. His face paled fish-belly white then colored beetroot purple.

Out on the road.

Jones's laughter rang in his head the entire length of the drive. On stepping back into the dusty lane, it quickly evaporated. The memory and good feeling Eli had experienced was boxed somewhere and stored for later at what he saw.

Michael's glasses rested in the dirt. He looked down at them for some time. Then, as he moved off for home, he crunched them underfoot.

2

Fern moped the blood from her brother's face.
'What are we going to tell our mum,' she cried.
Tears strung in her eyes and had soaked her cheeks.
She could barely see what she was achieving, which
was smearing Michael's blood over his face.
'Whh can't say,' blubbered Michael.
'She's gonna freak out. She's gonna kill us'.
'We tell her we were playing,' said Dom. 'We say we
were playing in the woods and Michael tripped on a
tree root.'
'But...'
'That's what we stick to,' Dom yelled, spinning on them.
Fern nodded ardently. Dom always knew what to do.
'Wahat a'bout Eliye?' asked Michael.
'We get him back.'

The footpath took him through the setting sun.
It took him home. He couldn't help but snort at that
idea.
He had removed his blazer from his pack and thrown it
on. He knew it was odd with the heat, but it covered his
collar. Better having sweat patches than them seeing
blood.
Meadowlake was not like the lane. It was an estate for
one. Typically, the house's looked like red-bricked
clones. There were trees, though these had not been
allowed to grow into an impenetrable wilderness. They
were dotted irregular along the pavement and were well
kept. He still thought this was funny as the lane was
considered the wealthy area and yet it's the
middle/lower classes that had upkeep to deal with.
Someone had spray-painted a tree trunk. In red it read
THE RENEGADES ARE THE SHIT.
Eli stared at the cloned buildings, his lips thin in disgust.

Anything could be happening inside them. It was more than likely that nothing was.

This is Hazel, after all.

Once he was sure he got the right house (on one occasion accidentally entered the wrong one), he trudged inside, sighing.

What met him was a suffocating and clammy fog. Kate was in the kitchen ironing. He hoped to pass unnoticed, but he couldn't help himself.

She stood in a cloud of steam. She wasn't beautiful like Eli's own mother had been. His mother had a fragile beauty like a glass ornament never to be touched. Kate was beautiful in a simple, heartier way, one Eli could see, even as she stood there choked by mist.

The kitchen windows were open behind her. Even with this, Eli could see perspiration dewing her neck beneath her short blonde hair. She was standing perfectly for the sunlight to hit her right and maximize her honey skin tone. She was there, and it made him ache in his chest and turn what initial disgust he had into sickness.

She was there and her sister, his mother was dead.

'Eli,' she jumped.

'I didn't hear you come in. How was school today?'.

He stared at her as the world on the edges of his vision wavered and drew close.

'Fine…just fine.'

He leaped up the stairs as noisily and swiftly as possible.

'Are you alight,' called in her too bright voice.

'Yes,' he called back, controlling his own.

His bedroom was at the top and to the left of the staircase.

Immediately, he dropped his bag to the floor. He unbuttoned his ruined shirt. Kate hadn't seen the filth that stained it from where she had been standing.

He whipped it off without taking his blazer off first. He ripped the two apart, threw the shirt to the floor and kicked it under his bed.

In the bathroom, he locked the door before stepping into the shower. The water between his feet was the color of red wine as he washed. He stepped out after it had cleared completely. He then took off the soaking plaster and reapplied another from the medicine cabinet.

With the towel wrapped at the waist, he darted into his room.

Kate Wilson had stopped ironing.

Her entire attention was aimed directly at the ceiling above. She could hear Eli moving about up there, and she knew something was wrong. She didn't go up or call out. She didn't even notice the iron's weight in her hand until her arm began to cry with it.

A dried and fully dressed Eli looked out from his window.

It was open, and he could hear children laughing close by. He lifted a book from the shelf below. The novel was one of ten that sat as neatly as trophies.

They had been his mother's most prized possessions. One was a library copy that she had stolen having not wanted to part with it. Money had been a problem in their house. It wasn't that they didn't have any but that his father, Sean, restricted her usage of it.

She got by fishing pennies from his chair when he was at work. She kept the few coins change she had at the end of the weekly shop.

She never had to save for him. The one thing Sean Allen loved more than his chair and his TV was lavishing gifts on his son.

He had told the man Jones that his name was Eli Donoghue. Donoghue was his mother's maiden name; he didn't want anything to do with his father after everything that had happened.

With her money, Rosa Allen bought novels. Really, she purchased the escape they offered.

She never begrudged him for his father's attention. Eli had hated himself anyway.

He had swiped the ten she had kept hidden before he was taken from the house. He hadn't understood why until reading *The Shadow Of The Wind* on his first night in this room. Now he knew of their power. How he could sink into them and disappear and not be himself for hours at a time. They were nothing if not magic to him, and more than that in each reading, he felt as if his mother was near, watching him.

He took the battered copy of *Stephen King's I.T* to his bed and read.

Night spread onto the porch.

Jones was doing what he had been doing for the past month. He was getting drunk. He was drunk, and he expected he would be thinking about his redundancy soon.

Yes, then after wallowing on that for a while, I'll start fretting about my retirement package. Twenty-nine years and it's already running low after a month. You at least expect it to last two considering how much time you put in, how much life you lost.

Can't beat a good fretting.

That lands us on Brandon's proposal.

Which is a lot of fuming and crushing beer cans?

Except...Jones wasn't thinking about any of that. He is thinking about the kid and how cold and old his blue eyes had seemed. How they had melted, practically lit up when Jones was playing. He had felt it too.

It had been a while since he'd played like that.

In a darker part of the night, Dom crept into his garage. If his dad knew what he was planning, he would be done for. Thankfully, the old guy has the TV cranked to its top volume. Dom can even hear it here as he stands in darkness.

It hums from the wall behind him as the second loudest thing in the Coyle household tonight. The first is his heart. He could feel it hammering in his fingertips, pummeling within his throat, thundering in his ears and even aching in his balls.

He slips along the car stationed inside the garage, hands out.

He hasn't switched the light on for fear of being noticed. The orange streetlights ooze through the garage window. He can see the workbenches well but not the alley between the car and the wall. Nothing prevents him from his destination in the end.

As silently as he can, he searches the bench drawers. An eagerness slips into him as each drawer is opened. He knows it's here and he begins rummaging faster and carelessly.

Tonight, Dom has the devil's luck. He finds it, a rag that conceals a thin, cylinder object that he unwraps. He feels for a button, and the blade flicks out with a dry snap.

He holds it aloft in the light and feels his lips pull back to show teeth.

3

'Come on in, Eli,' said The Camera Lady.
He took a seat on a sofa that looked like a turd that's
been in the sun. There was also a limb plant and a
funky smelling rug that made up the contents of the
school counselor's room. Mrs. McCall sits opposite
A.K.A The Camera Lady.
Eli had referred to her as such ever since his first
session. Not because she was expressionless. In fact,
The Camera Lady was extremely expressive, at least,
in poorly hidden irritability and disinterest.
He had conjured that name because of her scribbling
pen. It recorded everything.
'And how are you feeling today?' she asked.
'Fine,' he said. The word was fast becoming his
catchphrase.
The Camera Lady's pen scratched at her notepad.
'It's been a week. How are you assimilating with your
classmates?'
Most pre-teens his age would have frowned at hearing
such a question. Eli's vocabulary was significantly
larger than most pre-teens, and he smirked instead.
He couldn't help himself.
'Fine.'

'Eli Donoghue,' barked Mrs. Thompson.
'Huh.'
They were starring, some snidely as Eli jolted to
attention.
'Well.' Her head jabbed sharply, a gull spearing a fish.
He stared, probing the froth of his mind for a safe
answer.
'Have you been paying attention at all?' she sighed.

Giggles erupted from the surrounding classroom. Eli's eyelids fluttered, but not much, Mrs. Thompson's own held them.

She was a petite woman. Yet, standing hands on her hips, her jagged cheekbones like cliff edges below scorning eyes made her seem more.

'No, I was … daydreaming,' Eli confessed.

From the corner of his eye, he could see Fern. She wasn't smiling as the others were, but glaring, her pale face twisted in a sneer of hate.

The shameful heat he felt cooled and hardened away.

'Well, pay it,' snapped Mrs. Thompson.

He fell silent, the shadow of yesterday descending upon him. As the class reverted back to the lesson, Eli grew deaf. Instinctively, he crushed his blazer to his plastered neck.

All three bullies had walked through the school gates with the morning tide. The tide had seen Michael's swollen, blackened lips and parted.

The chatter started then.

He knew about the chatter, about the teeth people had. He had been Michael. Except his mark hadn't been physical. It had been joining a school mid-way through its year, of moving through the throngs of already sealed relationships, of being forced to stand before his registration class and be introduced, making him feel like a specimen in some zoo.

It had teased the student bodies' curiosity. His refusal to fully disclose himself had agitated it.

And when two teachers decided to gossip around eager ears, his story had gotten out. Well, almost. The story that cycled the school contained only grains of truth. Michael was getting a taste of what he endured.

'It was his dad's fist for breaking his Xbox.'

'It was from fighting Dom over Fern. Dom loves her, apparently'.

These were two of a dozen different rumors Eli had heard.

He could sympathize with him. Nothing could make him forget yesterday, but still, he understood. Perhaps he would have felt more if he hadn't been distracted by...

'Alright, class,' called Mrs. Thompson. Her authority lost by the final chiming bell.

The weekend dawned like a promising fantasy as it rang. Around Eli, there was a cacophony of snapping books and zipping bags.

Well practiced at isolating himself, he let his classmates rip ahead. Though, on this occasion, it took some effort. He hoped to stop by Jones's on the way home.

'You were pretty far out today,' said Mrs. Thompson.

Eli looked up to find himself alone with his teacher.

'Where were you?' she asked.

'Nowhere, Miss,' he said and added, 'just daydreaming.' The question jarred him slightly. Embarrassment was a small part, but mainly, he felt evasive the way he would over a toy when he was younger and had friends. Yet this didn't feel right. He wanted to keep Jones a secret because he did not want to spoil it.

Mrs. Thompson spied at him from above the cliffs of her cheekbones. Oddly, they seemed softener somehow.

'How are you finding the school? You've been here, how long is it now?'

'Two months,' he said. "I find it fine'.

'I know you see, Mrs. McCall ... '(Mrs. Thompson exhaled hard) 'but if there is anything you would like to talk about that perhaps you don't think you can with her. You know ... '

Great. Another one. Exactly what I need.

'Thank you,' he said his face flushing red. 'I'll keep that in mind.'

He left the class with his head down.

Acidic bleach poisoned the school corridor's air. Eli made his way to the staircase with his nostrils burning. He took them two at a time, trying to recall his previous giddiness at hearing Jones play again. But it was crushed beneath his hatred for Mrs. Thompson's pitying tone.

He wished she had just continued on being her bitchy, scornful self.

Doesn't she know I just want to keep my head down?

He reached the bottom step and closed his eyes to let out a breath. The staircase was deserted of any fellow students, allowing him to do this without fear of being judged.

He recalled the song Jones had played for him yesterday. The one that had been unwinding softly in his head ever since. Filling him, so there was no space for other concerns. With it was the delight that he had been invited to hear more.

When he opened his eyes, he felt the weight of his annoyance float from him. He had been expunged. All that remained was the memory of Jones's song, cycling in his head.

It made him feel lighter on his toes.

The frictionless floor echoed his footsteps as he headed to the exit. Sunlight streamed from high windows of the double doors where his freedom waited on the other side.

There, stepping into the sun, they fell on him.

Dom was leaning against a brick wall, waiting.

He had a daisy in his hands and was plucking its petals off.

'Hello, Eli,' he said. 'We've got a bone to pick with you.'

On hearing his voice, the meat on Eli's bones clenched. Figures leaped from the shadows behind him and seized at his arms. Michael's bruised face leered at Eli.

'Got ya,' he cackled.

Eli fought, dragging a breath into his lungs.

Dom pushed off the wall and plunged his fist into Eli's belly. Instead of a scream, a great woof escaped him as he folded over.

'Let's get him away from this door.'

They half-carried, half-dragged his body to the boiler house. A grey building obscured from the schoolyard where he could hear the shrieks and the cheers of everyone else.

No one would see them. That realization electrified Eli with terror.

He couldn't stop them as he was thrown against the building's steel door, but despite his pain, he lurched to his feet. He tried to run and was intercepted by Michael.

Eli elbowed his jaw in a bid for freedom and perhaps would have achieved it if Dom and Fern hadn't grabbed him and yanked him to the ground once more.

'Shit,' spat Michael.

'Are you alright?' asked Fern.

'Yeah.'

Michael kicked Eli between his legs and the world spun as a blurred kaleidoscope; brilliant sunlight, blue sky, shining steel, and yellow dirt.

'Get him up,' said Dom.

Hands gripped his arms, pulling them from his groin. He was hoisted to his feet.

'Hello, there ... you doing alright? No ... don't fucking look it'.

They chuckled ecstatically.

By far, the worst feeling came next. Eli vomited so violently his body was retched forward, his eyes shut. His throat and tongue were laced with its taste.

Dom easily avoided the outpour. He drew close, wrapping his fingers around Eli's neck.

'You're one dirty bastard, aren't you.'

The fist connected with Eli's lower left cheek, followed by another across his upper right, causing his head to snap from side to side. A knee buried itself in his gut, and he dry-retched.

'Go on, Michael give him a lick.'

Fingers yanked his head back by his hair before a smaller fist smashed into his lips. Dom and Fern cheered, as Eli tasted blood.

'Hurts your hands,' he heard Dom say.

He did not look up; not wanting to know where the next blow was going to come from. As he did, he felt Michael and Fern's fingers pinch his arms.

'What are you doing with that?' asked Fern.

Her voice was puzzling. Eli lifted his head from its flopped position. It took effort, but he managed. His entire upper body was a sagging, weak mass in his capturers' grip. The legs beneath felt like quivering stumps and seemed a million miles away.

Dom held a long, thin object. At its end was a blade.

'Teaching,' Dom said in reply.

He was marveling at the knife.

'That's why we come to school to learn. I'm gonna teach Eli that he shouldn't have fucked with us'. The knife rested against Eli's cheek.

He was not scared, surprisingly because he was here and there was no need for that now. He could tell that Michael and Fern were as their grip of him had slackened.

'Is this the type of knife your mother used to cut her throat?' asked Dom.

The question caused his eyebrows to rise.

'Actually, it was a kitchen knife,' he said. It hurt to talk but not too much.

'And it wasn't her neck but her wrists she cut. I would know. I found her body sitting in the bathtub. Ever seen a dead body Dom or even your mother naked. It's not pretty'.

The knife had pulled away. Though Eli was sure, Dom wasn't aware he had done so. His face was losing that sadistically jubilant look. He was now frowning.
Why won't he be? This was what they had always wanted. They wanted to hear the story. Every insult, every cruel remark, and thrown punch was from being pissed off at me for not telling them what they wanted to hear.
'Won't recommend it,' said Eli and coughed a laugh.
Dom's frown deepened. Eli's legs felt closer now.
This was his chance. He kicked out and struck Dom hard between the legs.
His actions immediately caused Michael and Fern to let him go and distance themselves from him. Their shocked faces gaped as their leader cupped his balls. Dom tried to snarl something, even made to move. As if from nowhere and for the second time in two days, an adult appeared. Red painted fingernails latched onto Dom's neck and threw him backward onto his ass.

'Ellen … for goodness sake that wasn't very sensible,' shouted Mr. Miller.
He waddled up behind Mrs. Thompson, his tweed jacket flapping. Eli's History teacher did not turn to him as her focus was fixed on the ground.
'What do you think you're … ' yelled, Mrs. Thompson. Her throat caught as she spotted the knife. Her eyes fixed upon Dom. His mouth opened and closed as if he couldn't draw breath. The teacher wheeled on the twins.
'Get away from him,' she said lowly.

A crowd was forming, encircling the scene. Mr. Millar (Eli felt a spike of loathing in seeing him, knowing he was one of the gossiping staff members that lead him to his notoriety) was trying to calm them. Mrs. Thompson was yelling at the three while her high heel stood over the weapon. Eli barely heard her. Dazed, he seemed to have developed only selective hearing where the loudest noise was that of the murmuring crowd.

'Are you okay?' asked a light, unfamiliar voice beside him.

He didn't answer nor turn. He was watching the three cower.

A hand slipped into his left.

'Heather, take him inside with Mr. Miller, would you,' said Mrs. Thompson.

The hand responded by firmly leading him from the scene. He still did not turn from seeing their faces until he was being guided through the muttering crowd.

He looked at his feet so he wouldn't meet anyone's eye. A horrifying idea sprung to him that someone would trip him now and he would explode. None did though the notion stayed with him until he was in the dark and cold corridors of his school.

'It'll be okay now,' his guide said.

Eli chanced a glance at her. What he saw was a girl his age. She had long, golden hair that framed a face smooth and untouched by any teenage blemish. He knew who she was; everyone did because of how pretty she was. Her name was Heather Elliot.

'Victoria … Victoria', called Mr. Millar.

They were at the school's heart, the receptionist's domain.

There was a creak of a seat, and a face appeared in the square window. That face was already contorted in a scowl the pupils knew well. It broke on seeing them. Mr. Millar whispered fervently to her.

'Alright,' Victoria said. 'Bring him in here, girl. I guess I'm acting nurse for today'.

Heather and Mr. Miller were shut outside.
Eli was told to take a seat. There was only one in the tiny nursing station behind the reception, and it was the type usually found in dentistry. He hopped on-board.
'Right, let's get that face cleaned,' said the receptionist, moving to a small sink.
She appeared to be someone who had to speak, no matter what she was doing. As if silence was to be feared. However, when she applied a wet cloth to Eli's face, he knew this was false. He could see her eyes. They were grey and drowning in concern.
'Please tell me you got in a good dig for this.'
Before she had been a jelly-faced receptionist with too much make-up and an awful perm. Now she could be someone's sweet grandmother.
'They'll remember me for sure,' he assured.
Victoria wiped a tear from underneath her glasses.
'Good…anyway at least now you don't look like a victim. Now you look like a badass'.
Make that a cool, sweet grandmother.

Heather had waited for him.
Seeing her surprised him that he was speechless. She surveyed him with hazel eyes.
'You look much better.'
'Thanks'
'Don't thank her, thank me,' muttered Victoria.
She squeezed his shoulder. Eli was again speechless, this time from gratitude.
'The Principal's waiting to see you,' said Heather.
He nodded and started walking. He didn't need to be led this time.

Heather must have lied.

At least that's what Eli judged from Principal Black's reaction to him. The man had propelled himself to his feet (an enormous task if there ever was one considering his size) and held out one ballooned flipper of a hand.

'Come on in, sit' he ventured.

Eli did as told. Black fell and quickly overflowed his seat.

'I have been informed of the incident that happened moments ago by Mr. Millar. You'll be pleased to know that the police have been contacted. It is a severely serious offense to carry a knife, let alone threaten to use such a weapon, and I assure you, Eli, we are taking this seriously. The three culprits are being detained currently, and I have spoken to them. Their future at this school will be determined later as for now they have all been suspended. I have also phoned your godparents and informed them about this incident.

'What,' Eli spluttered.

Black's eyebrows arched. They had plenty of space to do so as his head was completely hairless. It shined too, catching the light as if it were polished bone.

'It is policy, especially concerning a case as delicate as yours. Your school counselor and social worker will also be informed. Now before the police and your godparents arrive, I wonder if you could clear something up for me, and I want you to be honest. There is some dispute over what Dominic intended to do with the knife. That he intended to scare you on account of how bruised Michael's face is. Is there any truth in what they say? Are you responsible for what happened to Michael?'

Eli stared. When he spoke next, he did so with a voice devoid of life.

'He intended to cut me. That's what he wanted to do. As for Michael's face, I am to blame. That happened after he gave me this.'

With one hand he pulled his collar down and with the other removed the plaster.

'I … see … I think it would be best if we waited for the police and your godparents to be present to discuss this more. Ah Victoria, how can I help?'

'Mrs. Thompson wants to speak to you', said Victoria, from the office door.

Eli kept his eyes focused on Principal Black's shining thumb like head. The face within it brightened on hearing his receptionist's words.

'Excuse me, Eli.'

For a man the equivalent size of a walrus, he moved surprisingly swift.

Eli waited until the door was closed before leaving his chair. He opened it a crack. The Principal and Mrs. Thompson were speaking some ten feet from him. Without knowing what he was doing, Eli slipped through and quietly back-pedaled down the corridor.

4

Eli was unable to even label his feelings as he strolled onto Jones's drive.

He had run away. People would be worried. Yet as the gravel crunched underfoot and he heard the twang of a guitar he found he didn't care.

He stopped, craned his head to the sky, and sighed. It won't last, he knew. As soon as he left, Jones's reality would start again. That didn't matter. He was here as planned.

'Well, hi there,' said Jones, seated on the porch.

'I had a feeling you'd be back. Something just told me … sweet Jesus'.

The music died mid-song. Eli stopped walking as Jones rose to his feet, his guitar gripped by its neck and forgotten. He could not hold his gaze.

'Guess I won't be winning any beauty competition,' said Eli.

'Aye, … you look awful.'

Eli climbed onto the porch steps with effort, collapsing onto the bench.

'Was it the same guys,' asked Jones, his voice dropping an octave.

Eli answered him with a look. The guitarist's face had become a storm once more.

'This happened in school or on the way here?'

Again, a look conveyed his reply.

'I doubt they would have let you walk home. So, I'm to take it you fled. You do know I have to take you home. Ryan and Kate will be worried'.

'How do you know they're my godparents?'

'I'm not an idiot, and I know everyone in this town. Plus, Ryan and Kate are friends'.

Eli's tongue played across his bottom lip.

'So you know about my … '

'Parents,' Jones finished. 'No, that was their business, and I had no right to ask.'

He paused, absorbing this information.

'They wanted to know,' said Eli. 'Dom and his friends ... that's why all this happened. They wanted to know about the kid whose mother killed her self and how it was my dad's fault.'

He hadn't cried as they'd hit him or pressed a knife to him. Nor even upon seeing his mother's lifeless body in a tub of her own blood. He cried now, though and without sobbing. His teeth were gritted, preventing him from doing so.

'Calling her ugly, calling her fat. He said he'd leave her if she ever got fat and she believed every word. When he left, I thought things would be better ... but ... why? Why did she do it?'

Jones bent at the knees, his hands gently grasping Eli's wrists.

'Eli, let me take you home.'

They drove in not-quite silence.

Neither of them spoke, but there was a clonking noise coming from Jones's Ford. Eli was thankful, as its continuous rhythm helped him think. He needed a lie, an explanation that condoned his behavior for whatever hurt he had caused. However, seeing the police car parked behind Ryan's car jarred him.

No lie was going to be big enough he realized.

Reluctantly, he stepped from the Ford. Led by Jones, he trudged silently up the drive.

The front door was ripped open before they reached its threshold.

'I can't stand waiting around, I'm going to look for him.'

Eli felt as if he had been thrown into icy water. The shouting voice belonged to Ryan, who appeared to be speaking to a figure behind him.

He was exiting the house without looking forward, and at speed. Eli made to cry out, but Jones beat him to it.

'Whoa,' he said, and in a blur of movement had caught Ryan by the shoulders.

A feat that made Eli's eyebrows leap.

Though Jones was slightly taller than Ryan, he was also older. What exact age Eli, as of yet, did not know. Despite this, he had stilled his godfather with little effort.

'Jones,' gasped Ryan, having almost stumbled. 'What are you doing here?'

'Bring this fella home … I think he belongs to you'.

When Ryan's eyes fell on him, Eli wanted to shrink under a rock. There wasn't anger in them but relief, which, as he was roughly pulled into a hug made him feel guiltier.

'What the hell were you thinking,' Ryan whispered into his ear.

'Dorian Jones', said a perplexed voice.

Its owner stepped from the house; a police officer.

'Ben,' said Jones.

The two men were starring at each other like two duelists before the count down ends. The officer named Ben opened his mouth to speak but was silenced by Kate.

'What do you think you're playing at Eli, running away from school?'

Living with his father had taught him when to talk and when not to. This was the latter.

He said nothing as Kate copied Ryan and dropped to his level, crushing him in a hug.

When she was done, she held his damage face firmly between her hands. As she did the muscles in her own face clenched and unclenched.

'Bastards,' she said.

'I think we best take this inside,' said the officer.

They moved from the front step to the kitchen.

The officer lingered in the hall to speak into his radio. Jones shifted into a corner.

Under the kitchen light, Eli saw how haggard his godparents looked. As much as he had experienced fear, seeing them now had an entirely different quality. Ryan had fallen into a seat and seemed ready to sleep there. Kate snatched the cordless phone from the kitchen table, offering it to him. She was still in her nurse's uniform and looked like a vampire victim.

On seeing them, Eli glanced at the clock on the wall. It told him it was 4:22 pm. Neither would have been home by now during a typical working day.

Their appearance must not have had only affect on him as Jones spoke.

'I must apologize,' he said. 'I should have phoned to say that Eli was safe at mine and that I would bring him home.'

'Don't worry about it,' interrupted Kate.

'Yeah, Jones,' said Ryan. 'We're just happy he's home.'

'Your social worker would like to speak to you,' Kate told him.

He noted how her tone changed from speaking to Jones to him. He pressed the device she held to his ear.

'I'm here.'

'Hello, Erin, I mean Eli,' said a familiar voice. As always, she sounded close to despair.

'Sorry, I have another case called Erin. Unfortunately, I can't be there right now as I'm tied up with her. Look I know what happened and Kate's spoke to me. She told me what you've put them through this evening, running away is just not on. You worried them'.

'I know. I'm sorry. I just wanted to be alone'.

Eli heard a frazzled exhale from the other end of the line.

'How are you feeling? I heard it was bad'.

'I'm fine.'

'Maybe I should swing by tomorrow. I might be able to fit you in between … '
He heard yelling on her side.
'I've got go,' she hissed and the line cut dead.
Eli turned, setting the phone onto the kitchen table. The officer had returned.
What he said next forged a ball of dread in Eli's stomach.
'I have a few questions for you and Jones'.

'Here, this will help with the swelling,' said Kate.
She pressed a dampened cloth to his right eye. Ice churned inside.
'These would have been asked earlier,' sighed the officer, 'but you ran away, and we will get to that later.'
'As the incident at the school involved a knife, it has become a police matter. As such, I need a statement from you. First off, there has been an allegation made that what happened is the result of an earlier confrontation between Dominic Coyle, Fern and Michael McBride, and yourself. Is that true?'
Eli's clear eye rolled over the four adults. Nothing had changed. He was being asked to tell a story. Tonelessly as if reciting scripture he began at the beginning.
When he showed the gash on his neck, Kate gasped.
'You didn't tell your godparents about that, why?'
'I was tired of telling them things that they would worry about.'
It was a half-truth. Eli was tired of people wanting to know things to worry about.
'This is where you come in Mister Jones,' said the officer.
'That's correct,' answered Jones.
'Before this incident were you aware of Eli Donoghue?'
'Yes, Ryan had told me about him.'
'Ryan … you mean Mister Wilson. How would you describe your relationship with the Wilson's?'

Three different looks of anxiety and bewilderment played across adult faces.

'I did some work for the security firm that Jones worked for at the mill,' said Ryan. 'Jones was the one that recommended me to them to update their prehistoric computer system, and I took him out for a drink afterward as thanks. We had a blast. Since then, we've stayed in touch'.

'We've had him over for dinner,' added Kate sharply.

'What are you asking officer?'

'Nothing ... I'm just trying to get a clear picture ... of events'.

The officer was a big man made bigger by the bulk of his uniform. So far, he had scrutinized them all under his grey eyes that singled himself as an authority. They fluttered as Kate spoke.

'Ah, did you inform the Wilson's after witnessing Eli being bullied.'

'No, I assumed the kid would tell them,' said Jones.

'You should never assume,' replied the officer. 'Okay, final question, why Eli did you run from school and to this man?'

The officer's pen was poised on his notepad. His eyes tried their penetrative stare on Eli's one.

'Yesterday, on Jones's porch he played a song on his guitar. I'd never heard a guitar being played before, at least not outside a set of headphones. Jones invited me back, and I had been looking forward to it all day. With what happened I thought I was owed that'.

'You went to this man's house after only meeting him a day before.'

'I wanted to ask him to teach me how to play,' Eli lied. Though having said it out loud, he knew what he had said was true. He just hadn't realized it until now.

The notepad flipped closed, the officer's face grim.

'That's that for now,' he said, shoving from the table after some time.

'I believe the school board is meeting on the matter separately. You'll probably hear from them soon. As for us, if we have any further questions, we will be in touch'.

The officer's eyes rounded on Eli. They feigned a type of warmth selected by adults unaccustomed to dealing with children. One that causes them to lean forward, bending at the knees, that the majority of children recognize as when an adult is about to be condescending.

'As for you running away, we are letting you off. But I want you to know the extent Hazel's police officers have spent in searching for you … '

'What all three of them?' quipped Jones.

Eli watched curiously as loathing crept across his face for Jones. Then it was caged away.

'Yes … well … it was an extension search, taking lots of time and effort.'

'Okay, sir,' said Eli.

He nodded. Ryan showed him out and when he returned announced.

'I think that calls for a beer.'

'God, yes,' cried Jones.

Eli paid them little attention. His clear eye was starring at the space that the officer had occupied in the hall before leaving. He was wondering what his connection was to Jones.

5

Kate's stare grabbed his attention. She sat at his side and had done so the whole interview. Her hands obscured her mouth, and he wished her stare had been accusing, but it wasn't. It was another pitying look.

'I'll take a beer too,' she said ' ... and I think a takeaway's in order'.

'If that's the case I better get going,' said Jones. 'I wouldn't want to intrude further.'

He had reached his feet when three voices shouted him down. His eyebrows rose comically high. 'Alright then,' he grumbled.

As it was Friday night, the takeaway took some time. The adults filled it with awkward conversations that Eli observed but took no part in.

He hurt. The pain in his right cheek and eye had been replaced by an icy numbness. His left cheek felt dented while pain ran about his jaw. Below all this, his gut's constant ache had subsided to a weak whimper and felt made of jelly instead of flesh.

He was also woefully tired. Tired in a sense that his spine and shoulders were anchored by numerous weights. Yet his mind was alive and puzzling over the enigma that was Jones and his connections to the police officers strange looks of contempt.

'Eat up,' nudged Kate.

Eli blinked. A plate of steaming food had been set before him. Curry spices itched at his nostrils and a reply voiced from his stomach. He was ravenous.

Though he did little to cure this, picking up his fork, he pathetically took the smallest amounts on its prongs.

The night pressed in from the kitchen windows as pale blue.

'This is a sober occasion,' sighed Kate after the adults had finished their meals. 'Maybe you could cheer us up with a tune?'

Eli straightened in his seat.

'Well, I dunno, I do have an old acoustic in the car,' Jones stammered.

He met Eli's eyes, and something worked within his face.

'Sure, why not.'

He returned from outside, carrying a case of peeling, faded leather. The guitar, it housed was not slim and polished as the red almost heart-shaped guitar Eli had seen the day before. This was made of creamy wood and fat.

Jones seated, strummed its strings, producing a wholesome and full sound.

'I'm not much of a singer, but here we go.'

The song was not humble. Nor was it soft-footed or tender. It was raw, lusting, and undeniable causing them to nod and tap their feet. Jones sang in a voice far from pretty, more a rustic, hinged drawl that kicked Eli awake.

At some point, Ryan threw his arm around Kate's shoulders, and she embraced his side. When the song ended, he clapped, and she whistled shrilly. Eli hiccupped a laugh.

'What do you think?' asked Jones.

'What was that?' Eli replied.

'That was *Get Rhythm* by *Johnny Cash,*' said Ryan, shaking his head.

Jones's tongue clicked, and he said 'kid you need some education and I'm gonna give it to ya.' He launched into another song.

For an hour, they listened enthralled.

Eli was introduced to songs by *Bob Dylan, Bruce Springsteen, Muddy Waters, The Beatles* and numerous others that he did not know. He was held enrapture to their words and music through Jones. With it, the stale atmosphere of before had been exorcized. The only cause for it to conclude was himself yawning.

'I think it's time for bed,' said Kate on seeing him.

The remark bought nostalgia to his sleepy brain. It was something his mother, and he supposed all mothers said to their child at bedtime. The child's response is to deny and internally curse for letting his tiredness show. This was happy thinking, and it made him smirk as he was headed upstairs.

'Come on, I'll lend you a hand.'

'Why, I'm twelve, not two.'

'Because you look a mess, you're still in your uniform.'

Eli's retort was too far and too distant for Ryan and Jones to hear.

They remained in their seats, sipping their drinks. Jones followed Ryan's eyes to Eli's now empty plate. Seeing, Jones's curious look, Ryan's eyebrows jumped. 'Rosa, his mother had problems with food thanks to that asshole husband of hers. We've struggled to get him to eat for the past month'.

'You never knew?' asked Jones.

'What? About him?' Ryan shook his head, 'no, I mean on odd occasions we suspected they were arguing, but we put it down to just that. We never thought it was as bad as it was until it was too late'. Ryan drained his beer bottle. 'Thank you for tonight, Jones, playing for him really did some good. Better than anything I've done'.

'Hey,' said Jones.

Ryan's head snapped to attention. The voice that spoke was not the low grumble that Jones had used all evening. This voice was gristle and rage.

'It's a shitty situation. You should both pat yourself on the back. I have my own son, grown-up now, but I will tell you I didn't handle anything in his life as well as your handling having that kid just now'.

Jones looked away while Ryan stared at him.

Footsteps thudded softly from the staircase as Kate returned. She was dressed in a hoodie and pajama bottoms, her short, platinum hair gave her face a haloed look. It was still damp with tears.

'He went to sleep as soon as he hit the pillow. I could hear him snoring'.

She glided into a seat and pulled her feet up with her.

'I think I'll walk home,' said Jones, standing and stretching.

'We could call you a taxi.'

'Nah, fresh air will do me wonders. I'll walk back tomorrow and get the car. I'm sorry for what happened today. I should have phoned yesterday and told you about those kids'.

'It's fine,' said Kate. 'You couldn't have known what was going to happen.'

She walked him out and caught him by surprise at the door with a hug. Kate's head reached his torso, yet her arms were strong. She retracted from him, giving him a smile made more stunning by her tears.

'Thank you,' she said, and he felt her eyes on him as he walked away.

Neither noticed the police cruiser parked down the street.

6

Ryan was waiting for her in the kitchen.
When she got close, he slid the tub of Ben & Jerry's across the counter.
'Is it that time again,' she said and smirked weakly.
She walked into the frame of his arms. Her eyes were on his.
Their noses touched. Ryan kissed her hard enough that when she broke for air, he could hear the unsteadiness of her breath. Her hand plowed through his hair, yanking, gripping, and having endured five years working in care homes was piston strong.
With one quick tug, her bottoms fell off. Ryan's took longer as it involved a giddy, fumbling of a belt.
'We will wake him,' he whispered, already descending to the floor.
'Not if you're quick,' she said.
He was.

'The ice cream is only half-melted,' she said.
'You wanted me to be quick,' he replied.
They were in the living room with their backs propped against the sofa.
The ice cream had been a discovery they had made in their college days.
'Isn't that what you ladies do when feeling blue,' Ryan had said.
Kate had lost her job and out of immediate terror of being penniless wanted to stay in.
'Open some ice-cream, put on some music, massage each other … ' he had jabbed.
She had laughed and made to slap him. A tradition was born.
They ate in a world gone quiet. The house, it seemed, had ceased its ritual of creaking boards and gurgling pipes, serving them a reprieve from the day.

'We did good tonight,' said Kate.
'We did,' replied Ryan. 'But what do we do now?'
He wanted to ask more. For the past month, his brain
had become a cement mixer with his unvoiced thoughts
tumbling inside.

They had been together for ten years in which the
subject of having children was discussed frequently but
unrealistically. In truth, they were happy as they were.
Then Eli was thrust upon them.

Ryan had gone along with it because he knew Kate's
reason. Eli was her sister's son. The sister that Kate
had been so close to growing up and had somehow
drifted away from in adulthood. There was guilt there.
Guilt that on hearing what the boy had endured had
intensified it.

Ryan admitted he did feel a correct protectiveness over
him on hearing the truth about Rosa's marriage.
However, he would not say he had bonded with him.
These thoughts would never be spoken. If they were,
they would crack what fragile glue was holding Kate
and him together these days. They were his burden.
Instead of divulging his own worries, he asked, 'what do
we do now?'

'The answer is the same as always I don't fucking
know,' replied Kate.

Ryan smirked: this remark was another of their
relationships little quirks.

'We're due to see Eli's Principal tomorrow,' she said,
stabbing her spoon into the ice cream. 'If he suggests
we hold him back a year again I swear I'll throttle him
after all the effort we put into getting him into that snob
school.'

'I'd enjoy seeing that,' Ryan remarked, licking his spoon
greedily.

This time it was Kate's turn to smirk. However, it quickly
faded away.

She gasped, saying, 'I don't think Rosa would be too impressed with me for this.'

'This isn't your fault,' Ryan told her, seeing her expression.

He wrapped his arms around her shoulders and felt them shiver. He pulled her close.

'She'd be pulling her hair out,' she said against his chest. 'Remember how she used to do that when she was anxious about something, which was all the time.'

'I think of Rosa sometimes,' he said.

'You do,' said Kate.

'Yeah, I think of that time last August when they came and stayed. Remember, she told us Sean couldn't come cause of a work thing'.

'Yeah,' sighed Kate. 'Guess we'll never know if that was true or not.'

'Does it matter,' Ryan remarked.

'What I think about is how tired she always seemed. She never said as much, probably cause she didn't want to alert us to anything, but that's how she looked. She was like that for what…four days, and then we took them for a walk up one of the trails outside of town. You know the one that runs on the hill overlooking Hazel. Eli was giggling and running through the long grass. She was chasing him. I've been thinking about that smile she gave us, looking back after she had caught him for the hundredth time'.

'At the time,' said Ryan. 'I had thought she looks happy. For some reason, whenever we talk about your sister, I think of that image'.

Kate curled further into him.

With a smile on her face, she said, 'I remember that too.'

'I remember her looking at Hazel and saying she wanted to move here.'

She looked upward into his face. Ryan leaned down and kissed her lips.

'Come on, bedtime,' he said.

'Ahhhh, dad,' she whined.

'Don't call me that, you know that dirty stuff turns me on,' he told her.

They wandered together to the staircase, the ice cream tub empty and left on the floor.

Eli's left foot impatiently pumped as he sat.

Straining, he could make out a few words from within the Principal's office. Words such as 'terribly sorry,' 'uttermost seriousness,' and 'promptly and efficiently' were being used by the chipped tones of Principal Black.

At one point he heard Kate's response, 'I certainly hope so.'

That made him grin.

It was weird being in school on a Saturday. More bizarre that he was in regular clothes and the building was so still around him. Though, Eli did not feel uneasy about being here even after waking to find his bruises were purple/black and his eye bloodshot.

He was too stunned from the announcement at the breakfast table.

'Jones popped by this morning.' Ryan had said from nowhere.

The mention of his name made Eli swallow a mouthful of bacon and eggs wrongly.

'Well,' said Ryan after Kate had administered a hard thump to his back.

'He came to get his car, and we got to talking, and we agreed, that is if you want to, that he could give you guitar lessons after school.'

They would begin on Monday. This information improved the weekend considerable despite yesterday's horrors.

The present stretched before him as an endless opportunity. Especially as his godparents pleased by his sunny disposition offered to take him to Belfast. As if by cue, the Principals door opened. The room's three occupants shuffled out with their eyes on him. Eli's own went down the line and lingered on Black.

'Eli,' he said. 'Your godparents have told me that you understand the severity of your actions. I would like to say that if you at all felt that the school was not fulfilling your needs in regards to yesterday's events I apologize if this was the case'.

As true to his natural Black sounded like a robotic thesaurus. Eli felt his eyebrows trying to rise from his head.

'Ahh ... thanks.'

'And I thank you to, Mister Black,' said Kate.

Black's delicate, defensively tilt of the head told Eli all he needed to know about this surprise apology. Ryan gave his own to Black, but it was one of smug pride.

In the car, Ryan giggled to himself.

'What? He deserved it,' said Kate.

That was as much as Eli ever learned as to what was said in that room.

The fabric of Belfast, to Eli, seemed of times and designs meshed upon one another. He had spent little time in the city and found he was alone in gazing at the buildings. Some were grey, metallic and modern and others built from carved stone and crowned by gargoyles and inscriptions.

They wandered the city's heart, losing themselves in the crowds.

Ryan and Kate showered indulgences on him in the form of *Ray Bradbury's Fahrenheit 451, Neil Gaiman's American Gods* and *Alan Moore's Watchmen.*

After this, they parried their way to a coffee shop. As Ryan and Kate conversed Eli regressed into the vivid and sleazy illustrated world of superheroes.

He spent much of that Saturday that way.

Sunday was different. The clock ran, and he stared at it in panicked nausea at returning to school. What escape his books offered couldn't settle him.

Kate gave him the chance to stay off. 'We will just call in and explain, but it will still be there no matter what you've got to go back.'

Her words ruled out that option.

The walk to the gates that morning, Eli spent intensely examining the pavement. He felt eyes upon him and wondered when his hair would catch flame. His focus was so intent on the ground that he practically walked into someone.

'I'm sorry,' he blubbered.

There was a hand on his chest that he recognized.

He looked up, and his throat immediately locked.

Heather Elliot was grinning at him, her hair like gold in the strong sunlight.

'It's amazing,' she said. 'But you actually look worse.'

Words evaded him, and in that long pause in which his mind whirled, he realized something: that Heather had been waiting for him.

7

'I thought you wouldn't have come in,' she said.
'But I waited anyway. I wanted to see if you were alive or something, which you are, and that's great. I'm rambling, sorry. It's just … it's good to see you'.
'It is,' said Eli in awe.
'Yea,' she frowned, and her hazel eyes were crushed by its anger.
'Dom and those guys shouldn't be getting away with how they've been behaving. It wasn't just you that they picked on, there were others. But nobody stands up to them, and I was thinking I hope you do come in because that would be standing up to them'.
'That not hiding would show them up.'
It wasn't the sun highlighting her hair. Or how being in its shadow her eyes that he knew to be hazel now appeared to be dark chocolate. It was that she wanted to talk to him that was dizzying.
'Thank you,' seemed the logical response to both the situation and her words.
'Sure, come on, I'll walk you in,' she said, brightly.
Eli had to dash to keep up.
'Have you heard anything about those assholes?'
'Suspended for now,' he said.
'I expect they'll be expelled eventually,' she said then added, 'for the knife.'
Her voice dropped an octave causing him to study her. The memory of the knife surfaced in his mind. He saw blade catching the light becoming a silvery shard amongst the emerald grass.
Eli responded to Heather with a nod and a look.
Perhaps one that gave too much away as 'how was your weekend' was the next question?

As he made to answer the morning bell rang shrilly. Heather's hand gripped his right wrist. 'You can tell me later. See you in class'.

Then she was gone, sauntering off to her clique of friends.

He doubted he would 'see' her again. *Not a girl like that*, he thought.

It didn't matter. The sense of accomplishment bubbling in Eli's chest was enough.

He was, however, wrong.

In English, Mr. Logue revealed that the class would be paired to write short stories. As partnered names were being called, Eli sat innocently unaware.

'Eli and Heather,' Logue seemed to boom.

His hand-applied too much downward force, and his pencil's head snapped.

Heather navigated between tables to him like a breeze. Her dimpled smile inflicting internal torture to his insides. He wished he could melt through the floor.

'Hi,' he squeaked.

'Hi, again,' she said.

Coughing, he added in a deeper tone, 'what do you want to write about?'

'I don't know,' she said, falling into a vacant chair beside him.

'I like horror films if that's any good.'

Eli didn't. He liked horror books because the horror and the characters were always better developed, but as Heather had asked, he said he did.

'Do you have any ideas?'

'Well ... '

When Mr. Logue had spoken to the class, Eli had thought of the *Ray Bradbury* book he had finished at the weekend. It was about many things, and one of them had been books themselves. The idea stirred unseen in the dark canyons of his brain.

'What about a library,' he said. 'That's guarded by a creature that lives off books because books have power, and there are two kids who become trapped in the library and have to battle the creature to get out.' He watched Heather rock back in her seat.

'Not good?'

'No, sounds great, let's do it,' she beamed.

The story would begin with their characters caught in a torrential downpour after school. Seeking shelter they run to a nearby overhang and by accident discover its door is unlocked. Eager to escape the cold, they enter the building's warm and dimly lit interior. The library is a marvel to them until they realize the door was locked.

Eli's fresh pencil scratched across the page. He wrote fast to keep up with ideas that erupted from nowhere and branded themselves white-hot on his brain. It was sheer exhalation. As the class seized the opportunity to be lazy, he was flying on the fumes of creativity. With it came the joy and freedom of a newly discovered delight.

'I think we need to rewrite,' said Heather, her face flushed.

It was true, their first attempt was barely readable due to Eli's adrenaline rush.

Having massaged the cramp from his hand, he rewrote their story. When it was finished, he fell back in his seat and sighed.

'Better be quick,' Jones joked. 'Won't want you to take too long a break.'

'It's my business,' replied Ryan. 'I can take as long as I want. Plus, not I don't have many repairs today, people seem to be treating their computers well at the moment.'

He held the door for the chuckling Jones. A bell twinkled above as it closed.

'Good, because we might get sidetracked.'

Both men stood still staring with broadening grins. The room before them or more its contents commanded their reflection.

The long, narrow space was neatly filled with musical instruments. Pianos smiled at them in rows, light spliced off the golden surfaces of brass devices and a massive drum kit reigned overall at the shops' rear.

'You could be right there,' said Ryan.

He needed no introduction to the store, this was The Gallery, Hazel's one and only music shop. Though, Ryan mostly spent his time here on the floor above (an archive of CD's and vinyl) he couldn't help but be impressed at what he was seeing.

'Blimey, it's about time,' exclaimed a rasping voice.

In his amazement, Ryan had not noticed the thin man polishing a piano.

Now that he had he could not take his eyes off him. He was ugly in the sense that a prizefighter's fist is, gnarled flesh, skin taut over knobby bone and white scar tissue.

'You've been out in those woods so long I thought you had gone hermit,' said the man.

Jones exhaled sharply through his nostrils. Yet, he took the stranger's hand and shook it friendly.

'My absence is simple … I don't like you very much,' said Jones.

The stranger snorted. Quite a task considering his own nose was a considerable beak like the bow of a ship. Ryan felt its wind on his clothes.

'I'm not complaining. You always bought a foul smell to the shop. I lost custom'.

The two men regarded each other. Neither had released the other's hand, and both seemed intent on crushing the others. Yet smirks broadened on their faces.

They burst into laughter.

'Ryan, this is Lawrence Reed, or as we prefer English,' said Jones.

'How do you do,' said the stranger.

His accent alone qualified as an explanation for the nickname. It was a raspy, dry form of Kent that recalled to Ryan old war movies in black and white.

'He's the owner of this shit hole, which we have chosen, out of lack of choice really to visit. Ryan's the reason we are here, his godson is interested in the guitar'.

'How old is the little fellow?' asked English.

Ryan had to have him repeat the question.

'He's twelve.'

'Should get him a drum kit instead, that age it helps to thump at something.'

'I think he is heart's set,' said Ryan, slightly abashed.

'If you're sure,' wheezed English. His chest heaved awkwardly conjuring an image of ancient, dust-coated accordion coughing for life to Ryan.

English ambled to the shops' rear, allowing a view of his snow-white ponytail.

'He's a heavy smoker, don't be alarmed,' whispered Jones.

'You told me about him, you were in the same band,' Ryan whispered back.

'Yeah ... a long time ago,' Jones said, distantly.

'I think this will do. It's a little big, he'll struggle to make some of the chords, but that will be good for him. He'll grow into it,' said English, presenting them his find while a cigarette hung from his chapped lips. They were pulled into an encouraging grin.

On their way out, Eli's gift boxed and in Ryan's arms, English called out.

'Given any more thought to Brandon's offer then, old boy.'

Throughout the purchase, that voice had been jolly and humorous. As it spoke now, it did so without those things.

'I'm retired, remember,' replied Jones, lightly but not entirely convincingly.

'I can't believe we won a prize,' said Heather referring to the box of Celebrations they had gobbled.
'Not that your writing wasn't good enough,' she added.
'It's just that … there … actually was a prize.'
'What you mean my writing, it was a team effort,' chuckled Eli.
The last bell was already memory as they crossed the playground.
'Team effort,' she giggled. 'If you call me sitting talking a little while you do all the work I'm up for that. I'll see you tomorrow, yeah'.
She took off towards an Audi.
He waved goodbye, noticing the hundreds of others getting into cars or buses. Nobody walked home but him.
Hazel Grammar School sat on the town's outskirts. Its parking lot was tiny, barely accommodating to the cars that rolled up outside its fenced premises. Surrounding it was the woods and amid this tangled wilderness was a trail. One that was invisible until standing directly before it.
His route.
It was a long and winding dirt road through the place where the supposedly truly rich and Jones lived. The alternative route, which the cars used, didn't even have a footpath.
Some days he didn't walk home if Kate was off to collect him. Those days he had to admit were good. Only because he could pretend he was a part of an average family. Like the hundreds, he watched now.
An ache sparked within his bruised face.
Earlier, in Mrs. Thompson's class, she had cleared her throat loudly. Twenty-five students immediately ceased their crazed whispering and shy glances at him.
She had stood to survey them before the blackboard, hands on her hips.

'If you think Eli looks bad,' said Mrs. Thompson in a barely controlled yell. 'You should see what he did to the other guy.'

What followed was a chorus of relieved laughter from the class. The scandal that no student dared to address to any teacher had been spoken of. Eli couldn't help but smirk.

He had gazed at Mrs. Thompson, who had shot him a wink. Seeing, her wink again in his head caused him to smirk once more.

He turned from the school, no longer minding the walk as it meant Jones and his wondrous world of music.

After a few minutes, the sound of revving engines dissipated, leaving Eli alone.

The track expanded into the familiar dusty lane. Driveways ticked by, trails that either led to regal mansions where a bell tower wouldn't seem out of place. Or high-tech clinical buildings that appeared ready to morph into an iPod. Dense patches of forestry segmented these where wildlife buzzed, cooed or rustled about the undergrowth. All sounds that Eli found hypnotic and soothing to his slightly baked after school brain.

Who called these buildings home?

What were the fathers like?

What were the mothers like?

He pondered, becoming lost in vivid imaginings. Imaginings that cut short as he saw Jones's car was not alone in his driveway.

'Good afternoon, there,' shouted Ryan from the porch.

'What's going on?' His voice was timid and suspicious. Kate, who had been observing Jones's colorful flowerbed, turned.

'Seeing as we had Jones over last time, it was his turn to have us over.'

'Rightly so,' boomed Jones, stepping from inside to toss Ryan a beer can.

'And I will do so with great pleasure, beginning with whetting your appetites. Tonight you will all be dining on fine steak, a spread of wholesome vegetables topped with a whiskey sauce that might leave you needing AA. As it is the only thing I can cook that isn't a BBQ,' he concluded like a showman, arms stretched, palms outward.

The dinner despite what novice culinary skills Jones claimed he had, was delirious. The four ate on the lawn having maneuvered Jones's kitchen table there. The kitchen itself was insufferable. The sunlight was like hot oil and Jones's whiskey fumes, though salivate inducing, also resulted in dizzying spells. Jones avoided these by wearing a protective mask that made him look like a mad scientist.

Though, that did not prevent Eli from devouring his plate wordlessly.

'That's one growin' boy you got there,' said Jones.

'Sure is,' agreed Ryan.

'What … I was hungry,' said Eli, shrugging at the three staring adults.

'Jones I have a question,' he said. 'Something I was thinking about on my way here. Why are all the houses around here so ... posh. Why is your house different from every other one on this lane … I mean?'

'I know what you mean no offense taken,' said Jones, sipping his beer.

The alarmed look that passed between Kate and Ryan relaxed.

'My dad bought this land from a farmer long before any property investor took an interest,' explained Jones.

'His friends helped him build it, as that was their trade, doing so from whatever means they could afford at the time.'

'When the investors and housing companies came calling, wanting him to sell, he told them no, and I have continued to tell them in my own polite fashion. He told them this was his home and he intended to pass it on, which he did, to me. Really, he had no other choice, as my brother would happily bulldoze this place down. He's like … see that house over the there?'

He pointed his fork over his shoulder.

'The woman that owns it hates me. She's one of those class ones, believes people of a certain financial level should remain with their own. Seeing people like me reminds her that people like me exist'.

'Miserable cow them,' injected Kate.

'Absolutely,' Jones agreed.

'Anyway, some wealthy individuals saw the potential in being able to build whatever they wanted. The idea caught on, which is why no one's house looks the same. I think the only thing they weren't allowed to do was cut down the whole wood'.

'I think I remember that being talked about when they started building here,' said Kate.

'Don't ask me, I was raised in Antrim,' said Ryan.

'Aye, it shows … by your poor table manners,' replied Jones.

Kate and Jones sniggered at Ryan.

Eli watched them, moving to the edge of his seat. He wanted to ask about the policeman. But he stopped himself, thinking; it was a question for when they were alone.

The adults appeared not to notice this.

'Think its time?' Jones asked, giving Ryan a nudge.

'I think its time,' said Kate brightly.

She bounced from the table to the house. Her dress, a white-one piece fluttered above her working knees. She returned cradling a package the distinctive shape of a guitar.

Kate placed it before him on the table.

He reached out for it, hesitated, glancing at the beaming faces surrounding him. His face was clenched, but he struggled to make it so. Underneath, his emotions wormed.

Eventually, his fingers touched the wrapping in a caress. Then he was tearing it off, flinging it to the grass, each piece revealing the black leather of a guitar case.

He ran his fingers over it and unlatched the golden clasps.

Jones and Ryan were chuckling somewhere over his bowed head. Peering, at the acoustic guitar within the case, they sounded a universe away.

Jones slurped from his can and watched the pumpkin-colored sky.

He was thinking about the kid. Seemed he had done little else lately. He hoped he had liked the guitar, hoped it was enough to distract him, to get him to forget for a while.

He was thinking such thoughts when an expensive car coasted up his drive. Jones bought his fist to rest under his nose as a suited figure exited the vehicle.

'I see you've done a lot with the place in your reclusion,' said the suited man.

Jones stared at him as he would over the sights of a gun.

'What do you want?' he asked.

'Well, good manners wouldn't go amiss,' said the suited man, climbing onto the porch.

'Fuck off, how does that sound?' replied Jones.

A grin spread like a stain across the suited man's face. He draped himself from a support beam like a lap dancer and gave a propositioning leer.

'Don't tease,' he said.

His little brother seated himself opposite him with a sigh.

'Ah,' he said on spotting the cooler. 'You've been making the most of your time.'

There was a crack followed by a fizzle as he opened a beer can.

'What are you doing here, Roy?' asked Jones, staring out into the encroaching darkness.

'Just dropped by to see if you've given Brandon's offer anymore thought,' he replied.

'The answer is still no.'

His brother produced another sigh.

'Well, then,' said Roy. 'This is going to be embarrassing for both of us then. Trust me, I don't like having to give my big brother advice, but it's going to happen anyway. So let's get on with it and if you want to play the sulky teenager be my guest. Let's talk about what you've been doing with your time and your new friend. I suppose you're shocked I know … '

'Not really,' interrupted Jones. 'English told Brandon, Brandon told you, easy. Why do you care?'

'Dorian,' said Roy, reclining back into the seat.

'You know I hate my first name,' growled Jones.

He finally turned from the view to meet his brother's gaze. As he did, he took in the crispness of his brother's suit. It was entirely out of place for their humble childhood home. He was sure that was the very reason why it had been purchased.

'Because, Jones try as I might, and I assure you I do try really hard, I can't stop thinking about you. Maybe it's a blood thing. I mean I really could do without this worrying'.

'Sweet,' said Jones, burping.

Roy sighed for the third time, this one the biggest so far.

'It must have pulled on your heartstrings hearing that orphan boy's story. I know, didn't guess I knew that one did ya, but it pays to be mayor of a town know one cares about'.

'Guess it makes it easier to get away with things,' retorted Jones.

What sadistic pleasure Roy was gaining from this conversation ceased. His face said as much. The sarcastic and jovial demeanor that had been apparent since his arrival was whipped away. In its place was a frayed, petty and seething creature.

Jones knew it well from episodes together in their youth.

Roy Jones was never a content child. He had always wanted more, more toys, more attention, more control over the household that he was being raised in.

On one occasion Jones recalled how he had erupted into shrill squeals over a yo-yo. Both of them had been given one by their grandmother, but Jones's yo-yo had been green, and Roy's had been yellow. Roy had hidden under the kitchen table, screaming, 'I WANT MY GREEN YO-YO.'

Jones had offered to trade with his little brother. He had not understood what all the fuss was about then, but he never forgot the incident.

'You're wasting your time playing Good Will Hunting,' spat Roy in his face.

'Your gonna mess up that kid even more. What happens when he finds out your afraid to even go out your own door? Hmm no, what you need to do is to take Brandon's deal. Haven't you moped around here long enough, clinging on to … whatever? Your wife died long ago, Jones but your not. Quit acting like it and grow some balls'.

Jones's tongue played over the tops of his teeth. He did not look at Roy when he spoke next. He continued to stare at the dimming night sky, hearing only silence from the woods.

'You know I just remembered what an arsehole you are.'

Roy sniffed then shot to his feet, buttoning his suit's jacket as he did. His feet barely made a sound on the porch steps as he took them.

In the garden, his silvery hair glinted in the twilight. He paused, midway to his car.

'I like having conversations with you, Jones,' he said. 'I can say whatever I want and nobody will ever hear them.'

With that, he strode calmly across the lawn. His shoes gleaming like polished vinyl.

As his car reserved, Jones crunched his can and threw.

Roy Jones retrieved his phone from the inner pocket of his jacket.

With one hand on the wheel, he hit speed dial. No one was going to give him a ticket if he got caught. Not if they were smart.

The phone rang twice and was answered as if the person were waiting.

Roy knew that in fact, he was. He spoke into the device and said three words.

'Toy with him.'

8

'Have you heard anything about, Eli Donoghue?' asked
Fred Millar.

His voice was zany with barely controlled excitement.

'I've heard he's going to a meeting with the school
board tomorrow afternoon. The school counselor and
social worker are apparently going. Imagine having a
counselor and a social worker at twelve. Also, that boy
with the knife has been expelled. I wonder how his
father would take that, met the man once, wasn't
someone I'd say I'd cross'.

Victoria observed how Millar was leaning over her desk
between them.

'Actually, Fred I'm not really comfortable talking about
this,' she told him. 'I don't think it's very professional.'

Millar's eyebrows conjoined into one hairy caterpillar.
He opened his mouth to talk once more, but Victoria
had turned back to her work.

As he departed from her reception window, Victoria
grinned.

'I don't know,' said Eli.

He hoped that didn't sound like too much of a whine.
Not so much for Andrew (his newest friend) but for
Heather being near. The adults had assembled outside
his counselor's door. Whine or no whine, he tensed
each time one glanced his way.

'What's the big deal,' said Andrew. 'You go in, say your
piece and you're free.'

Eli wanted to strangle him.

'If it makes you feel any better, I'll wait on you,' said
Heather.

Her voice was smooth and sure and magnanimous. It got Eli moving. It wasn't walking more like the corridor had become a conveyor belt. Heather and Andrew disappeared, and he was alone before a semi-circle of serious adult faces.

'Are you all right, Eli? You look a little pale?' asked Black.

'I'm fine.'

'Then let us proceed.'

With a sigh, Eli entered the room first.

Eli's head didn't feel baked, but as if it had been subjected to a cosmic ray.

This made it challenging to follow Kate's rambling as he crossed the playground.

'That was intense, but at least it's over and done with; it's in their hands. Though, I don't think your social worker contributed much, especially as she couldn't get your name right. And what's up with your school counselor? She looked a bit sedated. Black seemed to be on our side, that's something, guess what I said sunk in'.

'Say what do you fancy for dinner, huh? We could get a takeaway again'.

'Ahh ... yeah ... is it okay if I walk home?' asked Eli.

They were by the car. Kate, clutching her clinking keys, paused and looked at him over its roof. He twisted where he stood, squinting to the female figure by the gates.

Kate's head rose as if by its chin. A muscle twitched by her right eye.

Eli shrugged upon seeing these things.

'Don't be late home, okay.'

'I won't, thanks.'

He watched the black Vauxhall peel away. A lone shadow beneath endless blue and a sun like a white coin.

'How was it?' asked Heather on arriving at his side.
'God awful,' he said.

They ambled home.
Moving as the young do, with no particular speed or
aim in mind. They weren't happy without cause but
happy because they had nothing to be unhappy about.
Eli found this strange.
It was still all their, his past, his present, and the
(fading) headache and yet it wasn't. It had become a
story that had happened to someone else, and they
had shut the book.
At least for whatever time they were together.
There had been no decision yet the pair had taken the
long way home, the route that the cars used (bothering
Eli none as he had no lesson with Jones scheduled).
'Look at that,' said Heather.
She was staring ahead. Eli was caught between looking
and noticing how the sun made her hair seem to glow.
Eventually and with sorrow, he turned.
There was a sign that read ROADWORKS AHEAD in
white. The words and their red background were dulled
under exhaust grime. Beyond was another only
positioned in the roads left-hand lane and further still
were a line of traffic cones.
Heather pinged the sign with a finger. The metal
trembled, producing a mini-gong sound. They were
alone to hear it.
'You know,' said Heather. Her tone was contemplative
and thus deadly to Eli. 'All those people are still back at
school. You could get your own back on them'.
'Heather Elliot,' said Eli, enjoying her tiny, devilish
smirk. 'What's a good girl like you thinking about
committing a petty crime?'

'Hey,' she shrugged 'I'm not the one that's supposed to be the troublemaker. In fact, I'm a little disappointed you didn't think of it first seeing as you've got a reputation'.

'What reputation?'

'The notorious one that everyone's gossiping about. Don't pretend you don't know of it'.

Eli held up his hands at her accusing finger.

'So,' she tilted her head to the side 'what you gonna do?'

They removed the sandbags that held the first signs stationary. Even then, it was a struggle to get one of them into the right lane. This they did chuckling despite themselves, the sign always moments from falling out of their grip. Then they plucked the traffic cones and dragged them into a crude line.

'There,' she said, hands on her hips. 'That should teach them.'

Like her, he surveyed their creation.

It's not the Barrens, and I'm not Ben Hanscom, but it will do.

They recommenced their leisurely pace, blazers balled inside bags, ties undone.

At some point (their conversation now passing in drips) Eli felt Heather's hand creep into his. He had been aware of the small distance between his and hers. To touch her hand, its skin furnace hot and moist, in his own jolted him with terror. Minutes passed before he could summon the courage to look. And what he saw was Heather's hand in his. His.

He looked at Heather. She kept her head straight, a smirk playing along her lips.

He straightened. Heat bloomed to a supernova temperature where they touched.

The comfortable silence was exchanged for one of agony for the rest of the journey. Yet Eli didn't want it to end.

As the scenery changed to suburbia, it was ever more evident it would.

When she said, 'this is me' his heart gave a depressed quiver. Heather didn't seem to want to leave him so disappointed (he guessed his face was a give away). She plunged at him, her lips meeting his in a kiss that was slightly too firm. Eli fell into the silk touch, the immense heat, and the sun-kissed scent of her.

Then she was gone, dashing indoors.

He recoiled stumbling on the curb, his mind feeling steeped in fizzy juices.

It had lasted both seconds and eternity and still seemed to be happening. After a while (Eli had no idea how long) he realized he was standing alone staring at her house.

He managed the walk home though he couldn't remember his feet touching the ground.

9

He glided into the Try 'N' Save car park, choosing a space close to the entrance.

Armed with a list and a trolley he proceeded into the-single-man-dash. An easy spot as those participating can be seen power walking around the aisles. It says I have ELSEWHERE to be and IMPORTANT things to be doing.

In Jones's case, this was rereading an *Ira Levin* novel. Things had been different when he had been with his wife, Rachel. Their visits had been slow, stress-free circuits. Their conversation's belonging to a couple deeply (perhaps even a little too much) engrained with one another.

Jones knew the past could appear rose-tinted, but he could not recall a lousy moment they had shared in this place. Remembering his history settled him.

Upon finishing, he joined the queue at Lois Campbell's till.

When it was his turn she recited, 'would you like a hand with … ' then cried 'Jones, what have you been doing with yourself?'

'Daydreaming,' he replied and flashed her a smile.

'You haven't been in over a week.'

He felt his lips falter askew.

'You know me, I make this stuff last.'

Three crates of beer beeped by. *There goes more of the retirement package.*

'I suppose you've been busy with your new job.'

'Job,' he asked?

'Your new one,' she said nodding. 'Your part of The Renegades again at least that's what I've been told. Do you remember the old days, I used to follow you guys around like a whipped puppy?'

'Sorry, but I haven't taken a job with the Renegades.'

Lois frowned at him. The recycled air coursed up his arms. He shivered, attempting to keep his face controlled while his insides rearranged.

'Well, that's what I heard,' remarked Lois. 'Debra Turner told me … I wonder what she was talking about. Anyway, what I am jawing on for, that will be fifty-four pound exact'.

'Fifty-four pound, right, right…'

Jones shoved his debit card into the reader. As it was read, he labored his items quickly into the trolley.

'See you next time,' Lois said as he retrieved his card. He responded with a curt nod and a grunt, already aimed for the exit. He needed to be home.

One of the trolley wheels was broken.

What had been bearable on the shops' smooth floor became tedious as he hit the pot-holed car park. Yet, Jones shoved on until he spotted the figure surveying his vehicle.

He knew him, of course, even if his back was turned. He knew him by the way he filled his uniform and by his scarped buzz cut.

This was Ben Cartwright, and he was an arsehole. To be precise, he was a lap dog with a superiority complex.

Jones changed from idle to approach.

'Still, playing with kids,' Ben greeted, charmingly.

Time trickled by at the rate of jam emptying from an upturned jar.

Jones kept quiet. Ben rocked on his heels, changed tactics, and sided by him.

'Brandon said he gave you guys decent pay. You think that would get you something better than this piece of junk. I heard you were on his payroll'.

Jones clamped his tongue from speaking what he really wanted to say. He could read in the gloating face that Ben wanted him to let loose. He was even leaning to receive a punch.

Jones responded low and slow.

'I think you have more experience of that than me.'

Ben's face became blank. He made to speak, but Jones couldn't help himself.

'If this is the part where you pretend to be Dirty Harry I gotta say I'm tired of repeats.'

The Ford tooted in sync with a flash of its taillights as Jones hit the unlock button. He proceeded to fill his boot with groceries. Although Ben had fled long before he was finished, he still felt eyes upon him. A familiar sensation that now sickened him. He needed to be home.

The line had been neat, but it was a masquerade. Lois's remarks and Ben's gloating were like the weights on a drowning man. His chest felt tight recalling what they had said. He tried to think not about them, but it was like trying to not think about pink elephants. He needed to get home, only there would he feel safe.

Tenderly, Eli inspected his face.

He touched the yellow splotches that were his bruises. They didn't look so bad amongst his new peach complexion, which was thanks to afternoon football with Andrew.

Heather called it his Simpsons look.

As long as they were healing, he didn't care what he was called.

They were the last reminder of Dom, Fern, and Michael. Yes, the student body continued to chatter. And yes the school board was in 'consultation.' But he had Jones and friends; the time in which he spent with them desensitized him to it all.

Eli stepped backward from the sink: not seeing the bruises.

'Hurry up, you're missing the good part,' hollered Ryan. Downstairs, *Top Gear* roared at full volume.

Kate hated it. She pretended to fall out with him ever since he discovered a liking for the show. Happiness curled across his face, watching it was the closest he felt to Ryan.

He descended the stairs, aware that sleep would come soon. Beyond was school.

He liked to say he thought of his friends equally and would have even acted affronted if someone forced the issue but really his thoughts magnetized toward Heather.

She had become a star, and he was her sole admirer. Though Eli would never articulate this. He found the image perfectly romanticized. Eli accepted it no matter how cringe-worthy it would be to say out loud. Once more, he never strayed far from the memory of their kiss.

He believed himself to be hers.

Slipping into the living room and his ritual seat, he quaked for the program to end.

He had seen her once that weekend in the doorway of her home. He had walked there with Andrew to invite her to the cinema with them. As he did, he had grown highly sensitive to Andrew's presence beside him.

Squeals and pounding feet could be heard from the house's interior behind her as she peered through the gap.

'I'm a bit busy,' she had squeaked, shutting the door in their faces.

This was not enough for his infatuation.

Tomorrow, he hummed in thought, *would be better.*

This proved to be sadly difficult as Andrew was alone at the school gates.

He shrugged and said, 'maybe she's sick.'

She wasn't. Eli found her encircled by a dozen cackling harpies she called friends. The memory of their judgmental stares and their grating laughter was enough to deter him from approaching.

He would speak to her in class when she sat beside him. Except only Andrew did. Doubt wormed at him. The same happened in the next lesson and in the next one. The doubt progressing that his teachers might as well be speaking from the bottom of a lake.

Eli chanced an encounter as they emptied out of a class. She glided past in tow with her flock, their movements reminding him of birds in formation.

'Heather, how was your weekend?' he asked.

'Fine,' she said lightly, coldly and without pause.

The birds cackled and that feverish doubt transformed into an understanding.

'Maybe she's in a mood,' offered Andrew.

It surprised Eli to hear hurt in his new friend's voice. They watched the flock swan on turning heads, their exuding presence suggesting their awareness and expectancy of this. Heather was at the front.

Eli felt something fragile tearing inside his chest as he watched her.

Images splashed before his very eyes, pictures of him and her writing, of their sweet kiss (his first) on that blistering day, of her hand in his as she guided him from Dom and the others. There were more, dozens, some small, like her crooked smirk of a smile, or large, like when she had waited on him on his first day back, bruised and battered.

Sandwiched between each image were others. These were of nameless staring faces. Eli recognized those belonging to the flock that had just passed.

He heard there chattering, crazed voices, all crawling at him for information.

'You okay,' asked Andrew?

He was fighting his tears. His jaw locked with the effort.

Through, gritted teeth, he heaved a response, 'yeah, I'm fine.'

'You're not really here today, are you?' asked Jones. This was after the fifth time attempt at trying to play *Johnny. B. Good.* The pads of his fingertips ached from the effort.

'Guess not,' he said.

They sat on the porch as they had done for all their lessons.

'Sorry,' he said. 'It's not that I'm not interested … '

'You've just got other things on your mind,' finished Jones. 'I know, I remember being twelve, so much responsibility. You know my mother made me do my homework the moment I got home, can you imagine that cruelty'.

Jones grinned over the body of his guitar at him.

What he had discovered about the guitarist was very little. He knew he had been married and that his wife had died, though he did not know how she had. He knew he had a son who worked in Belfast as a solicitor. He also knew his grin to be infectious.

Other than that he knew nothing.

Thinking such thoughts made him remember Jones and the officer again. He had yet to ask how they knew each other.

'Well, if we're not in the mood for practice, we shouldn't let the time go to waste,' said Jones, standing up and walking inside.

Eli followed, hugging his guitar to him.

The front of Jones's house was open plan, with the left-hand side functioning as a living room and the right as a kitchen. Though it was always impeccably clean, it was crammed with books, CDs and what Jones called 'vinyl.'

Jones had one of these in his hands.

To Eli, it was massive in comparison to the CDs he knew. There was also something about its slick coal-black surface that was mysterious.

Before he placed on the platform, Jones paused.

'Your distraction today, it's not over something about me?' he asked.

His worried tone made Eli frown.

'No,' he said blushing.

Please, don't ask me what it's about, he thought at the same time.

Jones didn't instead he nodded and said, 'good.'

'We might not be able to play, but that doesn't mean we can't continue your education,' said Jones. 'This is called *Summertime In England*. It's by *Van Morrison,* who is from Northern Ireland'.

What transpired in the next fifteen minutes and thirty-nine seconds would stay with Eli for his life. He knew little about music; in the same way, he knew little about Jones. He knew only what he heard on the radio. Sean and Rosa Allen had never been into music in a big way. Everything that Jones presented to him was new.

This was much the same.

He remembered feeling lighter, of being lifted by what he was hearing, though he moved not an inch during the song's entire duration. From reading, he knew the word beautiful could be used to describe a person or a place, but not a song. Yet as listened that was the word that fixed in his head. And when it concluded he found Jones's face grinning at him so broad his salt and pepper beard was parallel to his eyes.

'Yeah, man,' Jones cooed at him.

Eli learned another thing about Jones then. He was becoming his best friend.

10

Eli's chance to talk to Heather came at the end of lunch one day.

The bell had chimed summoning the student body back to class. Eli filtered into a position in the flowing mass and by some miracle found Heather in front of him. What was even more miraculous was that she was without the harpies.

He called her name.

'Hi, Eli,' she sighed after a pause.

To his delight, they folded into the same stepping rhythm. It was short-lived as Heather kept her gaze straight ahead, her books clutched to her chest.

'I was wondering if you wanted to hang out. We could walk home … '

'I can't, I'm hanging out with Jamie and Debra after school. I've got to get to class'.

The clap of her heels increased as she gained speed.

'Hey, I'm trying to talk to you. What the hell we're supposed to be friends?' said Eli.

'I've got to get to class,' she replied.

'And,' he yelled, indignantly.

The corridor captured his ferocity and amplified it with echoes.

Heather flinched from him; her gaze was sad and pitying. He hated her then.

Slowly and without an answer, she left him, disappearing into the gloom of the corridor. Eli made no move to follow, and in doing so, he knew he would not attempt to talk to her again.

As he added this embarrassing scene to his already overbearing feeling of shame, a door creaked open to his right. Whispering voices issued from within speaking excitably.

He stepped into the male bathroom and the attentions of three sixth years.

'Thank god,' sighed the one on the left, whose hair reminded him of a filthy lampshade.

'Shit kid you almost gave me a heart attack,' chuckled the one on the right.

'What are you doing?' Eli asked.

'Hey, your that kid that kills first years,' said the one in the middle.

He had a pin badge on his blazer that read, THE RENEGADES RULE. Eli had never met the three before but from the pungent stink of smoke, their wispy attempts at facial hair and their greased, long hair he could guess what clique they belonged to.

From experience, the Stoner's were not a group to be feared but somehow being recognized made Eli withdraw.

'No way, serious,' said the right.

Three pairs of beady, twinkling eyes exchanged glances. Eli's well-trained feet tensed to run.

'Hey kid, fancy skiving?' asked the middle.

Eli relaxed, they weren't interested in adding to his bruised face, they wanted to hang, and ultimately pry some information from him about what happened. With the memory of Heather raw in his head, he said, 'sure.'

Jones knew Harold was sixty-four.

The man that stood in his neighbor's doorway looked older. Jones remembered that the carer's car had been in the driveway earlier.

Without thinking, Jones's mouth took over.

'Hello, oh it's you,' he said, feigning disappointment.

'Pat said you'd be out. Be a good sport and bugger off down the shops would ya, your ladies in need of a good servicing and a good servicing is what I aim to give'.

Harold, who had leaped backward at the volume of Jones's voice, cocked his ear. Jones heard it to, a disbelieving giggle from the back of the house.

'You're a funny man,' grumbled Harold lowly.

Jones flashed his Cheshire cat grin.

'I came by to see if I could use your hedge cutters,' he said.

'Well come on in, I can use them to cut your head off,' said Harold.

Jones followed him through cool shadows to the kitchen chuckling.

'Coffee?' asked his neighbor.

Jones accepted, blinded by the sun's glare beaming through the glass doors at the kitchen's rear. As his sight returned, he spotted Pat haloed in light. Her figure was crone like, buckled into a motorized wheelchair, which she had jokingly christened her 'Death Star.'

He stepped forward and placed a loud, smacking kiss on her cheek. Pat giggled a schoolgirl's giggle, her shoulders squeezed tight.

'Get away you old dog,' she shooed. 'Shouldn't you be working? We were told you're playing in The Renegades again, congratulations. I was telling Harold I hope the Dollar's got wheelchair access ... though I won't be dancing to you like the old days. I was something then, if you'd have caught sight of me, well it could have been you putting this ring on my finger. I still can't believe you never saw us back in those days'.

A tear trailed a silvery line down her left cheek.

'Your still something, Pat' said Jones. 'I probably did see you both, but at the time, my mind was a little ... spacey'.

'Waster,' quipped Harold in his John Wayne growl.

'Sorry to say this but I haven't taken any job with them,' he told them.

Harold and Pat shared a glance.

'Well, that's what we heard,' said Pat. 'I'm sure you could get a job with those guys no problem, especially seeing as they're missing a guitarist. It would be brilliant to see you on stage again.'
Before he could respond, Harold interrupted saying, 'Jones came over to borrow the cutters again. We'll just go get them. The man has a schedule to keep'.
Thankfully, Harold led him away from Pat's inquiry.

'What's got you so frazzled then?' asked Harold.
They were in his shed, which smelt of hot sap and dust. Harold removed his hedge cutters from their place on the wall. As he turned to him, he said, 'it would be good for you, you know, get you out of the house.'
'It's all just a joke,' replied Jones a little too quickly. 'Anyway, I have Pat and you as a reason for me to get out of the house.'
'I hardly consider walking next door as getting out,' said Harold.
'You were right,' said Jones. 'I do have a schedule to keep. My dead wife's garden needs to be attended to'.
He grasped one handle of the hedge cutters. Harold held onto the other.
They were men of a particular generation, and Jones was relying on that oppressive upbringing that had taught them a man's problems were his own so Harold wouldn't press the topic further. In return, he would not ask what had happened this morning to cause his neighbor to look so glum. They did not speak any of this out loud but communicated by the harsh regard, in which they stared at one another.
Eventually, Harold let go of the cutters.

Ryan had the same idea as Jones did towards taking advantage of the days' heat.

This was standard practice in Northern Ireland after a few days of hot weather. People all across the country could be found attending to their gardens in a flurry of determination, not knowing when the rains would return, which were so frequent they had become cataloged by the population by their severity. The whole pursuit could be considered pointless due to the country's unpredictable weather, but that did not stop people partaking in this ritual every summer. Eli believed this was down to hope; that they hoped this year would be the 'good summer.'

It never was.

Unfortunately, Eli was quickly roped into the campaign. He was writing on the slightly moldy deckchair in the back garden when Ryan swaggered outside. He half-watched his godfather survey the unkempt yard, inhaling deeply like some mountaineer about to embark on a treacherous journey.

'You can help me with this, can't you?' Ryan asked on spotting him.

Eli's eyes met Ryan's after a slow, arched trajectory. His godfather's enthusiasm beamed down upon him like a second sun. There was no refusing it.

'Sure,' he answered after a pause.

'Great, you can cut the grass, and I'll weed the flowerbeds, come on, come on.'

Moving as if his body was reanimated from the dead, Eli rose.

The lawnmowers handlebars came to below his Adam's apple. The old machine spurted and farted black smoke as he shoved it against grass that had not just grown but colonized. Yet, seeing that Ryan was suffering just as much, he refused to complain or stop. All the naïve ambition in his godfather was lost, as the garden became an obstacle course. It fought back with brambles and thorns and relentless heat. And Eli oddly found he did not mind as the task briefly occupied him.

Breathless and filthy they collapsed onto the deckchair. Ryan reached and pulled Eli's notebook out from under him.

'What's this?' he asked.

'It's a story I've been working on,' said Eli.

'For school?' asked Ryan.

Eli shook his head and shrugged.

'Can I read it?'

A nod followed by another shrug.

The story was not long, and Ryan read in silence. When he finished, he produced his wallet and gave him a five-pound note from it.

'This is really good you should write more often,' was all he said.

Eli examined the bill and decided he would.

The hedge cutter blades chomped at the greenery, leaving a trail of discarded branch limbs.

Jones's muscles were screaming, but he refused to slacken. A constant regurgitation of congratulations roared in his skull as he attempted to drown them out with work.

He never heard Maria Hunter's approach. When she laid a hand on his shoulder, he jumped.

'Holy sh ... ' he cried.

'Watch out,' squeaked Maria, back-stepping.

The pair surveyed each other for a moment, each clutching at their chests.

'Sorry,' he gasped. 'It was my fault.'

An average person would have politely dismissed this. They would have said, 'not at all, I shouldn't have crept up like that.' Maria Hunter was not like everyone else. She was the type that expected apologizes, not give them.

As Jones was well used to her, he wasn't surprised by her response.

'A little more care perhaps next time,' she said and smiled a smile that could shatter an iceberg.

'I happened to see you working and wanted to come round and say congratulations. I think it's great to see you stepping back into the working world'.

Jones felt his hand tighten on the hedge cutters. He noticed she actually hadn't congratulated him.

'It's inspiring really seeing a man of your age attempt a second career,' said his other neighbor. 'Less chance of you impaling someone with those.'

'Yes,' replied Jones. His jaw was gritted.

'How did you manage to find out about my news?'

'Oh, I heard it in town from some fellow with a weird English accent. I couldn't really tell if he was putting it on or not, I thought he was a bit of a pervert actually. Anyway, he told me.'

'Well, thank you for your ... words, Maria,' said Jones. 'But I must be getting back to this. Might get the chance to nearly impale someone else'.

'Yes,' she said unamused.

Maria took a left at the end of his drive. He saw she was practically skipping.

Brandon Weir thought of the situation as a lit powder keg.

They were all waiting on it going bang, though no one would have thought this from how they appeared.

English and Lucy were playing chess on the shop counter. Karl and Shane were quietly arguing over who shot first, *Han* or *Greedo*. He was reading *The Belfast Telegraph*.

The Gallery had only a few customers. There were even less after Jones stormed in and the explosion they all anticipated occurred.

'Seventeen,' shouted Jones.

The four behind Brandon were already laughing loudly.

'Seventeen people have congratulated me in the last two days about joining your stupid band. What did you do, phone everyone in the telephone book? I don't take kindly to people dicking around in my life, Brandon. Will you stop laughing'.

'Look, Jones, it was just a joke, nothing sinister,' cooed Brandon.

He folded his newspaper closed and stepped away from the countertop.

'Tell that to Ben Cartwright,' muttered Jones, darkly. This jab made no dent in Brandon's passive expression.

'I can't help if some individuals acted inappropriately and anyway it worked didn't it, you're here.'

'We were only trying to help,' piped English.

'Now, at least your out of that cage you call home,' said Shane while scratching his rotund belly.

'Who are you to judge me?' snapped Jones.

Jones stared at them, his face a thunderstorm.

People create their own private lives with a select few. Though the people before him had never been allowed into his inner sanctum, they had not been just scenery. They had been his friends at a younger, more careless time. By some miracle, they all stood before him in a manner that said gosh-isn't-this-something-we've-made-it-through.

Through what exactly, Jones couldn't fathom. Age, he would later guess. Currently, he was struggling to control the fear seeping into him, constricting his chest that he was practically hyperventilating.

There was a reason why he had pulled away from them, why he had built a life with Rachel, his wife, which didn't include his old friends. It was in his nature to be excessive, and it had led to bad habits. Habits he could not risk being exposed to again.

'Hey, my offer has gotta be better than teaching guitar to some hoodlum,' said Brandon. 'How did you get mixed up with that boy anyway?'

Jones was quiet. Fury sizzled his fear into vapor, and he answered as a sweat-less, coiled instrument.

'That boy is none of your concern,' he said. 'Nose's have gotten too used to sticking into other people's business around here. I suggest you keep them out if you want them to remain uninjured and intact'.

'We had your best interests at heart,' said English, his voice timid, ashamed. 'It's not good for you to hide away out there in the woods all by yourself. Plus, this is what you were meant to be doing, playing with us again, not working for some security firm or retirement'.

'That's my decision to make,' Jones said to his old friend. 'Leave me alone.'

He exited the store in silence bar the crystallized twinkle of the shop doorbell.

'That's the legendary guitarist you guys won't shut up about,' said Lucy. 'He's got nice manners for a supposed friend, and that's checkmate English.'

'Mother ... '

'He just needs to blow off some stream,' sighed Shane. 'He's been cooped up too long, all that restless energy for the stage is bursting to get out he'll come round.'

'Didn't seem very energetic to me just like the rest of you,' retorted Lucy.

The debate that rose up next was nothing but a din in Brandon's ears. He stared out of the windowpane, believing that the conversation had gone exactly as it had meant to.

11

Jones watched the kid.

'No, no, no, you've got to be faster,' he said. 'Your fingers have to be like this, see? Timing, it's all about timing'.

Jones leaned backward, relinquishing his grip on his guitar.

'Where are you today?' he asked.

The kid's hands flopped onto his knees.

'Dom was at the school today,' said Eli. 'He didn't come in, he couldn't. The gates were closed, but a few people talked to him. I didn't, to be honest, I had forgotten about him. I hadn't forgotten about what he did, but I forgot to think of him, you know?'

He spoke again, voicing an afterthought that caused his forehead to wrinkle.

'I wonder what will happen to him,' he said.

'What do you think will happen to him?' asked Jones.

'He'll be expelled ... though the school still hasn't decided anything,' replied Eli.

'And that doesn't make you happy?'

'No, it does,' Eli said, quickly. 'It's just, I'll be there tomorrow and the next day and I just wonder where will he be?'

'My, my,' said Jones. 'I didn't realize I was speaking to someone of such empathy, how noble.'

The kid told him to shut up. He did, for a moment, in which he pondered over his recent experiences.

It had been a week since he had gone to The Gallery and had spoken to Brandon. As a result, it seemed, the congratulations from Hazel's populous had ceased.

Yet, his frustration occupied him more than ever.

It was the words of his old friends that his mind seemed to regurgitate to him, becoming ghosts that haunted his daily living. Shane calling his home a cage. The offer that Brandon made as he celebrated his retirement from Anderson's security firm.

Roy, when he asked him, *'what happens when he finds out his teacher is afraid to even go out his own door?'* They replayed maddeningly in his head now as he studied the kid.

Can I really do this, Jones thinks?

As he does, he already hears him self speak and is astounded by his fake jovial ease.

'A rude yet noble being apparently,' he hears himself saying.

'I am glad that you've said something as I am not blind to how early you've been turning up on my door. You've been arriving earlier every day for the past week. As if your capable of moving at some speed that time ceases to hinder you, remarkable. I thought, before telling your godparents of course, that I would inquire into this phenomenon.'

Jones gazed down at him with eyes that were dark and sorrowful.

'Eli, what are you doing?' he asked.

The kid's head hung low until all he could see was his guitar.

Jones felt his throat tighten.

'Don't try that sly appearance with me your not fooling anybody,' he snapped.

'There's nothing there for me,' Eli snapped back. 'Its boredom and they always staring ... '

'Well, they are gonna stare,' roared Jones. 'Face it and let them. They will always stare. Trust me, I've gone through some shit, just look at me, but here's a secret that nobody says out loud in school. They all think they're being stared at, who can blame them, kids are all hyped on hormones and the self-centered belief they're the centers of the universe. What's really the problem here?'

Eli gripped the neck of his guitar.

'This feels important. This feels like me. I can't be that there,' said Eli.

Another moment of silence passed as Jones observed the kid holding his guitar.

'But it is important,' said Jones, inclining with his head in the school's direction.

'What's not is how you feel, which sounds shitty but understand this. Those folks that you think are so interested in you are too busy worrying about what everyone else thinks of them to worry about you. Know that, and you can focus on what matters'.

'Knowing it is your secret weapon. Plus, and I know this sounds corny, but that place will take you places if you work at it. I'm gonna ask you for a favor. Give it a chance, keep your head down, and you might find there's something in it for you. Your past follows you like a shadow, Eli. That place can offer you a future beyond it'.

With reluctance and after some time, the kid nodded his head.

'That doesn't mean hiding down the street until we are due to hang out now cos I'll check.'

In the end, they shook on it. Jones's calloused hand swallowed Eli's tiny one that was growing rougher with each practice.

For the remainder of the lesson, Jones kept his cool. At least he believed the kid never suspected anything of his internal turmoil. He was clearly mulling over what had been said to him.

The sensation did not dissipate after the kid had left. Nor did Jones look away from the drive where he had strolled down, disappearing behind the greenery.

Tears beaded in the corners of his eyes as he stared. His chest heaved unsteadily for breath as his own words echoed in his head.

Jones's thumb wandered over the rough surface of his palm. It belonged to the hand that had shaken Eli's. It had been a firm shake, and the kid had given him a tight squeeze before letting him go. Jones was more than confident that he would give the school a chance. With that thought, Jones closed his hand into a fist. He stomped inside and made a phone call. When he hung up, his shirt was clinging to his sweaty torso.

Something had changed with Jones.

As to the cause or the why Eli had no clue. Nor had he noticed when this change occurred as school had absorbed his concentration for the past few weeks. This had nothing to do with his classes but his renewed friendship with Andrew.

It was a different friendship to the one that had existed before. The competitive edge of their previous exchanges having disappeared.

The mutual shunning of Heather, and to a more considerable extent, the entire student body, had created a consideration for each other.

Distracted by this, it was a surprise when he noticed how tired Jones now appeared.

Their lessons changed to and now consisted mostly of listening to music rather than playing. Eli kept this a secret from his godparents. Jones had refused to take any payment for music lessons, so it wasn't like they were out of pocket. Plus, despite Jones's fatigued state, they were still enjoyable. Though, the weird exchange that occurred between Jones and the police officer continued to play on Eli's mind.

Then they were the outings.

These were times when Jones was literally bursting with energy. He would take Eli fishing in the many rivers around Hazel, or to bookstores a town over. Most of these jaunts were trips to The Gallery to expand Eli's ever-growing collection of music. It was on one such trip that Jones proposed that they have dinner at Mia's Garden, a restaurant situated in Hazel's center. His friend's boisterous state changed to something Eli had yet to experience in his friend: anxiety.

This seemed to radiate from Jones as they entered the restaurant. Eli observed his friend's eyes bulge at the two women in charge of the places seating arrangements.

After he spoke, however, it became clear it was only one of them that disturbed him.

'Hi, Mia it's been a long time,' said Jones, tentatively. The woman looked as shocked to see him as he did her, her eyebrows disappearing behind her fringe.

She was beautiful. Eli had never used that label on anyone except his mother and Kate in his life. But he found it now necessary because he had never seen a woman like her.

'It has been,' she replied. Her voice was smoky and cool.

Eli's face burned. He had never mentally undressed a woman but now found he couldn't help himself, and there seemed plenty to undress.

Thankfully, he hadn't been noticed yet. Jones and Mia had only eyes for each other. He noted that the woman beside Mia had faded into the background as best she could.

'What can I ... we do for you?'

'We could do with a bit of refueling,' said Jones. 'I've told this young man that this is the best place in town for food. He's keen to see what the fuss is about'.

Mia's eyes fell on him. They were like molten chocolate. Eli felt his pelvis quake.

'Really,' she said. 'And what type of food do you like.'

All memory of hunger evaded him.

'I'm not really a big eater,' he mumbled.

'Well, we can change that,' she said and smiled. It was like being hit in the face with a soft pillow.

'Sarah, will you show these two to a table?'

Sarah materialized back into the foreground like an apparition. She politely escorted them to a table at the heart of the dining area. They ordered drinks, and she hastily disappeared.

'She's a friend of yours?' Eli asked.

'A long time ago,' Jones replied, stiffly.

Their drinks arrived.

'What are you doing?' asked Eli after the waiter had left.

'Just making sure nobodies spat in it.'

Cautiously, Jones raised the pint to his lips and took a sip.

'How come you've never mentioned your friend before?' asked Eli.

There was a pause in which Jones observed him with a heavy look.

'I don't think I ever told you this, but I used to be in a band,' said Jones.

'We got together at sixteen and were awful. We continued to be awful for some time, but we were friends, and it was a laugh, and eventually, something clicked. People started paying us to do gigs rather than boo us off stage. It was fun. Some of them still play together at the Emerald Dollar; it's a bar in town. They've asked me to join them again'.

Before Eli could voice his enthusiasm, Sarah appeared. She placed two bowls of steaming soup before each of them.

'Mrs. Green says that she still remembers what you like and that there will be no need for you to order anything,' Sarah explained before vanishing.

A spicy wholesome scent wavered off the food.

'I think I love this Mrs. Green,' said Eli, having tasted a mouthful.

A comic yet somber grunt escaped Jones. Noticeable enough that Eli regarded his companion.

'Are you going to join this band then?'

'I was offered the job almost two months ago ... '

Eli eyed him over his bowl, his spoon resting in the delicious liquid.

'I grew up in a house of music,' said Jones. 'My mother sang, my father played and taught my brother and me. Back then; it came to all of us, as easy as breathing'.

'I've watched the way you've taken to it, and I was the same. It's a new world in front you and all you want to do is dive in and explore. That's the way I used to see it'.

'You've told me the bad shit that's happened to you. So I'll be honest with you, perhaps selflessly honest, but I consider you a friend. Strangely, you might be the best friend I've had in some time.'

Jones took a long drain from his glass before continuing.

'When I played in that band I lost sight of that original idea,' he said. 'I started to believe that to be in that world, you had to do certain things, and it led to bad habits. We were pretty big. We didn't write our own stuff just did covers, but we played them like they were our own. We toured north and south of the border. I had this ritual every night; I'd checked my amp and lines. Just a little good luck charm, we all had them. Mine was practical considering the dives we were playing in. I stopped doing it, though, as the drugs I was on were demanding too much of my attention. They were my new charm'.

Jones finished his glass in one gulp.

'They didn't bring good luck. My amp sparked halfway through a show and set the stage curtains on fire. We got out … some of the audience didn't. I quit the band after that. It's taken me a long time to even pick up my guitar again.'

Eli's face was muscle. His blue eyes stared as sharp as a diamond's edge and as remorseful as an adult's.

Sarah appeared to retrieve their empty bowls. She replaced them with plates buried in pasta that he had never seen before and red sauce the color of gore.

'Beef ravioli,' she announced then departed.

'Why, tell me this?'

'I took the job,' said Jones, arming himself with a knife and fork.

Eli stared bewildered.

'Do you remember the conversation we had two weeks ago about keeping your head down,' he asked? 'I wanted to vomit telling you that because I am a hypocrite. I advised you on an opportunity when I was too scared to grab any. I'm still fucking scared. Life rarely works out like a story, not every choice is a dramatic episode, and it is quieter than that. I've watched you these two weeks keeping your head down, and I thought if you can choose something good for you then why can't I'.

'My first gig is in June. I'm already rehearsing like mad, which is why I've been tired. Would you like to come and watch it? Kate and Ryan have already agreed to be your chaperone's'.

'Hell, yes,' cheered Eli. 'What's your band's name?'

'The Renegades,' replied Jones.

Eli stared at him in disbelieve.

They slouched backward hoping their chairs won't break.

Jones moped at his lips with a napkin. Eli grinned with triumphant delight. They had conquered the main dish and prayed no one would mention desert.

Feverish whispering erupted from the podium where Mia and Sarah stood. They were careful not to look in their direction.

Jones followed his gaze and then winked at him.

'I didn't just bring you for the food,' he said. 'And your not the only one I wanted to invite to my long-awaited comeback.'

Eli watched him rise and suck in his bloated stomach. He observed him approach the two women who immediately ceased their conversation.

Jones muttered something to Mia he couldn't quite hear. Her response was to lash her palm across his left cheek with a mighty slap.

The restaurant fell into silence.

Jones sank back into his chair, nursing the side of his head.
'Maybe she isn't a fan,' Eli said, giggling.

12

Eli could not remember the night's beginning. There was just the show, an event hugged in writhing dark and colossal noise. It was a hot poker on Eli's mind: magical in its ability to diminish all surrounding memory. He vaguely recalled the troll-like bouncer's holding the door for them. Kate told him they had been escorted to a reserved booth. He could remember and describe the texture of the booth's leather as well as Heather's skin but not the escort.

He was gleefully lost.

There were so many people. Not just ordinary people. He had seen ordinary people earlier that day as he sat his last exam.

They had been nervous and insular, whereas these people were joyous and open. He watched them, noting their movements, the clink of glasses, and the occasional outburst of hacking laughter that topped the general murmur but above all, he observed the anticipation that loomed in the air. It was an intense static that he sometimes felt upon hearing that final Friday bell in school, only much more powerful.

Learning about The Renegades had been accessible due to their popularity. Yet the information he gained was completely unsatisfactory as his most significant source of knowledge refused to tell him anything. Jones.

'I don't want to spoil anything for you by giving the game away' he had said, grinning wickedly.

This left Eli to his imaginings, which were, sadly not as apt as he would have liked.

What did it matter, he was here now?

'What do you think the first song will be?' he asked his godparents.

'I dunno ... doggie in the window' replied Ryan.

Kate giggled while Eli shot him a scolding look. This was serious.

Though seated, he had a clear view of the stage directly opposite. The heads of those on the dance floor named The Pit, according to Ryan, were just below his eye line.

Black curtains withheld whatever sight he was about to see.

The Dollar itself was cavernous with its beamed church-like ceiling. Eli was peering upwards into the shadows when all light winked out.

The dark held him.

For a few moments before the first catcalls, he was alone.

He could no longer feel Kate and Ryan's presence beside him. His throat tightened as he breathed on the hot, moist air. Then it came out of the darkness.

A sound. An electrified sound that was as thick as syrup.

Instant recognition rose from the crowd as a cacophony of cheers. A beam of white light extended from the heavens.

There he was in the same clothes he had on when Eli first met him; rugged blue jeans and a white shirt, with his ruby guitar hanging around his neck. And Eli loved him. In that second, seeing him there, he realized he had always loved him.

He was playing a sleazy jig, legs pumping to the rhythm as the band collapsed behind him. Lights pulsed and shot rainbows. The group traversed the stage to the crowd's ecstasy. Their music was an intentional chaotic shuffle that Ryan proclaimed was the 'Start It Up by The Rolling Stones.

Making out the ear-to-ear grins on his godparent's faces made him realize his own. His cheeks were hurting, but he didn't care. He didn't want that feeling or the night to end.

As soon as he wished that the first song was over.

'HELLO, HAZEL,' bellowed the lead singer. A figure that looked like *Neil Gaiman's Sandman* had escaped the page to be a rock god.

The crowd rejoiced riotously at being addressed.

'WELCOME TO THE DOLLAR, WELCOME TO YOUR FRIDAY NIGHT AND A MOST OF ALL WELCOME TO THE PAAARRRTTTTTY'

The next few songs consisted of upbeat, energetic numbers. These ranged from a recent radio hit to *AC/DC's Thunderstruck*. Ryan put names to each song they played. At one point, Kate leaned in close so through the sweat-soaked air, he felt her breath on his earlobe.

'What do you think of it?'

He looked at her.

'It's brilliant,' he told her.

She ruffled his hair as he turned back to the show. He watched the crowd, molten shadows that danced beneath the sweeping lights.

Usually, Eli would hate being amongst such a mob of people. Not now. This wasn't a handful of individuals shackled by individual desires and selfishness but a collection of beings with a sole purpose: to see a show. Though, young Eli could discern from watching them sway and sing and scream that the ramifications of seeing The Renegades were a chance to let loose. That is how he viewed tonight having woken up this morning with an exam to attend. That desire was just as fragrant in the hot air as the musk of sweat. It was universal.

And even more than that Eli was apart. The thought thrilled him.

As the night spun on, several moments became branded in his memory. Jones, Shane (the bass player) and English (the drummer) becoming a violent cyclone of mounting noise as they jammed together. How the lights dimmed to one, and the crowd grew silent as Lucy (the pianist) performed alone. Her song was melancholy and redemptive.

Ryan sang every word then told him its name: *Not Dark Yet* by *Bob Dylan.*

The original would become one of Eli's favorites, but he would always remember that first listen in The Dollar. He would forever see that skinny woman playing like her soul was on fire.

He remembered Ryan's face and the feel of Kate's hand clasping his in the dark. He remembered seeing not just relief, but contentment on Jones's face as he played.   And he remembered wanting more.

Jones had been right. It was a whole new world open before him, and he wanted to dive in.

'How did I do?' asked Jones.

Eli raised his left hand, held it flat, and tilted it side to side.

'Little shit,' said Jones and laughed.

The Dollar was closed. The celebration for Jones's return encircled them, though they were being carried out with burnt-out energy by the band and staff. Like before, Eli and his family were being shown every courtesy by Brandon and had been allowed to stay.

Eli had Jones to himself at a table. Kate and Ryan were drilling Shane and Karl (the saxophonist) on the night's performance with a zealous hunger that Eli didn't share. He felt the same as Jones. Drained, yet content.

The two let their eyes roam through the festive fray. There was English in the corer, cigarette smoldering from his scowl. Beside him, a comical opposite was his wife whose weight could compete with that of a beluga whale. She burned them with a disdainful pout.

Brandon was behind the bar pouring drinks while joking with his staff. The Sandman like singer had vanished somewhere at the same time the pixie looking piano player had. Harold and Pat, other friends of Jones, were sat holding hands and drinking wordlessly despite the din.

'How was your exam today?' asked Jones.

Eli thought. He raised his left hand, held it flat, and tilted it side to side.

Act 2

The Big Crash

2010 - 2011

December – March

1

Mr. Logue shuffled his papers and coughed. 'I must apologize for the mess,' he sighed. 'It's been a rather busy day what with these parent/teacher meetings and trying to polish the school play. I'm writing it, and casting is set for when we all get back after New Year's in January, it seems like its all happening at once.'

Kate and Ryan nodded as if they understood.

'So, Eli, there isn't much I can tell you that you don't already know. His grades are high and steady, he's currently sitting on a B in most subjects, and he's the only student in lower sixth that is going to get an A in English. Let's see, every teacher reports that he is well behaved though quiet. Right now, Eli should be focusing on the future, his career, has he mentioned anything to you about it?'

Logue gazed at the couple trying to look comfortable in the classroom chairs.

They exchanged a glance that highlighted the blue file Kate held. They looked back and found the same teacher was waiting for an answer.

It wasn't like they had a problem with Mr. Logue that delayed their response. More that he looked like something on its last legs. His complexion was as industrial grey as the clouds in the window behind him. His face was a craggy Himalayan pass. And in the ebbing light, they could make out a crown of swirling dandruff above his unkempt silvery hair. In other words, it was hard not to make their first line of dialogue about the advantages of a holiday.

'Ahh ... yes he has mentioned it several times with us,' said Kate, uneasily. 'He's interested in writing.'
'Journalism,' beamed Logue. 'Well, I think that would be an excellent choice considering ... '
'No, what my wife meant was fictional writing,' interrupted Ryan.
Kate offered the blue file to the teacher.
Logue sucked in his cheeks, his grey eyes flickering between them in a debate. At last, he took the file from Kate but did not open it.
'I thought he had quit that,' said Mr. Logue. 'A few years ago I would catch your Eli writing in little jotters. The ones I confiscated were pretty good if I remember. I guess he got better at hiding them'.
'That's a few that well we think are his best ones,' said Kate. 'You should read them.'
Logue's eyes rose from the file to Kate. They were desolate and cold.
'We think he's got potential,' added Ryan.
'I'll take a look at these,' said the teacher, smiling.
He bent to the side and placed the file within a leather satchel.
'I'm going to be blunt here,' he said, leaning forward. 'That type of career is difficult to plan. There is no official course, no qualification that you can get that allows you suddenly to be publishing fiction. Even if you do manage to publish work, it's hard to make that sustainable. To be honest, it's not a realistic ambition.'
'If he is serious about this route I'd recommend that he work towards a more realistic goal in the meantime that will provide him with the means to pursue writing. That's going to be difficult because he's got to work at it like it's a second job. It takes dedication, and even then there's no guarantee'.
Logue smiled in an attempt to uplift his negativity. 'Speaking from experience if he fails, becoming a teacher is always a fallback.'

Kate inhaled severely and to the point were chords bulged in her throat. She glanced at her husband, reading his eyes she knew she was going to be the one to speak. She just needed the perfect words.

'My husband, myself and Eli are aware of all those things,' said Kate, speaking with all the sternness an experienced nurse could employ.

'But, and, I am putting it bluntly this is Eli's choice and where you failed we might find he will succeed. You should take a look at what's in the file'.

Silence ensued, in which, Kate could feel her husband's need to laugh was palpable. When it came to teachers, no one knew Kate's dislike more than Ryan. He pleasantly watched his wife locked in a staring contest with Logue. Logue blinked first.

'Well, I will happily look over his work,' he said, casually.

'And I will give him what advice I can. Is there anything else I can help you with?'

'I think that's everything,' said Kate.

Feigning sincerity, Logue bid them a good evening.

The empty corridor echoed their footsteps.

Ryan made several expressions to catch Kate's attention. Eventually, he gave up, cleared his throat, and said, 'I guess, we can look forward to Eli not getting that A in English.' Kate snorted in response. Her eyelids slightly fluttered at him as she readjusting her chin, so it broke the air before her like the prow of a ship.

'I can imagine what he thought when you put him in his place,' continued Ryan.

What he imagined was utterly correct. Logue was repeating the same sequence of words in his head as they exited the school building. Three words.

What a bitch.

Logue's keys slide into the elegant lock.

The lock belonged to a regal home, his inheritance. The elegant lock required some jimmying to work.

'Honey, I'm home,' he yelled as the door slammed closed. 'And I need a drink.'

Nothingness and no one replied to him.

To describe Logue's home as tidy would be like saying his desk was a paradise for the obsessively compulsive. That isn't to say it wasn't clean. It was clean in the parts that could be. The other parts were either buried or obstructed by climbing spires of books ranging from Greek philosophy to Russian cookery. He liked to think it gave the impression to any guest that reading was how he spent most of his time. The dust - a fine carpet of neglect - was enough for most guests to know these books were seldom explored. Logue cocooned himself with the words of mostly dead authors. The words themselves were as dead as they went unread except for the one that was haunting him. The author was *William Shakespeare,* and the story was *King Lear.*

The haunting mainly occurred in the study where Logue poured himself a drink. What he really craved was sleep, but that wasn't an option.

Clutching, his satchel he carried his drink to his writing desk. He took a sip while his eyes traveled across the desk's landscape. Balled paper, open books dissecting *King Lear's* themes and his computer hid its mahogany surface.

Logue emptied his satchel onto the desk. In his head there fizzed an acidic hatred.

It's all rubbish, he thought.

The catalyst for this awful idea was a night of heavy drinking and bragging about his literary skills to his colleagues. Unfortunately, the next day, a sober headmaster tasked him with his proposal: to modernize and write *King Lear* in a school setting.

He had yet to complete a single scene. But that's not what he had told Black.

His drink flowed through gritted teeth.

He made to set his glass down when his eyes caught something blue. He reached into the satchel, his fingers discovering sleek plastic.

The study's soft light revealed the first lines of a story through the clear sleeve that Eli Donoghue's godparents had given him earlier.

'Okay, Eli, let's see what you've got,' he sighed.

Logue sank into his cushioned chair. As he read, his cluttered surroundings faded from his notice, and a twinge of a smile grew on his lips. At one point a chuckle escaped them.

On finishing one story, he would greedily start another until there were no more.

He lit a joint and stretched out in his chair. His mind no longer fizzed but was honed to a single point: possibility. With it, he soon evaporated into dreamless oblivion.

2

The piano stamped out two progressive chords.
What followed was a roar of recognition from the
teeming audience. The accompanying brass section
(recruited for the festivities) heralded the chorus. The
crowd chanted back the words to their uproarious
delight.

Not a bad way to usher in the New Year's.

There are two types of performances in Jones's
opinion. The first is an intimate affair between the
people on stage playing in sync with a furious
determination to perfect and explore. These were
shows that featured the most improvisation, where the
crowd is featureless. The second type is where he can
see each distinctive face.

Tonight was such a show. Jones could pick out Eli and
Andrew performing awkward shuffles by the bar. He
could see Brandon serving as well as every individual
face.

Unusually, this disturbed him. It wasn't until the song
had ended and the show and his eyes scanned the
Dollar for the hundredth time that he understood why.
The person he had spent the night looking for, who he
had invited, wasn't there.

The applause could have flattened a forest. The band,
having given an encore (the setlist was comprised of
what the band considered the best songs of the
decade), returned to the stage to bow. Jones did so
vaguely, his mind spaced out from the current goings-
on.

'One hell of a night,' growled English in his ear.

'Huh,' Jones replied, eyes wide and longing.

Far from any noise, Mia held a thumb to a light switch.

Her gaze peered into the well of black that was her restaurant's dining area. She was alone, having let the staff go home, and the place was silent.

Come on, her mind said, *there's one more task to do.*

Yes, and then it's bed and back to another typical day without a stupid tradition.

She floated from behind the bar through the darkness to the kitchen side door. Her shoes clipped and clopped on the tile. The last rubbish bag awaited her.

'The company I keep,' she said.

By accident, she threw open the door with too much force. It slammed into the buildings' outer wall. The deafening silence, in which, she dwelt was shattered by the noise.

Her shoulders flinched.

The winter temperature teased at her skin. The alley beyond the threshold was dimly lit with plenty of shadowy recesses. She waited the standard Hollywood horror film time for any lurking would-be-murderer to strike and then waited some more.

Outside snow danced lazily. Mia closed her eyes and looked up. Icy, wet kisses rained on her. One landed on her eyelid, melted and ran down her cheek like a tear. A childish laugh escaped her.

Without thinking, she lifted the bag to head height and threw. It dunked into the bin with a wallop, and it was at this moment she heard the crunch of snow.

She swiped at a stray strand of fiery hair, staring at the alley's mouth.

'Hello, Jones.'

He stepped sheepishly into the light, a bottle of whiskey in his hand.

'I tried the front but didn't get an answer. I was just ... '

'Creeping around outside my home,' Mia interrupted. 'In this, in the middle of the New Year's morning.'

She wasn't surprised to see him. For some reason, it made sense that he would be here.

'What were your intentions?'

Jones seemed at a loss for words, something that pleased her.

'You know I can't think of a single excuse,' he said shrugging.

Mia's tongue rolled in her mouth while her heels ground at the snow.

'I think that bottle is cold enough,' she said. 'Come inside.'

She led the way. Her mind concentrated partly because this was her home and partly because she felt apart from the situation. As if she was an observer, not a participant.

Jones took a stool at the bar. Mia stood on the other side and poured. They both drank it neat. Steam rose from them as they did due to the restaurant's warm interior.

'I was looking for you tonight at Brandon's,' Jones announced.

'I was here.'

'You couldn't have got cover?'

'If my staff have to work, then why shouldn't I,' she said, sighing stiffly.

'That's a fair boss.'

Mia refilled their glasses and asked, 'why are you here, Jones?'

He stared into the golden liquid as if hoping it would provide the answer. His finger tapped on the rim of his glass.

'I am sorry for how we turned out, you know,' he said, gravelly.

'That's great, just took you thirty-three years to say that,' Mia remarked bitterly. She chewed at the inside of her mouth. 'How's your wife, how's your family?'

She could feel the chords on her neck strain beneath her skin.

'My wife's dead,' he said, his voice hollow. 'As for my family their visiting next week. You know that we've booked a table here, Nina's looking forward to building a snowman. I'm back with The Renegades, I'm back trying with life just like you always said for me to do.'

'You never listened to me,' she said. This time she stared into her glass. 'But you listen to that kid.'

Her lips felt like they had betrayed her in uttering those words. She no longer felt in charge but shackled to a railway line that's about to branch out over a perilous chasm.

'He comes here you know with that big friend of his. They buy ice cream, I don't think it's right'.

'What, the ice cream? Then why sell it'?

'Of course, not the fucking ice-cream,' she snapped. 'That you are his friend.'

Jones replied gently. 'I've had five years to think about that. I haven't once wanted to indulge in drugs. I won't let him down for that shit'.

He tossed his drink back.

'So you've changed, good for you. Are you here to get your old girlfriend back? She's grown up too, she might not even be the thing you want anymore if you get close enough to see her'.

Jones stared at her, angry for the first time.

'Bollocks,' he growled and tossed his drink back.

'I see you, this place and yeah you've done well, but you didn't show tonight. Just like you used to when you were pissed at me. You've not changed that much. Anyway, I've interrupted you enough; I'll let myself out. You can keep the bottle, add it to the ones at the bar'.

She called out to him as he walked away like a gunslinger from a western.

'Why are you so interested now?'

She hated hearing the desperation in her voice. Worse, she hated hearing the longing in it. 'Because we don't get to live forever ... might as well be happy in the time we've got.'

He left her to listen to the front door lock click and the gasp of air as it opened and closed. It was sometime before she rounded the bar to lock it again.

3

Eli held little expectations for his first day back. It was school, which meant the same repetitive drudgery of classes. He endured them with a long-ago developed tactic of not looking at the clock as best he could.

And it all played out as expected until the final bell. Eli wanted to sleep. His mind buzzed with notions that were more like drunken bees.

Chair legs scarped around him, pages were being shuffled. Mr. Logue was barked orders to a class already evacuating the room. He gathered his things but without urgency.

He was due to meet Andrew and walk home. Jones's family were visiting, meaning guitar lessons were on hold.

After five years, Eli had grown into a gifted musician that no longer required lessons. But he still strolled to his friend's house each day.

To him, that time on the porch with Jones extended beyond guitar tips. The closest he could come to articulate why their exchanges seemed so was that they felt like preparation. If asked for what, he would have replied for life.

Yet this thinking did little to sway his dampened mind. He had been invited to dinner with Jones and his family tonight. Nina, Jones's granddaughter, would be there. She was his age, and other than the notepads she carted about, her greatest enjoyment was to make his life hell. He must admit she was rather brilliant at it.

Before succumbing to the history of slights she had dealt upon him, he heard whispering. The source was a collection of male students huddled behind him. Eli had many talents, one was the ability to ignore people, but their whispering proved difficult.

One male detached and made his way toward him while grinning.

Eli knew him as Justin Blackthorn. He was on the rugby team with Andrew.

As expected he was tall, Labrador blonde and blessed with the looks of a hateful television presenter. The type people wanted to spit at.

'Hi there, it's Eli, isn't it,' he said, cheerfully.

'Our friend Andrew was telling us that you can get into the Dollar.'

That sleazy grin widened inhumanly.

'He said that you got in on New Year's Eve … and you got him in. Is it true that you know the owner and The Renegades? That you're let in every weekend without charge? That they let you on the stage? They even serve you drink for free?'

Eli knew people talked. In school halls, they did so with boundless imagination. From the glint in Justin's eyes, he could tell this particular affliction had struck him.

'I know the owner and the band, yes,' Eli said, slowly. 'I don't go every weekend without charge, I definitely don't get on stage, and I don't get served.'

Justin bobbed his head at the last part.

'Well some of us were wondering if you could get us into it this weekend.'

He nodded to the huddle. Eli leaned over Justin's mountain-sized shoulder and recognized the popular, the rich, and the snotty.

'Like with Andrew,' added Justin.

Betrayal anchored his stomach, dropping it to his pelvis.

'I don't think so,' he said quickly. 'Andrew got in because the guys got to know him.'

'Come on,' Justin groaned. 'Don't be a dick, don't hold out us.'

He said this while tilting his head and rolling his eyes. Rage surged beneath Eli's skin. The old temper, forged from a thousand knocks nestled deep within him, seized and piped into his muscles, his bones, breath, and eyes.

'I'm not,' he stated. 'And I can't get you in.'

Justin laughed a mocking grasp.

'You're not even going to try?' he asked, lightly.

'Listen, everybody knows that the only fucking good thing in this town is that bar, and those bouncers don't let anyone in underage. Except ... for ... you, now I want in'.

Justin loomed, and Eli answered by clenching his jaw harder. He was half a head shorter than him, but that didn't matter.

He had inherited two attributes from his father, Sean Allen. The first was a stocky build infused with wiry, surprising strength. The second trait was a ferocious temper that attacked without thought or fear of consequence.

'I'm not helping you,' he said in a voice of barbs.

Justin laughed the same disappointed twitter. His eyes darted nervously. Eli wondered if anyone ever had said no to him before.

'Is there a problem here, boys?' interrupted Mr. Logue.

'No, sir' said the boys in unison.

'Good, Justin would you mind, I want a private word with Eli.'

Under Logue's gaze, Justin departed with his battalion. The teacher held a familiar blue folder that captured Eli's attention.

'I read it,' he said proudly.

Sly humor haunted his craggy face.

'And I have something I'd like to speak to you about.'

'Sorry,' apologized Eli to a dirty look.
This was the fourth person he had bumped into.
What is going on? They're coming out of nowhere.
Logue wants me to help write the play, I've got to read
his notes, his scenes and give feedback on them. I'm
going to be writing the play. I' m ... oh Christ here's
another.
'What the hell are you doing?' spat a sixth-year girl.
'Sorry, sorry,' Eli volleyed at her, already ahead.
Glee tickled his nerves. He could not stop grinning.
The rushing throng parted, and there was Andrew,
waiting. He was leaning against the wall, and from his
size, it wasn't hard to imagine he was keeping it up.
For five years, the same faces surrounded Eli. They
were growing up, and for himself, this had meant acne
and what Kate christened 'chin fluff,' which he shaved
once a week.
Andrew hadn't so much grown as evolved from a
blonde butterball into a gladiator-sized hulk. Despite
this change, his good nature and easy-going
personality remained.
Until now, he had always been thankful for Andrew.
Grateful that he wasn't abandoned as his friend's
popularity rose due to his achievements on the rugby
team. But seeing him now rekindled the rage from
earlier.
'Did you brag to Justin Blackthorn,' snapped Eli.
Andrew, who had headphones in, removed them
slowly. His face was despondently blank.
'Excuse me,' said Andrew.
'Justin Blackthorn, were you bragging to him and you're
rugby pals about me getting you into the Dollar on New
Year's Eve?'

'I wouldn't say bragging,' gasped Andrew. 'Some of the guys were talking about what they'd gotten up to over the holidays. I did the same, that's all. I didn't mean anything by it. Why? What's happened?

'He wants me to get him and his friends in.'

Andrew's face grimaced.

'He does have a small obsession with the place ever since the bouncers refused him.'

'You didn't think of that before you told him,' spat Eli, venomously.

'I was just making conversation,' replied Andrew shrugging. 'It was an honest mistake. I didn't think he would ask you about it. I'm sorry'.

Eli's tongue wormed against his cheeks.

'It was supposed to be a private thing,' he said. 'I don't even know if I'm legally allowed there and now the whole schools gonna know, which might mean not being allowed back.'

'I'm sorry,' repeated Andrew before adding. 'It was an accident.'

Sighing, Eli relented, the rage in him was already dwindling to a black regret.

'Whatever happens, happens, come on, let's get out of here.'

They trekked over the playground, Eli a step behind Andrew. He had his head bowed, his eyes on his shoes and his mind circling in worry.

The chorus of car horns returned him to reality.

The noise belonged to a parade of student cars that looked violated. They cruised forward, hugging the ground due to their lowered suspension. Light sprang off their tinted windows and blindingly boisterous alloys. Smirks and headshakes made their way through the shocked onlookers.

The faces inside screamed out from open windows, along with the thud of rampant trance music. Eli recognized a few. Naturally, Justin was in lead position.

'If I ever insult someone's vision like that you have my permission to kill me,' said Andrew.

Eli gazed at his friend, their widening grins dissipating any tension.

'I'm still pissed at you,' Eli told him as they turned toward home.

'You can't be pissed at me, I'm too lovable,' informed Andrew.

They observed the progression of vehicles leave. Their destination would be Belfast to burn money in overly expensive restaurants in a desperate bid to be adults. For some reason, this made Eli sad. He was a teenager; he saw no reason to act like he wasn't. Yet, sometimes he thought this thinking was wrong.

'I'll find you more loveable after killing you a few times in Halo,' he told Andrew.

'That is not likely,' replied his friend.

He didn't like to admit, but it was impossible to stay angry with Andrew.

4

The night beyond was still.
The porch light was on, an oozy beacon of yellow stretching out. It lifted the darkness to show Jones's garden entombed beneath the snow. He could see through the trees, their branches; wet, bony claws, on both sides, but the right held his attention.
There were no lights on in that direction.
'Harold's still at his son's,' remarked Eli, gravely.
'Pat's passing hit him pretty hard,' grumbled Jones, his voice gravel and time.
'Their lives were built around each other. Now that Pat's gone, he's lost without her. That is the unfortunate part of life that no one wants to consider: the loss of a partner. There is no plan for that, but he's with his family, him and the dog. Where he needs to be.'
Eli didn't think to ask further.
A canvas of cloud blotted out the moon. The overall impression on him was an isolating, empty, and eternal feeling. A night were hard questions seemed to stretch out.
Hesitantly, Jones lit a cigarette. His reluctance due to the plume of aftershave radiating from Eli's Bruce Springsteen inspired dress-style.
The others were inside, and the house voiced their movements.
'Tell me more about this job offer then,' said Jones, puffing smoke.
'Its great,' said Eli.
'Well, your talent for words certainly has no bounds. What's wrong? I tell you my first job wasn't to write a play, even if you're not getting paid its several steps up from that'.

'Nothings wrong,' said Eli. 'I've already got some ideas it's just having read Logue's stuff, I thought he'd have more done.'

'Ahh you're just nervous,' said Jones, standing. 'Your gonna do brilliantly. I have faith in that, more so than were this could head'.

Eli could have thrown his arms into the air and cried, 'Hallelujah.'

Jones knew of Nina's distaste for him, but his reference was towards the bizarre creature that was Hanna Jones, Nina's mother.

Throughout her visit to her husband's hometown, Hanna's disposition was that of the ruling class reluctantly visiting the barbaric and savage lower classes.

'She's a city girl,' Jones had said. 'That's only now realizing there's a world outside the city.'

They hide their amused glance as Jones's son Martin joined them.

'Should be ready soon,' he said. His voice was a grave imitation of his father's.

Unfortunately, that impression transcended the rest of him. Besides Jones, Martin was simply a smaller, lesser copy.

At least he does me the courtesy of glancing in my direction, thought Eli. *Hanna never looks, just acts like I'm a bad smell, following them.*

'Are you struggling with that Dad?' asked Martin.

'It's been a while since I wore one of these is all,' replied Jones.

Martin's hands skillfully knotted the tie around his father's neck. Their eyes avoided each other.

Eli felt sadness radiate from between them, deeper and colder than the fallen snow.

'There,' said Martin. 'Good to see someone look after you.'

Eli pretended not to exist and was unsuccessful. Nina and Hanna were emerging from the house. He caught Nina, asking, 'why is he here,' just loud enough for him to hear.

This was going to be painful.

'This ... is ... painful' whined Peter Brett to no one. With oily fingers, he rubbed the bridge of his nose. The grease there redrew his attention to what owned the air: a reek of petrol and sweat that meant work and joy to him.

No hope of joy in this.

He looked at the computer and the account books before him.

This is not part of that joy.

The business had been busy lately with the harsh season. Worst winter in three decades people said. Peter didn't know if that was true, but it was a gift in his eyes with the economy the way it was. But accompanying that was tracking the money.

Something his father had never understood. Peter had replaced him as the owner of the garage after cancer claimed him.

How long had it been since he last thought of him? Years. Now an image came to him of summer sunlight through the garage doors and himself, but younger, dressed in ripped jeans and a blue t-shirt that read *Bad*. He was positioned with his back to the light, fixated on his dad negotiating life into some rust bucket. There his dad would speak to him, teaching him all the secrets of the world.

Peter felt his whole life ranged from this scene.

Really it hadn't been years since he thought of his dad as this memory was always in the back of his mind. Where his father, licked with sweat and stinking of grease and petrol, hung over the engine of a car. He wasn't some dying specter but in a body that was tireless and bright and painted in filth. Jim Brett.

The world clouded and trembled in Peter's emerald eyes.

His father never smiled much being a reversed type. Yet he had smiled for him. He would look up from whatever junk he was working on, catching Peter's gaze and smile a genuinely brilliant grin.

That's enough of the books for tonight, I think.

Peter rose, stretching like some cat that's slept too long in the sun. Joints creaked in him to which he thought, *only thirty-three.*

Peter shut down his computer, drew on his jacket, and dosed his desk lamp. In doing so, darkness swallowed him. A knot squeezed in his chest.

Beyond his office, however, there was still some light. Stacy Robinson's desk lamp was on. So was her radio. She often left it on for him when he stayed late. And she left it at low volume, so he would only hear it when he was going.

Peter reached for the off button, leaned beyond and twisted.

The music grew to fill the garage, transforming it into a Coliseum of sound. Each surface reflected the soft sway of music, sounding like an ocean's calm swell. Goosebumps spiked across his arms as he drank it in.

What type of twenty-five-year-old likes classical music?

Though he could have lingered, he switched everything off. Restoring the garage to its humble, honest state. Outside, the cold smacked into his chest as he locked the building.

Coughing, as the thick icy air entered his lungs, he peered around. Light streamed down in cone shape from the lot's overheads. His tank, a 4x4 Land Rover Discovery sheathed in snow, was alone.

He trudged toward it, pulling his coat tight around him. The wind clawed by, rattling the lot's chain-link fence like a toddler wielding a toy.

Peter scarped the key into the car door, his hands shaking. There was more scraping as he inserted the key into the ignition.

The car shuddered into life.

He lived on Belmont Road. This required him to utilize the town's main streets for the quickest journey.

Pavement, streetlights, shop fronts flickered by.

Mia's Garden rested ahead in the snow. Its fairy lights glowed through the Rover's water beaded windows. A family was shuffling along the pavement outside.

As he drew closer, their image caused his tired mind to crack. And from that fissure in his brain, something sleazy and cruel slide out and spoke to him.

(There's a nigger).

He kicked hard on the brake, causing his tires to screech.   Emotions flooded his body, reducing his awareness to what he could see beyond his windscreen.

On the pavement, the family hadn't noticed him yet. They were a family of four, a husband and wife, a teenage daughter and a grandfather. Then there was the white teenage boy in their midst. The boy was laughing eagerly at something the tallest of them, the grandfather had said.

What was he?

Was he an adoptive family member?

Was he the boyfriend of the girl?

Was he an abducted victim?

(It's disgusting is what it is, mixing of colors).

This was the same voice again.

What was damming about it wasn't that it was just twisted with anger, hatred, and a meticulous need for violence, a demand that implored Peter to act out with his hands. What was really horrifying was: it was his father's voice.

A sudden lurch in his stomach and he knew it was going to happen. With wide eyes, he watched the speedometer decrease even further.

The Rover's engine juddered violently and died.

He had stalled right by the entrance to Mia's. And they were looking.

Cars drove by in a barrage of ridiculing horns. Quickly, Peter fumbled at the keys as upper teeth dug into his bottom lip. He could taste blood.

The car engine shuddered, shuddered, and then growled. He yanked the gear stick into gear and torn away.

'Jesus, did you see that,' said Martin.

'Some people shouldn't be allowed to drive,' stated Hanna.

'Can't be helped sometimes in this weather,' said Jones.

He earned a scathing look that rattled a sigh from his lungs. Martin and Hanna turned away, stepping arm in arm through the restaurant doors.

Jones gave Eli and Nina a dispirited look and followed.

The house lay ahead through the naked trees.

Gravel churned under the car as he approached. It was no comparison to the volume of Peter's own breathing: a grasping, hopeless expulsion of hot air.

What the fuck was happening?

Peter didn't know.

Desperate thoughts began to germinate in his mind. He had recognized the tall one, Jones somebody, he played guitar in that bar band. He even lived nearby.

Why had he stirred such a reaction? Where had that come from? It had something to do with those colors black and white he knew, that terribly pale and young and susceptible boy laughing at that man's joke.
A paralyzing question scratched at his brain.
Am I going crazy?
Peter gunned the tank's engine the last few meters up the drive.
The house was a one-story design. Beach wood furnished with floor to ceilings windows. His business had indeed been fruitful.
The car's cabin had turned into a sauna, soured by his fretful sweating. He needed out, and that impulse drove him to bail from the car even before it had entirely stopped. He wasn't even confident he had switched the headlights off nor cared.
He was sprinting, his keys jangling as he scrambled for the right one. There was a click as tumblers merged with house key's teeth.
He shouldered the heavy door and squeezed through the gap.

Being a single teenager, Eli had extensive experience with lulls in conversation.
Despite, this he was not prepared for his current dinner.
Five faces stared at each other in silence while the restaurant's music played. Waitresses and waiters darted about as customers engaged in small talk and dining, giving the restaurant a busy, energetic atmosphere. One that was incapable of affecting their table.
As if to make it worse, Hanna Jones took control.

'I'm sorry,' she said although her tone suggested otherwise. 'I don't understand why he is here? Is there a reason why you can't you enjoy a dinner with your son without inviting strangers? You've hardly seen him or your granddaughter, and yet our time has been spent mostly with this ... tag along, no offense, dear'. Eyes danced from face to face.

The majority of Eli wanted Jones to defend him, yet he knew this would make things worse. He motioned to the edge of his seat, drawing breath to speak.

Jones was, however, quicker in responding.

'Eli, is here because I wanted him to be,' replied Jones, casually. 'He is my friend. I asked him here for support because although I have been looking forward to seeing all of you and having you's visit, I must admit I am slightly nervous'.

'Friend,' repeated Hanna. 'What man of your age is friends with a child? What do you have to be nervous about? This is your son, your granddaughter'.

Eli sank into his seat's lining as best he could. He did not know what was going to happen, but from Jones's face, he knew it wasn't going to be good.

'Yes,' replied Jones, his casual tone somewhat amused. 'I have no feelings of nervousness around them. I just needed a little back up around a harpy such as yourself'.

(Hello, son).

The voice was warm, inviting, and ever so familiar. Yet, a playful hostility slithered underneath its warmth.

Peter's face contorted, sobbing as he marched into the living room.

(Nice place son, a bit sterile but you can clearly see you're loaded).

He crossed the carpeted terrain at a stubborn push. His aim was the drinks cabinet by the far wall.

Bourbon slopped over the rim of the tumbler as he poured.

'Fuck,' he mumbled, tossing back the glass.

Liquid plopped in his mouth, baptizing his tongue in a fire. He continued to drink, his arm repeating the same action until a hazy, stupor took his brain.

Racist. That was the word society used.

It had never occurred to him that it included him. Yes, he had charged them types more for his services.

Though these incidents, he could never recall much.

He tossed more hellfire down his gullet. Then, gripping the bottle, he took a seat.

The living room bordered him; it's space mournfully barren.

Three walls were black stone while the fourth was a strip of glass to Peter's right obscured by lime curtains.

The floors only occupants were three leather sofas, arranged in a box shape before the opposing wall.

Perched on that was a 152-inch Plasma TV. Attached below was a selection of electronic toys that he regularly escaped into.

The benchmark definition of any male bachelor, he thought bitterly.

He had no family, no lovers, and no one, just his work. And he loved that, loved working with his hands and providing a service.

Peter's fear and panic had faded with drinking. Seated on the cold leather of his sofa, he was confronted with the despair of his home. It gave him the courage to ask.

What had overcome him on James Street?

The answer came instantly. Thrust to Peter by the slimy other housed in his mind.

It was the memory of working with his father, but it was different. Like maturity had hit, and he saw the harsh reality with all childish fragmentation brushed away.

This time he could hear what was being said to him, unlike previous remembrances.

As an adult, he listened to his father, teaching him all the secrets of the world.

Tears bloomed in his emerald eyes.

He starred at the dead TV screen, not seeing. His eyes recoiled to the past. Tears slid down his oily cheeks to his collar as his lips shook.

'Your home early,' said Kate, hearing the slam of the door.

'I walked home, Jones and Hanna started arguing,' deadpanned Eli.

'Christ, before or after the dinner?' asked Kate.

He was on the stairs now, trudging upward and not looking back.

'During,' he replied.

In his room, he collapsed face-first onto the bed. The mattress flopped under him, making his backpack jump. After considering it, he pulled out Logue's writing.

Why did he have to open his fat mouth?

He would have been fine if Jones had kept silent. Sighing, he withdrew the pages from the folder. The paper was stiff and had an official air to it.

He reread them with a deepening frown digging into his brow.

Logue's material provided a general plot description, some pages about characters and themes, and two rough scenes. Guiltily, he thought they were awful.

This wasn't the story Logue had so passionately promised. It was derivative and clichéd. It read as it had been written: by an adult pretending to see from a teenage perspective.

Eli starred at the opposite wall for some time his gaze hard and concentrated. He hoped his friend was okay as he switched on his laptop and started to work.

'Why?' Nina cried.

Hanna did not answer. She had her daughter by the arm and was trailing her into the red bleed of their car's brake lights.

Martin had removed himself from the scene by buckling into the driver's seat.

'Why are we leaving? Is it cause of Eli? I want to stay, please mum can't I stay?'

Those had been Nina's words.

Jones stared at the vacant space where his son's car had been. He had shouted for Hanna to let the girl go but had done nothing else.

Branches snapped to his left, and he turned to see Maria within the trees separating her property from his. Her eyes gleam feline-like in the dark.

He knew immediately that she'd spied the whole thing.

'I think their gone, Jones,' she said, critically.

'Fuck you, Maria,' he responded.

5

The living room had been tipped on its side.
Or so it appeared to Peter hanging from the sofa's
edge. Early morning light hung from between the lush
curtains. He could tell by its limp, grey quality.
He pushed himself up and swayed. A wrong move as
the entirety of his being seemed to shriek in pain.
'God,' he moaned.
The hammering slush of his hung-over brain reeled in
his skull.
He leaped for the kitchen. His feet skidded on the tile,
arms fanning out as he slammed into the kitchen island,
bowed forward and puked into the sink.
'Jesus Christ,' he roared.
When his expulsions eventually stopped, his throat felt
coated in hot glass. His heart throbbed in his temples,
and it was joined with a voice repeating his name.
*(Peter) (Peter) (Peter) (Peter) (Peter) (Peter) (Peter)
(Peter) (Peter).*
*(That was some faggorty performance Peter, worthy of
applause).*
'You're not real,' he uttered.
Yet that smarmy voice was as real as any voice in his
head.
*(That's not very nice. I taught you manners have you
forgotten)* said his father.

(I've had a look around in here and I'm a little disappointed, to say the least. You've let your mind grow foggy, Peter. Oh, you remember that we talked. We talked endlessly, you and I, as father and son do, the father passing on his hard-learned wisdom. You've forgotten what that wisdom was though. You're a creature without context, no clue as to why he thinks and acts as he does. That is no way to treat a father's legacy. Well, those memories will be coming back. The brain, like any engine, just needs a little tuning every now and then. You had a taste last night, what do you think?)

Peter trembled as he clung over the sink.

How long have you been in there, lurking in the back of mind?

(Peter, I've always been here. Now let's talk about what you saw last night).

He didn't want to, he wanted a wash. His skin felt so filthy it felt irradiated.

The voice did not follow him as he undressed and stepped into the shower.

It's a trick, just some drunken trick. Stress-related, that was it. Too much overtime at work, too many late nights and too much booze piled on top.

Steam swirled in the air. Peter closed his heavy eyes and swayed in the cocooning mist.

Exiting the shower, he noticed his reflection in the mirror opposite. He looked better than he expected, his eyes were bloodshot, and he was a little pale.

(You can't wash me away, son).

Peter nearly screamed and would have slipped on his wet feet if he hadn't latched onto the sink basin. The voice within was chuckling sadistically.

(Do you think what you saw last night was right, that white boy familiarizing with those niggers? We know what they're like, Peter. You've forgotten the details, but you know it in your gut. You know not to trust them. They steal; they'll take anything, anyone).
The voice was sneering now, grinding, spitting words at him.
(So why didn't you do anything? Don't blubber to me, I know how weak you are. Still, even you should have felt the need to teach them a lesson. They have no right to be around our kind). The voice paused and grew calm. *(It's all right, shhh).*
Tears slid down Peter's quivering cheeks.
(You can still make your father proud. You know where he lives, and it's not too far from here).
The fibers beneath his skin attempted to leap free as the house phone rang. Peter stared at his tear-stained reflection. The image bounced back at him depicted a naked individual, corpse white, his sex a pathetic, shrunken thing.
The voice, that nauseating, sleazy presence, was gone. With a towel wrapped around his waist, he staggered to the phone.
'Hello,' he mumbled.
'Peter,' spoke a concerned female voice.
'Stacy?' Peter had to ask.
'Yes … sorry, you don't sound like you … '
'Bit of a cold I'm afraid,' he lied. 'Not surprising with this weather and the way I've been working of late. I was just about to call you'.
'Oh, it's fine. I mean you're the boss after all. I only phoned out of worry. I thought for once perhaps I was here before you but then after everyone else arrived and I know its silly so don't tell the others, but I guess I got a little scared'.
'It's fine, it's fine, just need some bed rest. I'll see you when I see you'.

Peter smoldered the end button. He had wanted desperately to shout at her 'help me, help me' but he hadn't. Something, the thought of his own madness prevented him.

Who can I call now? John and Patrick but they're at work and would probably phone for the men in white coats before he finished explaining his situation.

Susan?

He hadn't thought of Susan in years. Yet his mind's eye reeled backward.

Peter saw her sandy hair, waves of it, her smirk, and her chocolate eyes. He had told her once that he could have dived into them and not come up for air. She had laughed at that, a don't-be-so-silly chuckle. That had been Susan, always composed, giving little yet so vibrantly alive.

Peter had never known love like her.

They had met in university, the one time in his life he had lived beyond Hazel. And he had bought her home to meet his father. The entire thing went better than planned, it had been perfect. That is until Susan had left.

'I'd end it now before she has you putting a ring on her finger or a bun in her oven' said Jim Brett as casual as reciting the newspaper.

'That woman is just like your mother, she'll use and abuse you.'

He hadn't argued, not even replied to him. His disappointment was too much.

It played out in the end. Peter found himself stressed to be even in her presence. He shrank from their conservations and soon their dates until she had eventually ended it. There was no pain when she delivered the news, only relief.

New tears sprang in Peter's eyes as he stood.

The voice had been right. The memories were flooding back.

'We're meeting here,' said Eli, disgusted.

'School policy prevents the meeting of pupils outside of school without the proper structure,' recited Logue.

'In case you happen to be a sexual predator,' said Eli.

Logue stared, his expression unamused.

They stood like two envoys from opposing armies. Between them, dull in the grey/white smear that had become the sky, was Logue's untidy desk. Eli's proposal lay on it.

'I've read it,' Logue said, hoisting his fingers into his belt like a cowboy.

'Putting it simply your idea to modernize King Lear is to not modernize King Lear in its entirety but select some of its themes and put them in a secondary school setting.'

'Yes,' Eli answered instantly.

Logue's bushy eyebrows stayed cemented in skepticism. Then his gray eyes flickered.

'That's it.'

'Look, you can either do what everyone's expecting you to do, which is the same old thing they've seen a thousand times over to a thousand different stories. And you and I both know what happens when people walk away from those things. They say that was fun, but … it's … not … as … good as the original. So let's give them something original'.

Logue's expression remained unforgivably set.

'Give me a few more days to write the first few scenes.'

At last Logue's face muscles began to move. It was like tectonic plates pulling apart.

'I want it to be noted that I know how absurd this thing is,' he said.

Eli's eyes ignited into fireworks.

'God, this is a mistake,' Logue muttered. 'Go on, then you've got permission.'

She had gotten to the door when he called her.
'Mia.'
His voice quietly alarmed and reproached. Mia sighed.
Jones could see from the bed. She was naked,
barefoot, and divine in the darkness, which shrouded
her. A shaft of moonlight stabbed from the curtains and
when she turned, hit across the skin of her side making
it pearl.
He heard her heave a breath.
'What are we doing?'
Even in the dark, he knew that stance. Mia stood,
posed with a grief that was his doing, carried on her
shoulders from half a lifetime ago.
'Mia,' he whispered.
He had wondered what it had been like for her. To
witness him wallowing in self-pity after the fire at his
last gig, watch him retract from the world to this cabin.
He lay, his bare body as dark as night and felt
powerless.
'We can't start over,' she wept. 'It isn't right. We lost our
chance'.
'No,' he said, firmly. 'No' firmer still.
He slid forward to her. She rocked on her feet, a thing
that was snow and pearl and fire at once, that had heat
and life and yet always seemed so beautiful to him that
it shouldn't. The darkness masked her face, but he felt
her eyes.
'We didn't lose our chance. I ruined it … me … and I
am sorry. I … let my self down with the drugs, with
everything. I let it crush me and then push you away. I
was scared, scared to even try to fight for anything that
mattered in case I would lose it again'.
He rose from his knees, pressing his face to hers.
'But I'm not anymore.'
They embraced in the strip of silvery moonlight. This
was the first of many nights where safe in the dark, two
people met to explore over the years, renewing.

6

The week zipped by in a flurry of pandemonium.
Eli wrote every day, every night. A drive had been
installed in him that was as hard as iron and as hot as
magma. He was compelled to write, to make characters
flesh and let them live and breath on the page and to
shine a light on their path ahead.
Everything else in his life became secondary.
School became an interlude between sleep and the
play. Lessons were spent imagining character back-
stories and mentally editing scenes rather than listening
to teachers.
Andrew had a front-row seat to his madness. On seeing
his tired disposition, his friend remarked, 'I see you've
gotten your first taste of heroin.'
Eli didn't reply as he was elsewhere.
Logue's deadline came swiftly, and once more, they
met in his class after school.
The teacher had the newly printed pages clutched in
his hands. Even though they had been read, his eyes
continued scowl down at the words.
Eli would not have been surprised if the ink decided to
jump from the page.
'Okay, if we are going to do this I have condition's,'
barked Logue.
This seemed to be the only vocalization that they were
going ahead with his idea. Eli's nerves, which had for a
week been a jangled, fevering mass flared with delight.
'Condition one: no swears.'
'Come on, if you want to tell a realistic story about
modern teenagers ... '

'I agree,' interrupted Logue. 'But stop painting the dam thing with them. This has to be PG13, or it will never fly. Condition two is we meet twice a week, one for corrections and the second to review the play's progress. Is that a deal'?

Eli held out his hand. Logue studied it as if he might be disease-riddled.

'God this is a mistake,' he said as they shook.

The second time was better.

Out of the night and the cold and the dark she came to him, a mirage of wild flame and heavenly snow. They collided on the porch and toppled inside.

Jones landed first, his hands merged with her hair. Mia straddled him, panting. She scratched at his shirt and plunged to his lips.

When they were done, he cradled her to him.

She sat between his legs, bare before the crackling fireplace. Sweat glistened on her, on her white back and breasts that heaved for breath. His heart walloped lethally against her.

'Feels like your having a heart attack.'

'I might,' he gasped and nuzzled the nape of her neck.

'Mister Jones,' Mia giggled, and it was a beautiful sound.

Ever since their first time, he had felt starved. Blood inflamed in his veins with a wanting he had only known in his youth.

All week he had wandered like a ghost through his life, waiting to hear from her. He knew it would happen again, but he would be a liar if he didn't admit he'd been nervous.

'You kept me waiting,' he said, his voice deep and breathless.

'I wanted to come but ... '

She smiled almost to herself and leaned into him.

'I wanted to wait too until I could wait no more.'

He tightened his hold of her.

'What were we talking about last time?'

'Rachel, I remember reading about the crash,' said Mia. 'It was probably the first time in years I had ever contemplated speaking to you again. Did you love her?'

'In my way,' he said while staring into the fire. 'It was not like you. Rachel and I ... were two lonely people; we were each other's excuse to hide from everyone'.

'Did you ever play guitar then?'

The ruby guitar sat in the living room's corner.

'Sometimes, never for anyone else, just for me,' he said gingerly.

'Listen, we don't have to do a point by point catch up ... ' began Mia.

'We do,' said Jones. 'I want you to know I didn't choose her over you.'

'I know that,' she said, stroking his face.

Then after some time, she asked, 'what happened between you and Martin?'

Mia felt Jones's cheek stiffened beneath her touch.

'I think when she died, the grief allowed Martin to really see me. I think that's when he learned his old man had never really been happy in his marriage. They may have left a week ago, but truthfully I lost him decades ago, and I don't think I can fix that'.

'Can't fix everything, focus on what you have got now.'

Jones's eyes lit with curious bemusement.

'Aren't you supposed to be the negative one?' he asked.

'Maybe you're rubbing off on me,' she said then her toned turned severe. 'You know what I have been for the past week ... happy. Dwelling on the past, it's just a waste'.

'No more dwelling,' he concluded.

They nestled closer, sheltered in their lovers embrace, and watched the flames dance.

Memories more than the moments haunt people.

In his opinion, a person is his or her own treasure trove of collected experiences, good or bad. When the world shrinks away and night thoughts settle in, they niggle at the mind. Memories are dragons that never cease.

They are the ghosts of a life.

Peter had been discovering a lot of old memories lately. This particular one had bed covers in it. They were navy blue with red racing cars woven into them. They were as warm as any loving hug and as velvet as sleep.

He stirred beneath them, tiny and balled. He squinted against the waking light, reeling between dreams and reality.

The bedroom was dark, too dark for the morning. Yet light existed as a stalk of brightness thrust from the hall, illuminating half his room.

Shapes materialized within the dark half. Plastic robots shelved in military order, their eyes jewels of bloody crimson. Big Sam, his forever guardian, a titan sized bear of gold-honeyed fur was still on his throne in the corner.

In the stalks center, slumped in his desk chair, was his father. His chin bowed on his chest, his pink scalp visible amongst lonely wisps of lingering hair.

The light hit him like a spotlight, enveloping round the contours of his frame.

'Dad?'

He lifted his head. A sloppy grin pried his flabby cheeks wide.

'It's Peter,' he cheered, throwing his arms out.

The grin was stationary like a scar.

'What's going on?' Peter asked from the bed.

The scar's edges sagged. It made his father's lips look like they were bleeding.

'Nothing, your mums, gone out with her friends, is all.'

His father's eyes fled his. There was a pitying sadness in them.

He noticed then how still the house had been. It was the stillness of a knife pressed against bare skin before the plunge.

'Do you love your mother, Peter?'

Jim Brett's gaze was worn but hard. There was a familiar, stringy and soggy flavor on him. He answered with an honest, 'yes.'

'She ain't like any other,' his father slurred. 'No sir ye bob … not like her friends, nothing but a gang of whores. Oh aye, they'll sweet talk ya alright, fuck ya raw and ragged for what they can get out of those husbands of theirs, vultures, leeches'.

He barred his teeth, spittle wept from them.

'Patricia now she's different, she something else' he cooed. 'Oh, no doubt she can be sweet if she needs to be. She can be docile like a woman should. Then she can be this treacherous, cunning cunt,' he snarled, swaying in his seat.

'She gets her hooks in, twists you by the balls and just grins at you, that wolfish fucking foul ass grin. They laugh at me, all high and mighty, noses upturned … they laugh,' he said, his voice fading.

'I hate her,' he uttered, gasping. 'But goddamit I can't get rid of her.'

Emotions warred beneath his father's skin. Peter watched as his lips quaked frantically, his eyes staring hard as tears rolled down his rosy cheeks.

'Don't ever end up like me, son.'

James Brett seized his shoulder, pinching the soft flesh between his tiny bones.

Peter remembered hating his mother from them on. For making his dad feel so sad.

He also recalled that the feeling was almost mutual. Patricia Brett had regarded him as a pet she did not want. She would feed and water him, but the rest of the time she kept a cool distance.

Thinking of the cold Peter dug his hands deeper into his pockets. He shuffled slightly, hoping to gain some heat in his feet. Snow crunched beneath him.

'What am I here to see?' asked Peter.

Firelight flickered in the front windows of the house before him. Smoke trailed from the chimney as the only indication that someone was home. Though Peter knew it was anyway. He had seen the woman practically tackle the man known as Jones on his porch.

(Patience, son) replied the ghost of his father.

7

Even Logue's resilience did not last that long.
It took a week, a mere two sessions but he caved. The note Eli received sported a severe warning and the words sketched in vicious slashes 'TO HELL WITH SCHOOL POLICY.' Below this, in the more careful script was the teacher's address.
Just around the corner from mine.
An eerie notion he considered the whole walk there.
One look at the house, and it affirmed his hesitance.
It was a grand home of red brick and white windowpanes. In its windows were lights that were soft and welcoming. The snow, which had begun to lessen, crusted the two square pieces of the lawn. A cemented path sliced these apart to the front step.
Eli paused beneath the looming ashes that ornamented the estate. He licked his lips, surveying the silent street and finding himself alone.
This is too freaky, he thought.
The front door thundered under his knuckles. Eli was tethered on the balls of feet that were ready to run as it was yanked open.
'Good evening.'
Logue added to the oddness by lunging forward, balancing on the door's handle. His regular grim face was now flushed in rosy coloring.
Eli snorted at the burnt odor that whiffed from him.
'Welcome, welcome, Eli,' he said urgently.
'Nice house,' was all Eli could think to say.
'It was my father,' drilled Logue, rolling his eyes.
Eli handed his snug coat and scarf to Logue's urging hands. He racked them and stomped deeper into the house. Eli followed, unsure.

The teacher's study gave a bad name to the word mess. Spine bent and dog-eared books lurked in all four corners of the room. Dust sanded the air. There was a desk, which appeared to be the only thing not layered by tombs. It was bare but for a mahogany box where Eli assumed Logue kept the source of the house's funky smell.

'Let's get to work,' Logue, prompted.

They had to as auditions were confirmed for next week. They kept the same routine. One meeting where Logue would criticize and Eli would rewrite. The second meeting solely dedicated to discussing the progress of the play.

Sometimes this turned Logue's study into a boxing ring of words as Eli defended his work. Both were unable to move forward until a compromise had been met.

Most of his work Eli did in his own room. Achieved, thankfully, by Kate and Ryan providing food every night at his desk.

There were moments of frustration and doubt as to whether his work was excellent or unworthy to be even printed on paper. What got him through was the sheer joy in piecing words together. In those times, his brain felt like it was making all the right connections.

He found himself smiling as he sat. At some inside joke, half-forgotten.

The week past to the sound of punched laptop keys. Mixed with this soundtrack were the albums that blared from his CD player such as *Astral Weeks, August and Everything After, For Emma, Forever Ago, Blood On The Tracks, 21, By The Way, Sigh No More, A Rush Of Blood To The Head, American Slang, Brothers, Lungs, Darkness On The Edge Of Town, Fleet Foxes, Gold, Hail To The Thief, Absolution, Grace, The Suburbs, Only By The Night, Time Out Of Mind* and a further mile-long back catalogue.

Sometimes, Eli sang along, most times he worked without even hearing them.

'!!!AUCTIONS!!!'

'FOR THE SCHOOL PLAY TO BE HELD AFTER SCHOOL ON THE 8TH OF' 'FEBRUARY IN THE MAIN HALL.'

'A PRODUCTION CREATED BY MR LOGUE AND ELI DONOGHUE'

Logue was less than happy about the posters. Not because they were nineties wave sheets (neon pinks and oranges) but because the auditions were upon them.

'We haven't even got set pieces sorted for fucksake,' was one of his many complainants.

Eli ignored him, focusing on his job.

However, Logue wanted him at the auditions. He suspected this was in case anyone had a problem with the script. Eli was confident in its quality. At least he was until seeing who was amongst the potential candidates.

Justin Blackthorn sneered smugly at him from the line-up.

'Okay people lets try to calm down,' Logue soothed.

The gathered volunteers continued grinning and sniggering.

Stale sweat and flecks of dust clotted the air. Outside of P.E. classes, the Main Hall was only used for assembly. There had been a session thirty minutes ago, which meant the cathedral-sized space smelt like an unwashed gym bag.

'Was that you, Eli?' asked Justin, wafting his hand in front of his nose.

The lame joke received a chorus of laughter. Eli, to the right and behind Logue, felt his collar burn.

Heather Graham was also auctioning. She did not laugh and continued to look angelic while invoking fiendish thoughts.

Eli had not spoken to her in five years.

There were many rumors about her. Most focused on the fact that her boyfriend was in his twenties. They had always seemed as ways for jealous onlookers to dirty her image to Eli. And Heather appeared mature enough to not care.

She carried that maturity and in doing so was regarded as something as rare and mystically as a unicorn. This only added to her appeal.

Eli had more cause than any, but he never partook in the rumor mill.

This was because he was frightened of Heather. For she had hurt him in a way, he never knew he could be. With that memory came the awareness that she could do so again and with the public embarrassment of it.

The other students were like a firing squad before him, each clasping a printout of a scene.

'Okay,' Logue said again, louder.

'You're each going to read a scene with me. State which character you're reading for before we start. You've all got your copies?'

An awkward shuffle of pages followed. Eli fixated nervously on their faces.

The sniggering grew quiet as a dozen eyes surfed over lines. Then it died completely.

'Are we actually going to say this,' asked someone at last?

It was Justin Blackthorn. His script was flipped open to the second page.

The teacher paused, taking stock in his disbelieving eyes.

'Yes.'

A clatter of hissed whispers erupted.

'And who wrote this?' asked Justin.

The teacher turned and nudged his head in Eli's direction.

'He did.'

Naturally, Justin bagged the lead role of Alan Heggarty.

'You've got to hand it to him,' Andrew had said. 'He wanted it more. He's still obsessed over this Dollar thing. My thinking is he neither wants to bargain, threaten, or lead you on'.

'Encouraging,' Eli had replied.

To everyone's surprise at the auction and (more surprisingly) awe Justin had bought tenderness to his character. Alan was very like him, except he wasn't an arsehole.

He was popular, played rugby and swaggered about his school corridors with childlike gullibility, content in his bubble that everything will remain the same. That bubble soon breaks when Alan's best friend James, commits suicide, the play's big bang event.

Justin's baby blue eye's had reeked with dazed sadness and relentless questions in his auction. They held the world and made it believable.

Once the scene ended, Justin was back, and Eli had to scuttle from the hall.

The running started after that. Eli made every effort to never be cornered by Justin.

With his cast plundered from the schools' population, Logue propelled himself into his part as director. He kept the play's pedal pressed firmly to the floor.

Eli judged that Logue was secretly enjoying himself. Rehearsals happened four times a week in the main hall. Each time Eli witnessed his words made real on that stage. Never had he known such unfathomable pride.

Not everyone had Justin's discovered talent. Yet roles were dished to those that at least could remember their lines. Heather received the lead female role.

To add a little light to the play, Eli had written some comic relief. And he could only think of one person to perform it.

'It's easy,' Eli assured.

The look he received was a shot of mocking absurdity.

'Are you serious?' said Andrew.

'Read the lines, think about how you would say them and do that.'

'You're serious?'

'It's fun and hey if it isn't, you can stare at Heather for hours,' Eli shrugged.

His giant friend hounded after him with contemptuous eyes.

'You're serious!'

When he auctioned, Eli waited to hear the laughs. The hall, it's cream stonewalls were ghostly in their power to magnify sound and usually rendered the place feeling like a mausoleum. Not with Andrew reciting his material.

The walls came alive.

The cast where all huddled in their seats before him. He was timid at first; this Thor sized sixteen-year-old until the first volunteered snigger. After that he gained ease and stuck his groove, leaving the cast in stitches. Eli didn't tell him. He'd written the part thinking, 'what would Andrew say.'

As for the writing, he captained that alone. Or so it felt like with Logue's new responsibilities piling higher and higher.

Their twice-weekly-therapy sessions now met without any disagreement.

The grey teacher would sit in his leather chair with a strange smile on his lips. He reminded Eli of Jones when we first got back with The Renegades, tired but content.

Unlike Jones, Eli sensed they would never be friends. *I'm a tool to him,* he thought and knew it to be true. Eli didn't care because, in a way, he was using Logue to. He wrote for himself because he needed to, but Logue presented him with an audience for his stories. Knowing Logue's opinion made him feel less guilty for stealing a handful of joints from his stash box.

On stealing them, he walked to Jones's. As always and despite the cold temperature, Jones greeted him from his porch.

'And what brings you to my neck of the wood's?'

'Thought I'd give writing a break tonight … and party,' Eli shouted back.

He held up a single joint. Once Jones discerned what it was his signature thunder-like laughter escaped him.

'Where'd you get that?'

'Stole it from my pothead English teacher,' Eli said, mounting the steps.

'Is he the type to catch you on it?'

'You mean to punish me for the stealing the slightly illegal substance to which he's got a vault load and would potentially make his career questionable if found out,' Eli quipped and then added. 'I think I'll be alright.'

'You go ahead, kid,' said Jones.

Hearing him, Eli realized his own stupidity.

'I'm sorry. I didn't realize … '

'It's fine,' Jones interrupted, 'that stuff I have no doubt is piss, but I won't stop you. In my opinion, everyone should try something dangerous once to at least learn to stay away from it'.

Eli borrowed Jones's lighter. As he inhaled, his throat burned, making him splutter. Jones patted his back and chuckled, 'kids these days, no stamina.'

8

(You know where he lives).
Those words had led him to the shadows and the cold.
Peter wished he had bought a coat.
Snow shimmered down as a white haze, gentle and soundless. Trees stood stark naked, deadwood in the black night, their limbs like milky bone.
Out here, the cold had teeth, and its bite raked through the skin, flesh and bone, numbing, grating. This was a cold country it warned. Yet, Peter showed no sign of leaving.
The festering in his mind won't let him.
The house was hunkered in drifts of white. A weave of snow crowned its rooftop. A lantern on the porch shone like a yellow diamond. Its windows were dark, betraying nothing.
(He's in there) gnawed his father's voice.
Peter saw it too. Smoke trailing languidly from the chimney.
He was atop a ridge to the left-hand side of the house. From his perspective, overlooking the entire scene, it recalled to him the idea of the American wilderness. Or what he knew from films. He edged closer, eyes manic and wide, cheeks taut.
Light catapulted from the nearest window.
Peter's heart raced in revolt, sticking in his throat.
Jones moved in the light, nude and black as dirt, a pelt of coal color hair on his chest. He danced nimbly around a kitchen island, his lower half obscured by it.
Peter was a statue, caught and shitting himself.
Maybe it was the jaw-dropping nakedness of his enemy. Perhaps it was the coursing terror of being caught, but he stumbled butt-first to the snow.
Swiftly and without grace, he kicked backward, panting.
Doing so till his skull thudded against a tree trunk.

'Fuck' he grunted.

Below another nude figure appeared. This one was female and predictably exquisite.

Peter watched as she plucked a rosy apple from the table's fruit bowl.

She was the color of milk, but for the pink of her nipples, lips, and her furious scarlet hair. Her body curved in places that would make men drool.

She tasted the apple, coyly smiling to Jones as she chewed.

'Oh no,' Peter cried.

He felt wrath rise from the other, spreading like fiery bleach over his brain.

(Look at those dirty fuckers) howled his father. *(A filthy nigger and his whore … just … just like your fucking whore of a mother. That's what she was really doing all those nights she was out with her friends. She was seeing HIM).*

'Please stop,' Peter whimpered, terrified.

He knew this was beyond some breaking point now. Seeing, Jones with the boy, had been bad enough, but this woman was too much.

Pressure bugled painfully against his skull. The other demanded action.

Even amongst this lucid tempest, Peter was too afraid to move. But he could imagine.

He saw himself push open the front door. No need to be to quiet as he stepped inside, the two would be in the back rooms immersed in their depravity.

There was music playing, the song of wood and mattress within the house.

Peter's fingers clenched on the spanner he imagined he held. His footsteps were like knocks on a door. He entered the bedroom like a wraith.

The nigger was bucking his hips violently while she was sprawled on a bed of red silk, bare and milk-white and helpless. Her legs were seized in his arm and held stirrups fashion as he charged again and again. The room stank of rot and torment.

Over his apish grunts, she didn't make a sound. Her body took his beastly thrusts, but he could see her eyes over his filthy shoulder. Her soul had long since vacated them.

(DO IT).

Peter rushed forward and swung with all his weight. At that moment before his arm finished its ark, it felt serene to obey, to give into that righteous anger.

The spanner landed, colliding with the animal's crown in a gush of blood and gore.

Something had happened to his lips as he had been imagining. They were grinning.

Eli loved to stay behind for rehearsals.

To be amidst the on-going production was to see the cast practice, regurgitating words he knew by heart. Even hearing the natter of the H.E girls as they painted backdrops or the squeak of feet on wood as the stage crew messed about backstage. It was energizing.

In those moments, his fear of Justin disappeared.

He took to writing in front of the stage, hoping to absorb some of the flowering excitement. On one memorable occasion, this proved to be a bad idea.

In reflection, he was dimly aware that the rehearsal had ended. However, at the time, his writing commanded his attention. He didn't even notice the music playing from his laptop until the person interrupted his thought by saying, 'I've seen them live.'

Eli's fingers stopped their dancing.

The voice was silk and honey and slightly timid. It hadn't spoken to Eli in five years, yet he knew it.

Heather Graham stood to his right, script in hand.

Awkwardness didn't suit her, but awkward, she appeared.

'At Glastonbury last year,' she added.

'Lucky you,' he coughed, sense fleeing him.

Her jaw rolled at his cheekiness. An epiphany punched him, the useful type that gives warning after you have said something stupid.

'What are you working on,' her voice now hard.

She wanted to say something else. And Eli had prevented that he knew. He turned to the screen, his hazel eyes, bright seconds before were now dead and dour.

'Figuring out the ending, whether anyone dies or not.'

'A little levity won't be such a bad thing,' she said.

'Not realistic.'

Seconds ticked by, each more arduous for them as if the years behind were dangling above their heads.

He had yet to look up from his screen.

'Still pissed then,' she replied. 'Thought you'd have got over that by now.'

'Usually starts after an apology, which I have yet to receive,' he said. 'Do you expect me to what … to run after you like the rest of the school because you decide to talk to me again'?

'Fuck you, Eli,' she said, turning heel.

Andrew drifted to his side.

'Wow, I think that was the hottest thing I've ever seen,' he said.

Eli watched her merge into the throng. Throughout the years he had envisioned many confrontations with her. They had all ended with him feeling a lot better than now.

'What were you talking about?' asked Andrew.

'Nothing,' was all Eli would say.

9

'What ya thinks wrong with the big man?' asked John.
'Could be a woman,' Patrick suggested, impassively.
'Just cos your wife rules your world doesn't mean it's
the same for the rest of us. Nah it's not that, what's it
been now two months since we last hung out with him'.
'It was New Year's, so yes,' said Patrick.
John scratched his jaw below the seashell pattern of a
scar that covered the right side of his face. He was
gazing across the garage's interior to the empty office.
'Where is he anyway?'
'Where do you think,' replied Patrick irritably.
'Again,' remarked John. 'Jesus, maybe it is a woman.'
'It isn't,' proclaimed the third member of their group.
The two men jumped.
Yaro had always been a silent partner in their
conversations and was more inclined to contribute a
laugh or a nod of his bulbous baldhead. To hear him,
his voice so deep it sounded like it reached out from a
cave, was startling.
'This is something else,' said Yaro, slowly.
The same heavy thoughts cycled in all three heads.
'Well there you have it, Yaro-not-so-silent knocks that
theory down,' said John in his usual dire callousness.
'Then what could it be, where does go at lunchtime
every day?' asked Patrick.

Peter occupied a bench across from Hazel's Try 'N'
Save.
Any passers-by would have deemed the heart-attack-
sized sandwich he was eating necessary. He was far
too skinny. If they had looked a little longer, they might
have thought about phoning an ambulance.

Peter was aware of his physical appearance. He just had more concerning things to worry about, like the memory he found himself recalling.

It was of his father as he worked on an engine.

'You know this is Negi's car, doctor Negi's,' said Jim Brett. 'Their making curries doctors now, fuck-ing tripe. Dhank hue, very mucha Mr. Brentte he says to me. Wouldn't let those dirty, curry hands touch me, you never know what you might catch AIDS or something. They're all a bunch of diseased riddled rats them curries. Of course, our current government just lets them walk right in. Lets them infiltrate and breed while shipping all our jobs to their countries I hear. Cause it's cheap. Giving them power, our power, shitheads. Well, the curries ... they ain't that bad against the niggers. They come here, all yes sir, no sir, but their eyes, niggers got greedy eyes, not for money or power, for women ... white women.'

Peter, the small six-year-old version, listens with rapt attention.

His father's hands also captivate him. They move like instruments made of flesh and bone, precise, skilled, and durable.

'That George Lewis ... is some size of a nigger. You know him?'

Peter blinked. His father rarely asked questions, only for an audience.

'He cuts grass,' said Peter, innocently.

'Does he?' his father hummed. 'Funny, I caught him doing just the same to your mother's lawn. The howls of her ... like a fucking alarm bell, on my bed to'.

For the first time, Peter's attention is diverted. A perplexed earthquake assaults his features. This is fleeting; his father often says things he doesn't understand.

The memory is cut short.

Orchestrated with such accuracy that it could only be fate's middle finger, Jones exits the Try 'N' Save opposite him. He is carrying plastic bags like dumbbells.

(I wanted to kill him, Peter) confessed his father, mournfully.

The surface of Peter's tongue feels coated in ash.

(But I couldn't in the same way I couldn't leave her, or even confront her. I was weak. And knowing that black dick had her shrieking like a banshee every time I left the house poisoned me) the ghost of his father spoke softly.

(What do you feel when you see that white boy and nigger together?) it asked.

(When he's pumping that monkey rod into the white slut? Anger? Hate? That's me, Peter, that's what she made me, and that's what he's making you. You know you can't lie).

'I know, dad,' said Peter.

(But we've both been lying to ourselves, all this following him around, daydreaming fairy tales. Fairy tales are for pussies. They make us feel better for a little while, but really there's no comparison to reality. Look, he will be going down that alley, his cars parked in the lot on the other side lets make our dreams come true).

'Why, dad?' asked Peter tonelessly.

He felt a hesitation in his companion.

(Because it's right. Look at the world, Peter, look what it's given to him, look what it's taken from us. The loneliness, the empty house, the fake friends, we deserve better).

In the same tonelessly voice, Peter agreed.

(Lions only stalk for so long. Eventually, it ends, and it's always with a death).

He agreed. It was just easier.

Peter choked down the last of his lunch.

Anticipation tickled in his intestines as he crossed the street; stopping at his 4x4 to retrieve a wench from the toolbox in the passenger's footwell. This he shoved inside the sleeve of his jacket.

Jones passed by on the pavement; Peter spied his darkened image through the Rover's tinted windows. His breathing grew rapid in seeing him so near.

He followed him as neatly as a shadow.

The alleyway was a narrow canyon where light rarely penetrated. What it did reveal were overloaded bins and discarded cigarette butts. It was the town's unofficial shortcut from the street to the more spacious parking lots. Though commonly used, it was empty.

(An ideal place to hunt) whispered his father.

Sweat greased his fingers as they gripped the end of the wench. Peter could smell wet cardboard. His intestines were no longer excited but heavy.

The alley, despite being a narrowed fissure of shadow, now seemed too open, too bright.

(DO IT).

Jones was humming to himself unconcerned.

(DO IT, NOW).

His fingers tightened on the weapon.

Jones heard an all too loud scrape of a shoe.

Thoughtlessly, he stopped humming, stopped moving, and glanced behind. A man rocketed past him with his hands shoved deep in his pockets.

It is enough for Jones to see that he is far too skinny and not much else.

Eli had finished writing the play and intended to celebrate.

The hall was in darkness. The only lights were those raining in columns on the stage, allowing him a view of a slightly off genuine teenagers' bedroom.

Ready To Start by *Arcade Fire* emitted riotously from his laptop.

The play was three weeks away, but he wanted to see the stage alone. Before the hall became filled with proud but disinterested family members.

He wanted to see it in the quiet and the dark when it was still his. He wondered if his mother would have been proud of his play?

The choice for darkness was inspired by a tactic Logue used to focus his actors. And it worked. They didn't have a cast of Bale's or DiCaprio's, but this strangely elemental atmosphere proved to be fertile soil for their creative efforts.

He heard a sound come from behind the stage backdrop.

'Who's there?' he called.

Fright punctured him.

Already his legs were moving, mounting the stage steps loudly.

The stage lights blinded him to the hall. He was in his character, Alan Heggarty's bedroom. There was his bed, which really was a table with a duvet and low mountain of clothes thrown over it. Having changed his perspective, he could see the backdrop was made up of panels that weren't connected. Between these were abysses of darkness.

The sound reoccurred, something half-heard or half-imagined. Eli faced the particular abyss that he thought was its source.

The dark fell from the figure as he stepped closer. In a split second, before he recognized who it was, he thought it was Dominic Coyle.

It wasn't. It was Justin Blackthorn instead.

Peter clambered inside the cold interior of his car.

(You weak little motherfucking pussy) yelled his father.

He chucked the wench into the toolbox with a crash.

(You had him).
Peter shuddered on seeing his greyish hue in the rearview mirror.
(You're a pathetic weak waste of flesh).
'I'm sorry, dad,' said Peter, pulling out his phone. 'But I think I need to spend time with other people. I don't think you're very good for me'.
His eyes were the worst. Red veins laced his corneas in bright forked roads. Beneath each eye were black/purplish smudges that look like dead flesh.
He sent a text to John and Patrick.
They weren't really his friends. They were the great pretenders of friendship. They offered him their company, and if they need a flavor, he provided. This had never bothered Peter before as their hangouts were about wasting hours. Filling in the time between work and sleep.
His phone beeped.

FROM: PETER BRETT

Fancy the Old Arms tonight?

JOHN MAGUIRE

I'm in, Patrick has to ask his wife if he's allowed first.

PATRICK KELLY

Shut up!!!!! I'm in!!!!

(YOU'RE SUCH A DISAPPOINTMENT, PETER).
'Thanks, dad, good to know,' he said.

Eli's legs dangled from the stage's edge.

Justin's legs did the same beside his. It was bizarre for Eli to see having been avoiding him for so long. Turned out Justin wanted to talk. After twenty tedious minutes, he realized he was trying to apologize.

'Can I just say we're all really impressed with what you've done here. My dad is a big reader, pretty sure he knows more about this stuff than Logue … '

'If he's read *Where's Wally* he knows more about literature than Logue,' said Eli.

Justin regarded him with raised eyebrows and a smirk. 'I let him read your script,' Justin continued. 'He couldn't believe it. There's not much to do around here. I know that better than anyone and doing this, fuck I'm mushy, but I think everyone else feels the same. Doing this, it's learning there's more out there. Being Alan means something to me. Is that too mushy?'

'Completely.'

This time Justin laughed a loud bark of a laugh that made Eli pleased to hear. Perhaps he was the mushy one?

'I came to that audition as a way to taunt you, and now all I can think of doing is saying sorry.'

There was no overbearing presenter persona here, no wolfish leer. Justin rode the hard line of sincerity, an irksome task for any teenager.

Eli found his dislike for him disintegrating.

They sat on the stage's lip, viewing the hall like kings overseeing their kingdom. *The Gaslight Anthem* roared about *The 59 Sound* from his laptop.

'Do you think its any good?' asked Eli, sounding sincere and meaning it.

Justin whistled. His lips spreading in a Cheshire cat grin.

'I think that when it's opening night, they're not going to know what hit 'em,' he replied. After a pause, he added, 'you know I used to think you were a snob.'
'No, I'm just arrogant,' Eli chimed.
'I'm ignorant, please to met ya,' Justin parried lightly.
The doors to the hall clattered. It was Andrew with the other cast members. He managed to summarize the sight of them side by side by raising his hands biblically toward heaven and proclaiming, 'HOLY VAJAYJAY.'

10

Kate slapped a tub of Ben & Jerry's onto the kitchen counter.

On seeing it, Ryan's right eyebrow arched.

'Ice-cream … it's been a while.'

They pressed close then broke apart as what sounded like a herd of elephants descending the stairs.

'We're going to head on now,' said Eli from the hallway.

'Okay, what can I ask, is Jones cooking tonight at this get-together?' asked Ryan.

'Barbecue,' said Andrew.

'Barbecue, it's the last weekend of February,' cried Kate.

'Where's your sense of adventure, Kate,' said Andrew.

'Jones loves barbecue's,' said Eli. 'All week long he's been moaning about how it's been four months since his last.'

'What are you up to tonight?' asked Andrew.

'Just cooking a nice romantic meal for my wife and some … ice-cream' replied Ryan.

The corers of Kate's lips twitched as she held her expression.

Outside as they pulled on their jackets, Andrew said, 'Ryan sure does like ice-cream … maybe he was alluding to something else.'

'Oh god no, my godparents don't do that, they can't,' squealed Eli.

What proceeded for the entire walk was an incessant barrage of innuendo and jokes about the possibility for Eli's godparents' sex life. He laughed despite his embarrassment but thought Andrew went too far by mentioning a sex dungeon.

The aroma of glazed meat greeted them as they reached Jones's driveway. Figures contoured in the day's dying light around a barrel-shaped barbecue in the garden.

'Dude,' gasped Andrew unwittingly.

The object of his perplexed awe was Lucy. She sat sipping a beer with her boots resting on the porch banister. There was something coiled and feline about her, something inaccessible and punk that said I-don't-care.

Andrew's reaction came as no surprise to Eli as he knew of his friend's crush on the band's resident pianist. Half of Hazel was in love with her while he couldn't see her like that. Eli had grown up around her and thought of her as a big sister than a person to desire.

'Keep staring, and your eyes will fall out,' whispered Eli.

'Your eyes will fall out,' retorted Andrew.

His usual lightning-fast wit was dampened as Lucy regarded them. The left half of her face hidden by a fringe of dyed red hair.

'Hungry boys?' called Jones.

Jones, Karl, and Shane were the figures clustered around the sizzling barbecue.

'Eli,' said Lucy.

'I hate you,' whispered Andrew.

'And Andrew,' she added.

A small sound escaped from Andrew's throat. Eli didn't need to look at his friend to know he was near to swooning.

'Now the party can get started with the young blood here.'

'I will hav' you know I'm all young blood,' shouted Shane.

His enormous belly swung as he spun around to face Lucy and the house. Jones and Karl chuckled beside him.

'What are you mouthing on about now, Shane,' bellowed a shrill voice.

Its owner eclipsed the light from Jones's doorway. Her front was in shadow; this, coupled with her sheer size, impressed an ogre-like quality on them. Her voice only added to this impression. It reminded Eli of the way a terrier rips at a toy.

'Some people are trying to have conversations of their own. A little consideration would go a long way,' she said. 'We can hardly hear ourselves think in here let alone speak to one another with all you're cattle calling.' She lingered, scolding unseen but well felt, before waddling inside.

'Jesus, is it me or is she getting worse,' said Jones, lowly.

'I ca'nt understand how Englis' has stuck her,' said Shane.

The others told him to keep his voice down. They had all clustered around the grill, Lucy included, having stepped down from the porch.

Eli, who had affection for English, had spent the least amount of time with his wife, Jane. This had been mostly due to English's actions. He seemed to know the suffering his wife bought on people and was continually shooing them away as she approached.

'I never asked this,' he said to the group. 'But how does someone like that end up with English?'

'Nobody knows,' said Lucy, shrugging.

'They met after the band broke up in our twenties,' said Karl. His voice was a gloomy boom. 'When Brandon got The Renegades together again, this was before Jones was included, though I do believe Brandon sought you out.'

'He did, and I politely told him to fuck off,' replied Jones.

'That was back when it just felt good to be jamming together again,' said Shane.

'Indeed, it did,' said Karl. 'Shane, English and I were always close.'

'Always up to mischief is more like it,' said Jones.

'True, and like all of us, we hadn't seen each other in a while,' said Karl. 'So we thought we'd do the nice thing and invite English's wife to those first few rehearsal sessions, you know, so we could get to know her and vice versa'.

'Bloody disaster,' muttered Shane.

'Oh, I remember those days ... we sucked something fierce,' added Lucy.

'And we all know why,' said Karl, looking to Shane.

'Because of her,' he said.

Five voices hissed him quiet. Once Karl was sure that the giantess from inside was not rising to interrupt them once more, he continued.

'She hated every single second of it and turned up for everyone. Brandon almost threw in the towel on the whole idea of our comeback if I remember correctly'.

'Why?' asked Eli, unable to contemplate such a thing.

'She freaked everyone,' Karl answered.

'Nope, not me,' said Lucy, 'that bitch has got nothing that can scare me.'

'Yes, she has, sweetheart,' said Shane. 'She's got you living in her converted garage because English championed the idea to her, but they only reason she okayed it was so she can be the one to put the squeeze on you.'

'English, wouldn't allow that to happen,' replied Lucy. For the first time, her I-don't-care manner slipped to show genuine concern.

'He wouldn't do that,' said Jones.

'I don't think he would either, maybe back when all this craziness started he would have sat by while she did something like that, but English has grown some backbone since then,' said Karl.

'I'm sorry, but, how exactly did she freak you all out?' asked Andrew.

'Not all, Andrew, not all,' said Lucy, causing his face to blush.

'Well, at first it was just English that seemed to have the problem,' said Karl. 'He kept losing the tempo on songs, missing beats, and he kept looking off to the side to where she was sitting. Being good friends, we didn't know how to tell him that he sucked. And from the look on his face, we could tell he knew he did. So we kept on playing, and sure enough, we all end up looking where he was looking, looking at her staring back with the most … '

'What? Was she angry?' asked Eli.

'She was sad,' said Karl. 'She had the most sorrowful face I've ever seen. I've had years to ponder over it, and I think the reason why Jane looked at us that way was out of jealousy. She had had English all to herself for so many years, knowing now the relationship they have, I don't think she can stand him having any ounce of enjoyment that isn't created by her. That's why he didn't hang out with us so much in the beginning, especially with you'.

Karl pointed to Shane, who shrugged.

'All I did was tell her to piss off that one time.'

'He's improved though over the years,' added Karl. 'Every time we would schedule a rehearsal, she would schedule something else on that day for English to do, now he just ignores whatever plans she makes.'

'You don't know the half of it,' said Lucy. 'He's been speaking out more and more often at the house of recent, I can hear them arguing even though there are fifteen feet of space between their house and my digs.'

'Maybe she thinks English is cheating on her,' offered Andrew.

'She has already suggested that theory a few times about me,' said Lucy, toasting her beer bottle to the sky. 'Why else would he offer me a place to live?' Andrew blubbered out an apology.

'I have no doubt that is exactly what she thinks,' said Jones. 'I don't mean that English has been playing away, but if Karl is right, and I believe he is, Jane's view is that English spending anytime with us is a form of cheating on her. She is a jealous person, as you said, but she's also a very selfish and insecure one'.

'So how come Brandon didn't throw in the towel back then?' asked Eli/

'Ah, we found our groove all right in the end,' said Shane, his voice rising in volume. 'By chance, Jane was busy with her family one day, and English happened to stray from The Gallery to the Dollar, hoping one of us was there. Turns out we all were, enjoying a lovely session of day drinking. It was English that suggested we play something, give it one last shot, and the rest is history.'

He shouted the last word before anyone could hiss at him.

From Jones's came the sound of the front door springing open: she had risen.

'Shane Richards what did I say about your bawling,' she shrieked.

She was on the porch, glaring at down them all.

Her husband, English, stood at her side, and if he could have made himself, any smaller Eli believed he would have in the light from Jones's house.

This was not the night Eli had imagined. Over five years he had gotten to know these people, and he judged that all of them were good-natured, if only sometimes crass. What astounded him was Jane's inability to see them as the same. Instead, she treated as being worthy of ridicule and hate.

No one had ever stood up to her. Not because of the ferocity, which she regularly scorned and berated them with. But because of pity and affection, they all had for their friend, English.

'Guys, this is going to get worse,' Lucy whispered within their group.

'Your nothing but a dumb farmer boy bawling to the heavens,' Jane spat. 'Can't you see there are other people here … like … like the neighbors let alone me. They don't want to hear your heckling. No one wants to listen to a drunk to stupid to get a decent job … '

'WILL YOU SHUT UP?'

The voice shouted so loud it was unrecognizable.

Eli's head whipped around with the rest of them to find the speaker who dared challenge, Jane. On reading Lucy's face, he recalled what she had said about things getting worse. He followed her gaze to the porch and whom she was staring.

The owner of the voice had been English.

He stood by his wife, his hands' fists, and his chest heaving for breath. Jane's eyes bulged, seeming to become all white at his words. Her ballooned face sagged, her chins threatening meeting the tops of her vast chest as she stepped away from him.

The group watched her descend the porch steps backward as if propelled by the heat in English's eyes.

'That's enough,' he said to her.

Her mouth fell open, her jaw working to find the words.

'You dare speak to me like that, in front of people,' she stammered.

None of her previous ferocity could be heard in her voice.

'You're going to get into the car and leave,' English told her.

Lucy smirked from ear to ear.

'Please, English … I didn't mean to be rude … I'll be good, I promise,' said Jane as tears trailed down her cheeks.

It was then that Eli felt sorry for her, sorry that her insecurity made her own worse enemy, that she saw anything other than herself in her husbands' life as a threat.

'No, not tonight, not anymore,' said English.

He stood a wheezy, reed of a man above them. Eli had always thought it was a paradox that he could play the drums with such power. No longer, he was seeing that power now.

'Go home, and wait there, where we can discuss this later,' said English. 'I have a gig to do, and I won't have you here, bullying my friends.'

'I'm no bully,' she shouted. 'English, you know me I could never be … '

'Go,' he said, pointing to their car.

'Fuck you, you bastard,' she spat back at him.

Fresh tears sprung from her eyes, but they were hateful ones. She waddled to their car – luckily the last in the car – and took off in a cloud of gravel and dust.

'Best night ever,' said Shane, gleefully.

English was stagnant atop the porch, reeking god-like power. Lucy was the first to his side.

'Are you okay?' she asked.

'I could use a drink,' he said grimly.

'Shane will see to that,' said Jones. 'The food is almost done.'

'That was intense,' whispered Andrew as they followed the group inside.

'I know I had no idea it was that bad between them,' said Eli.

'Let's enjoy ourselves, she's gone,' toasted English.

He downed his shot before anyone else. Both Eli and Andrew were allowed to partake, and both their faces convulsed at the taste.

Later, Eli cornered Lucy, and he asked, 'is English is going to be all right?'

'Alright,' she said. 'I think English will better than he's ever been in some time if he sees this through and dumps her ass.'

'You think she'll be waiting for him at home?' asked Eli

'Oh aye, she will,' replied Lucy. 'Don't let her tears fool you into thinking she doesn't know what she is doing. She'll have the house a mess, and a suitcase full of her clothes right where he can see it when he's home'.

'Jesus, so this has been going on for some time then?'

'Well, yeah but it hasn't been this bad, I hope that means it might be finally over between them,' Lucy said. 'I don't mean that to sound terrible, but neither of them is happy. The thing is I know English can be content without her, I don't think she can be satisfied with anyone or alone.

Then on seeing Eli's face, she added, 'everyone has a story going on Eli, even if we don't know about it.' It made Eli wondered what other things were going on in the lives of his friends that he didn't know about.

In every town, there exists a bar like The Old Arms. People did not come there to socialize but to drink until their problems evaporated or their money runs out. As such, The Old Arms décor had not changed since it had opened. Its cedar floorings were a century old and seemed not only to soak up split alcohol but light as well. This created the perfect gloominess for its customers to wallow in.

There was no jukebox or even a stage for a live band. It wouldn't have been needed on this occasion as both Peter and John were providing entertainment.

'PUSSY,' they screamed and jousted a swaying Patrick between them. 'Pussy whipped, pussy whipped,' the two chanted ecstatically.

'Put that phone to good use,' demanded Peter. 'Stop texting your ball and chain and play some tunes.'
'Alright, alright, alright,' warbled Patrick.
The song he chose was *Purple Rain.*
'That doesn't really help your street cred,' said John.
Peter snorted while onlookers frowned. Outside there circle The Old Arms usual atmosphere of an unattended graveyard ruled. Neither of the three noticed.
As John taunted Patrick once more, Peter grew deaf to his surroundings.
(Peter) Said his father. This time he was speaking gravelly, tenderly.
(I'm sorry about earlier for everything I said. I used to drink here, but you already knew that didn't you. All those things I taught you, all those memories you forgot or lied to yourself about, you remember them now. I never wanted you to come to this shit hole. I know you like it cause your old man drank here, but I deserved to drink here because I was a cowardly man. I never wanted you to be like that).
Gradually, sound returned from the world around him. It was like someone was slowly turning the volume up. Without thinking, Peter started to talk.
'I missed this guy's,' he said. 'Just have been so distracted lately with … I found out something … unsettling, and I've been struggling with what to do with it
'Whatisit?' slurred, Patrick.
Peter pretended to avoid their gazes, pretended to nervously look in his glass.
'You know The Renegades … '
'They're awesome,' said John.
The glare he received from Peter made him silent instantly.

'I found out, don't ask how, that the guitarist is abusing some kid he's supposed to be teaching guitar. I thought about going to the police, but what would they do: nothing. It's my word against his, and I think the kid is too afraid to say anything.'

'Jesus, that is disgusting,' said John.

This was rich considering what John had some times shown Peter and Patrick on his laptop when drunk, but Peter kept his lips tight.

'What is the world coming to,' said Patrick.

'What would you's do in my situation?' he asked. 'I suppose you both are in my situation now that I've told you both.'

Patrick's face had faded to a snow-white. He looked like a frightened child. John, always eager to please, blinked sluggishly and shrugged.

'I'd teach him a lesson. I'd put fear into him,' he said. Peter leaned forward over the table.

'We could do that,' he said. 'He's playing tonight we could wait until the shows over ... '

'Guys, your not serious about this,' said Patrick.

'A kid is being abused,' John snapped. 'Even if the police believe us and do something they will only put him in jail for paedro's probably not even that, probably let him off with a fine and what, that kid gets to be the weirdo forever.'

It was so easy, really, Peter thought, falling silent. *They practically convince themselves.*

(Good boy, Peter, I'm so proud of you, son) said his father's voice.

Found in a notebook of Eli Donoghue's concerning what transpired on the 28/02/11.

I kept an article from that night. It was by some journalist who happened to step into the Dollar and chanced upon The Renegades. They ended up writing a review of sorts, nothing major there's been many wrote about them over the years.

It's not even that good.

The author tries to give the reader a sense of being there with ludicrously common adjectives such as 'tremendous,' 'powerful' and 'moving.' Has anyone ever felt the feeling of such words after reading them? I doubt it.

In its 250 short words, it does no justice to what occurred during those hours. How the old songs fitted neatly with the new. Or that *Bob Dylan's Summer Days* became a sleazy, gritty grind of a song. How the audience jived and bopped and slide up and down each other to its dirty guitar jangle. It became a song where you seek that person you longed to disappear with, in the dark. That's not mentioned. It doesn't say the crowd suffered three more songs of this nature as the band revved into *Slippery When Wet* by *The Commodores* before *Kiss* by *Prince*. How they revived the *Coaster's* song *Down In Mexico* that had Jones, Karl, Shane, English, and Lucy singing in jubilant sync like 50-style backing singers. Nor does the article mention that to prevent the crowd from turning into an orgy The Renegades covered *Coldplay's Viva La Vida's,* getting everyone to sing along. Or how the lights dimmed, and lighters starred the darkness as *Mumford & Sons Awake My Soul* was covered.

These are only a few moments in an entire catalog.

I can tell you we left Jones's bellies full and minds only lightly pondering English's melodrama, that as we neared the Dollar's doors, a focused levity overcame us. If it had ended differently, I would have kept this article for reasons geeky and greedy. Instead, it serves to provide me with a condemning reminder. We went into the Dollar like everyone else, propelled by our past, hoping to find a level of happiness. Life, as it usually has, had other plans for us.

Eli.

Outside the air was icy cold.

Its touch burned against his hot face and froze in his throat. He exhaled a jet of steam and tried to steady his shoulders from swaying. They seemed to want to dance. Somewhere close by John let out a high-shrieking howl.

The trio giggled together. John howled once more. The scar on his face gleamed silvery as he thrust his baldhead into the moonlight.

The howl was swallowed by the dark.

Around them was Hazel's closed linen mill, the factories standing as empty husks. To Peter, the way their towering outline merged with the deep black of the winter's night sky reminded him of a gothic castle long abandoned.

'This is where he used to work,' said Peter to the others.

He directed their attention to a derelict building on the perimeter of the mill's land. The fence that extended from this building had collapsed in several places, allowing them access.

'How do you know that?' asked Patrick.

'Cause I've been researching him,' Peter snapped back.

The ground at their feet was littered with objects. One of them happened to be a piece of piping that John lashed out at, sending it skidding across the lot. On hearing and liking the metallic clang it made, Peter retrieved it
They continued on.

The Renegades had a tradition.
Once the bouncers had escorted the last drunk from the Dollar, it became theirs. Or in actuality, Brandon allowed them its use and even free drink, which was why Shane was currently passed out over a table. Eli and Andrew were finding great delight in doodling on his forehead with a permanent marker.
Beside them, English was encircled in toasting arms.
'If you and Lucy need a place to stay, just say,' said Karl. To which Lucy responded by saying, 'it's that bitch that has to find a place to stay, not us.'
Jones observed all this while texting Mia.
'Whose awake at this hour texting you?' asked Brandon from behind him. 'Who would be texting you when everyone you know is here?'
Jones wheeled around while slipping the offending item into his jeans.
'Surprisingly, I do have a life outside of this place that you're not part of,' said Jones.
Brandon's eyes continued to gaze from a fixated position of curiosity.
'I thought I said having a life outside of the Dollar wasn't allowed.'
And there it was, thought Jones.
His words weren't quite a threat unless you knew Brandon and unfortunately he did. Though, in this case, he believed it was more a suggestion of risk was being implied. Being in control wasn't enough for Brandon. He liked to make sure you knew who pulled the strings.

170

'There's your mistake,' said Jones. 'In this world you need it signed and in writing to make anything stick.' He drained his glass and turned away. It was like turning your back on a tiger you've noticed hunched in the undergrowth.

There had been a time when things had been friendlier between them. Though, Jones had always been wary of the large, quiet man who viewed everything with detachment and skepticism. It turned out he had been right to do so.

'Alright,' he boomed in an announcement. 'If I don't start packing up we'll be here all night.'

'Nothing wrong with that,' said Lucy.

Spryly, Jones heaved himself onto the stage to retrieve his guitar.

'Well, let me put it this way. The quicker we get this stuff packed up, the quicker we can all go back to mine for barbecue. I've still got half a cow to cook'.

'I'm up for tha,' shouted Shane sitting up, causing Eli and Andrew to shriek with fright.

Jones slammed his car boot closed, his guitar safely sealed inside.

'Where's your lady friend tonight? The one you're always texting when you think no one's looking. Don't you lie to me I know what you've been up to?'

He hadn't heard Lucy following him outside, which was typical. Trying to appear cool, he rested his rump on his car's boot. The pair contemplated each other bathed in the boozy amber light from above the Dollar's back door.

'Who told you such nonsense?' he asked

Lucy coyly stretched her arms, clasping her hands together behind her.

'The lady herself,' said Lucy gleefully. 'Having a secret isn't worth keeping unless you can confide in one person and then gossip endlessly about it. Be glad she has me as a friend as I can keep a secret. Not many can in this small town. Even if she hadn't told me it's pretty clear your seeing someone when you cancel on English's poker nights or Shane's cinema trips, plus your always on your phone nowadays'.

'Shit,' sighed Jones. It was all he could think to say. 'Has she told you … '

'Everything, yep,' she said and laughed.

His cheeks burned.

'And Mia should trust you even though you're telling me about it,' said Jones.

'Well, I figured since Mia's secret involves you, I could tell you,' she said. 'Plus I asked her, and she said to let you know as it would annoy you. Actually, the word she used was to tease you … aren't you heading round their tonight?'

'Nah, it's late, plus now that I've offered Shane will be planning to eat me out of house and home until he passes out on my sofa,' said Jones.

'You gotta love him.'

'Has English been confiding in you lately?' asked Jones.

Lucy tilted her head, making the crimson blade of her fringe flop across her eyes. Her coy grin remained but with an added pinched look at the edges.

'Well, after what happened early I guess his personal plight isn't a secret anymore so I can talk about it,' said Lucy. 'Yeah, he's been confiding in me.'

'I know what he means to you so I won't ask for details,' said Jones. 'You also know what he means to me, so tell me how serious was tonight's argument.'

'Very serious,' Lucy told him. 'It's the best thing for him, though.'

'I'll take your word for it,' said Jones. 'Come one we better get back inside before people start gossiping about us now.'

'Yes, the parties' heart and soul are being missed.'

They crossed the alleyway behind the Dollar. Jones was two strides behind Lucy when his world was violently wrenched from him.

The pain would come later.

For the moment he was sailing, his legs dislodged from the earth. The dingy alley, with its nauseating light, rose to a phenomenal height. His piece-of-shit car was on its piece-of-shit-side, and he was drifting by. Then the wet and hard tarmac charged upward to enforce reality. The pain came now brilliant and red from his back and ankles.

A bellow splintered through his lips and meshed teeth.

'BOOM,' roared an unfamiliar voice.

A shadow fell upon him as he lay. Its source loomed above him coated in shadow.

The figure bent at the knees, entering the light. The face of Jones's attacker belonged to a goblin; its skin was pulled taut over sharp bone while eyes were unblinking and lunatic.

'We're gonna gut you nigger,' it proclaimed, and Jones believed it.

The goblin man hunched at his side, inches away. Jones could smell and taste fumes off of his rank drunken breathe.

It is then that he noticed what is in his hand. A length of piping, which by the power of deduction Jones guessed had been used to trip him.

Suddenly, there's a scream, and Jones spun to see Lucy bear-hugged by another much fatter man who was currently pinching her cheek. A third man stood against the Dollar's back door, blocking any help that could come.

'Don't worry,' said the goblin man. 'We only want you.'

Things were going swimmingly.

The trip-up had been a perfect, cricketers' swing. A tsunami of satisfaction drowned him as he stared down at Jones, and he realized he didn't know what to do. He had dreamt and fantasied for so long that now the moment of his desires was before him, and he was clueless. It's sort of funny. Sure enough, Daddy came to the rescue.

(Make him suffer).

'My dad told me about people like you,' said Peter, almost tenderly.

He jumped to his feet and bought the pipe down. Jones managed to get his arm up in defense only to howl as pain erupted across his deltoid.

'Nothing but greedy, vicious people that take and take and leave nothing for the people that actually deserve anything.'

The pipe cut down again. Jones could hear Lucy crying now.

The goblin man grabbed him by the face and lifted him close to his own.

'All those friends …the woman … oh yes, I know about her, I've seen you bucking like dogs in heat. Wouldn't mind breaking her in myself,' said Peter chuckling. 'Why do you have that?' he asked in a whisper. 'Why do you get such things?'

The pipe end was jabbed into his stomach, and Jones coughed. The next jab tore something in him. Jones didn't have time to cry as a sledgehammer walloped into his jaw. Darkness invaded his vision, promising escape.

No, you'll die, hold on you old motherfucker, hold on for Lucy.

'Look at him, boys,' announced Peter. 'He's shit hot, this town loves him, and he's banging some white bird, and probably this skinny little dyke here as well. He has the world. Don't we deserve that as well? Don't we deserve women on our cocks?'

'You have to get them hard first,' gasped Jones, his voice choked in pain. 'Though, in your case, I imagine it still would be laughable to see.'

Peter's arms which had been raised in celebration fell. He stared enraged at the man that should be begging and frightened and is instead defiant with his words.

'Hey, I thought you said he was fiddling with some kid,' said John while holding Lucy.

'Oh, what does it matter anymore, you're here now,' said Peter.

With those words he launched himself at Jones, hacking at his body with the pipe and his feet. His blows fell with no rhythm or coordination just manic fury, each hit connecting with a meaty thump.

'Stop it,' Lucy cried to no avail.

When Peter finally stepped back, he was breathless and gasping. Jones was a ball at his feet in a growing pool of blood. In the alley light, it looked like oil.

Briefly, the alley became a pocket universe surrounded in edged silence. The only sounds inside it were Peter regaining his breath and Lucy's whimpering.

The other two men shared a glance, and she sensed their worry. This had gone further than it was supposed to her mind told her. Even though her eyes were fixed on Jones's body, a part of her brain, the region in charge of survival was still working, it seemed.

'Perhaps, we should go,' said her captor.

As he did, Lucy yanked his thumb backward. A yelp of pain escaped him, and she found herself no longer caged within his groping arms. She knew her success was only down to the fact that his commitment had wavered. But she didn't care. She was running and already feeling a stitch biting into her side.

'Get her,' she heard the man with the pipe yell.

She wanted to yell back, 'fuck you, bitch,' but she needed all the breath she could muster.

Tears blurred her vision. She was hyperventilating and not getting a decent enough lungful. She felt like she was running through water.

Arms folded around her waist, followed by a weight that bought her to the ground.

She met it face-first as two of them fell on her. She screamed and fought and flailed. One was laid across her, pinning her to the wet ground. The man's sharp rasping breath caressed her right ear. The other one was grappling with her fighting arms.

Together, they held down her arms at the elbows. Then the one with the pipe began to hammer at her splayed fingers, breaking the bone.

This time Lucy's screams were guttural, agonized.

'Hey, what's going on here,' yelled a muffled voice.

Patrick shoved his shoulder into the Dollar's back door as bodies became to batter against its other side.

'Shit, I can't hold them off forever,' Patrick wailed. 'Let's get the fuck out of here.'

'Come on,' yelled Peter racing by with John in tow.

The moment Patrick fled the door was flung open with a bang. What followed was the sound of many feet funneling into the alley. Some took off in pursuit of the attackers while others froze still. English was one of the latter.

'Dear God,' he said.

11

They were waiting, waiting for news, waiting for the guillotine to drop.

Everyone from the Dollar either stood or sat outside the ward Jones had been admitted to including Kate, Ryan, and for some reason, Eli didn't understand; Mia. Lucy had yelled at English to contact her, as she was loaded into the back of an ambulance.

The restaurant owner stared at the doors to the ward with eyes that had a glazed, lost look.

The drop of the guillotine blade came in the form of a nurse. She stepped through the ward doors, took one scan of the crowd and began to speak.

'You can see him now, but only one visitor at a time; he's had a lot of painkillers and needs his rest. Lucy is still speaking with the police'.

In the corner of Eli's eye, he saw Brandon step forward to speak when someone else spoke first. It was English who occupied the seat beside him.

He stared tenderly at Eli from underneath a set of wiry silver eyebrows.

'I think you should be the first to see him,' said English. A quick glance around the group led to various nods of approval. Eli ignored Brandon's frown as he stood, his godparent's hands patting him on the back.

Eli followed the nurse through the double doors, down a corridor and to a bay of six beds, all full. 'If you need anything, just call,' said the nurse, who was several inches shorter than him. She spun on her heel and left him.

Jones's bed was the first on the right.

He lay in its center, facing the ceiling. A monitor by the bed beeped, displaying figures that might as well have been another language. A bag hung from underneath the bed filled with piss that was bright red.

His face hadn't been cleaned properly.

Someone had hastily tried to clean away the blood but hadn't completed the job. It smeared Jones's swollen face, and Eli felt his heart fracture in seeing it.

It made him want to tear at those responsible that his fingers curled into fists. He wanted to use them on the people that had done this, he wanted to punch and beat and claw at them until his hands were bloody. The anger sizzled in him as he stared at his friend, tears silently falling down his cheeks.

'Jones,' he said, his voice a whimper.

His friend did not respond, though his chest continued to rise and fall without hindrance. The painkillers the nurse had mentioned were doing their job.

'The people that did this ... they'll get what's coming to them,' said Eli.

He had no idea how right he was.

Later, after everyone had left, Brandon made a phone call.

'Ben, I need a favor... now,' he said, 'I don't care what the time is, call me back as soon as you get this.'

He ended the call on hearing the ivory click-chop of expensive shoes. He pocketed his mobile and greeted Hazel's newly re-elected mayor.

'Where is he?' said Roy Jones.

Roy didn't wait for an answer but plowed into the ward. Brandon followed, gears ticking in his head as he noted Roy's flapping bed robe.

You look old tonight, Roy, and you're the younger brother.

Roy halted by his brother's bedside. A hitched creak escaped his throat as he stared at the mess that was Jones's face.

'It's bad,' said Brandon coldly. 'Physically, broken ribs, jaws pretty tore up, there was internal bleeding, but the doctors managed to patch it up in surgery. It's just a waiting game to see what his mental state is when he wakes. He's taken some hard knocks to the head'.
'Who did this'?
'I'm working on that. That's not the question you want to ask, though. What you want to ask is what do we do when we find the people that did this'.
Roy's eyes snapped from his brother to the man beside him.
'Your brother was doing his job, enjoying his life and someone took that from him and dropped him in that bed,' said Brandon. 'Whatever the reasons are, I'll find out, but we both know they won't justify this. Doing this is nothing but sadistic and calculated. They knew he was working tonight, knew where he parks his car'.
'You think someone planned to do this.'
'Don't be stupid,' spat Brandon. 'Of course, this was planned.'
Roy's throat closed. Even in grief, he felt wary of Brandon's fury.
'I'll leave it in your hands. You won't find any resistance from my end'.
Brandon nodded, slipping soundlessly away, pulling out his phone as he did.

It had been too easy to find them.
All it took was a right ear, Ben Cartwright believed.
Ignore the noise - musician attacked behind the Dollar - and listen to the quieter voices in the fray. Ben admitted that if he hadn't turned out to a crooked cop, he would have actually made a pretty good one.

He mapped a journey of compliments through Hazel from that night. He tracked these to their source, The Old Arms, where the bar staff was more than willing to help. This information was passed on to the 'right' person. What surprised him this time was he had not been ordered to destroy his findings only delay reporting them.

John Maguire might have lived if he had paid more attention.

His apartment building had a specific design fault. While the walls provided visual discretion, they did not, in fact, provide audible privacy due to their paper-like thinness. This was apparent as he heaved himself onto the landing.

'I can't believe this,' raged Mrs. Johnson from 211. 'I've been at work all fucking day, and you haven't even moved your fucking arse off that sofa. Look at this place'.

'What? You've only been gone four hours,' came Mr. Johnson's response.

A torrent of swearing exploded from behind the blue slate walls. Further along a child wailed in 210. This was either being ignored or wasn't being heard over the zing of bedsprings from the same flat. These were a small part of the maelstrom that made up his building. Some nights he swore he could hear if a mouse sneezed two floors above him.

Tonight, John gave it little consideration.

He was haunted by the memory of the girl's hot skin in his arms and the coppery scent of blood in the air. It had been plagued for days, arousing dark thoughts and lusts in his already stressed mind; particularly, when he remembered how she had trembled in his arms.

Enough, he thought, *no more thinking about this crap. I have tomorrow off, two bottles of vodka, a curry to order and then a long night on the Xbox. If murdering some teenagers online can't ditch this the vodka surely will.*

Pre-occupied by his hope to lift his guilt, he did not notice the whine belonging to the apartment's buildings entrance doors. Nor did he hear the clump of many boots as he continued down the dim corridor to his apartment door.

If he had, he might have thought it strange as he was usually the last home during the week. As it was, he inserted his key into the door and slipped inside, unaware.

John had christened his flat: his shithole.

The corridors' drabness extended into his living space. Paint peeled from the walls under the feeble light of bare bulbs. Damp and cold was its air.

He had thought of moving numerous times. But he never did, claiming he couldn't be bothered. Though, in his more honest moments, he thought places were like habits: sometimes they got their hooks into you and didn't let go.

With a wheezy, grumble, he placed his shopping bags onto the kitchen counter. The familiar tension in his lower back from another day's work spiked.

As he grasped the two necks of his vodka bottles, a charge of footsteps rocked the boards beneath his feet. They ceased with a sharp crack.

He spun to see splinters flying from his door as it was batted open. Men trooped into his home all dressed in black. He recognized their faces as Dollar's bouncers.

'Hello, John,' said the man closest to him.

'Alec,' responded John.

'Nothing personal but you fucked up, man,' said Alec. 'I'm sorry, but the boss is gunning for you.'

'Jesus,' he gasped.

'Just the way it is.'

Until this point, John had lost all sense of himself. As they lunged at him, he reconnected to the weight in his hands.

He tossed both bottles at them. The man beside Alec threw up his arms as both bottles smashed over him. Glass and vodka laced the apartment's damp air.

As the men cowered, John slammed the fridge door into Alec's face.

'Son of a bitch,' he roared, blood spouting from his ruined nose.

Alec fell backward, causing a bottleneck in the entrance to John's kitchen. The man behind him half-tripped/half jumped and seized upon John's leg.

Over balanced, he grappled onto the countertop, spilling items. He gripped something that felt like a weapon and slashed at his attacker's face. It was a potato peeler.

The crappy device caught in man's cheek and skinned him. The scream that erupted from him threatened to burst John's eardrums.

He ran, leaving the peeler dangling, it's blades still seized in the man's flesh. He ran from the kitchen and toward the living room windows.

Something like a brick wall tackled him.

Colors somersaulted as he was speared over a couch chair. They were on him in seconds. Fists rained down like meteors. John tried to kick out, to punch, to bite, to crawl but it was no use. They trailed him along the floor, mopping him into tables, the TV. He got one good lick, hearing swears as his foot connected. However, the begrudged recipient lifted the nearest object at hand, his Xbox, and hammered it down on the seashell-like-scar on his skull. Bone cracked. As the white box was raised over his head, he could once more smell the sickening coppery scent.

It seemed he couldn't get away from it after all.

'I'll see you tomorrow, Stacy,' said Patrick, refusing to look at her.

Instead, he bent his head and stared at his walking feet. Patrick not only being the type of person that feels incapable of keeping a secret but one that feels his face gives it away.

'Bye, bye, Patrick,' she replied behind him. 'See you tomorrow.'

'Yeah … see ya,' he said.

He had stressfully avoided Stacy's gaze all day. Especially when she questioned Peter's ongoing absence.

'What do you think is going on with him,' she had asked him at least twice?

Thankfully, her questioning was more an admission of her own curiosity. She had not yet thought Patrick might know something significant.

If she had, she would have interrogated him.

'Fuck you, Peter,' he said under his breath.

And he meant it.

In his mind, Peter's disappearing act threatened to link them to a brutal crime that was now the gossip of the town. He suspected Peter had himself shut away in his house continuing the bender that had made them all criminals.

How did I get into this, he thought despairingly.

Stacy's motor trundled alongside him to the kerbside. She gave him a final wave before turning right, and he reciprocated going left.

Tall hedgerows soon framed a thin road without a pavement. From ahead Patrick could hear the rush of the river and see the hump of the stone bridge he crossed every day. Beyond it was his home and Muriel, his girlfriend, or as the guys referred to her as his ball-and-chain.

She wasn't possessive like the nickname implied, nor was she demanding and he weak-willed. She simply enjoyed his company and still did after four years. The feeling was mutual, and though he would never admit it to the guys, it was with her that he felt the most content, most happy.

They didn't have much with him working at the garage and her beauty business, but they had each other. That's all that seemed to matter.

A point that was becoming even more apparent to Patrick after what he had been involved with. Why had he allowed himself to be dragged along? He now speculated that everything Peter had told them was a lie - that Jones was not some evil child abuser - but it had been his way of getting them on his side.

Thankfully, he wasn't dead, according to the local grapevine. That would have made Patrick an accessory to murder instead of assault. Still, the thought caused his mind to wallow low, even mounting the bridge where he had a view of the river below, could not take his despair away as it usually did after a hard day.

Today, the water surged over the rivers rocky bed, forming white.

It was then that he heard the car gliding up behind him. At first, his mind panicked, thinking it was Stacy, returning to question him some more. However, as the vehicle drew alongside him, he realized he didn't recognize it.

It was something similar in design and size to Peter's 4x4.

The driver window descended with an electronic whirl. Alec Johnston, one of the Dollar's bouncers, leered at him from within the window frame.

'How's it going, Patrick?' he asked and then added, 'off home to the Misses.'

'You are correct,' replied Patrick.

Despite his confident tone, his body felt enveloped in heat. The 4x4 with the black tinted windows matched his walking pace to cruise alongside him. It was a squeeze with the narrowness of the bridge and the vehicle's behemoth size.

Patrick could feel his hip scratching the bridge's stone as he walked.

'Dam, Alec, that looks nasty, what happened to your face?'

'Oh, this,' said Alec, pointing at his bruised nose.

'Some guy took a swung at me the other night when I was working at the door. You should see him what he looks like'.

The bouncer laughed without any humor. Patrick noticed that the 4x4 was full with several other bouncers that worked at the Emerald Dollar.

The encompassing sensation of heat was replaced with an icy caress at his spine.

'Can I do something for you?' asked Patrick.

'As a matter of fact, you can,' said Alec, leaning out the window.

There was a window or door open somewhere.

The heating was on due to the arctic chill returning for one last heehaw. Yet, there was an unmistakable cold current, which Peter could feel even beneath his robe. It tickled the skin of his pelvis, causing it to harden with goosebumps. The sensation was surprisingly delightful. As soon as Peter acknowledged this pleasure, he froze, awaiting judgment. The voice of his dead father, which had plagued him relentlessly, stayed mute.

In the kitchen, he found the glass sliding door to the back garden ajar without any memory of having of leaving it so. This was nothing new. Peter had spent the last three days drinking to forget. Often after passing out, he woke to find he had damaged or moved furniture with no memory of doing such.

As he grabbed the door handle, he paused and looked beyond. There was nothing out there, but snow and darkness and silence. He slid the door closed and made his way to the drinking cabinet.

Glass trilled on the glass as his pouring hand shook.

'I expected … well … something different' said someone behind him.

Peter choked on his whiskey, spinning.

The owner of the voice sat on the arm of Peter's sofa, a bemused smirk on his lips as his eyes took him in. He was large, huge even, dressed in dark winter clothes, his hands clad in black leather gloves. One of them held a revolver.

'What the hell do you think you're doing here,' spluttered Peter.

His words caused the home invader to glance at the detritus that coated the room.

'Let's not play dumb, now,' said the invader. 'From the state of this place, I think you've been expecting someone to turn up at your door. Probably not me, but the police perhaps; guilt is a corrosive thing for those that feel it'.

He spoke in such a soft, casual tone that Peter had to strain his ears to hear. Yet, that did not stop them from squeezing at his heart.

Everything the intruder had said was true.

'Do you feel it, guilty, I mean?' he asked.

Peter stood there, bathrobe open, revealing his naked chest and boxers, a glass of whiskey forgotten in his hand. The intruder's gaze searched his face.

'No,' he said, 'you're not, you're just afraid. You're one of those uncommitted individuals that lack the balls to follow anything through. I've known types like you, you feel bad after you've done something heinous, and you think it absolves you. It doesn't, it just makes you a pussy'.

'My name is Brandon Moran,' said Brandon. 'You might not know this, but I own this town. If you value the fact that your genitals are currently attached to your body and wish for it to remain so, do not lie to me. Understand?'

Peter felt hot liquid dirty his loins and run down his legs. He whimpered in disgust and fear.

(*Jesus wept. You're such a disgrace*)

What was that? Was that fear he heard in his father's voice as it tried to return?

Fuck you, Dad, thought Peter. *You got me into this shit, and you fucked off.*

With that, he boxed his father's voice and buried it in his mind. Even that didn't feel final, but for now, he was without fear of it.

'Can we focus on the moment?' asked Brandon. 'It is common knowledge that I own The Emerald Dollar, and as such, I own The Renegades. You and your friends hurt my people, people that are valuable assets to my business. The doctors say that Lucy, the bands' pianist, has severe nerve damage and is not likely to regain the dexterity that she would employ to hold a pen, let alone play the piano. And Jones,

Jones, if he does wake, could wake as a retard. In light of this information, I have murdered your friends. I was told they were much like you, as they died, pussies'.

'Oh yes, I know all about them, about your little drunken walk about town before you ended up at my bar. What I don't know is why did you do it.'

'He was hurting that boy,' Peter stammered.

'Now, now,' said Brandon, unperturbed, 'I don't believe that. Dorian Jones is such a saint that if he ever found out what I have done, and what I'm going to do he would tell the police, even though he knows it would never amount to anything. So do you want to reconsider that answer?'

Peter's mind whirled.

(*Tell him the truth and while he's listening do his fucking head in with your glass*).

He looked down at the glass as if noticing it for the first time. Then gazed at what Brandon held casually in his hands.

'Don't worry, I am not here to kill you, this … ' Brandon said, patting his gun, '… this is to ensure you cooperate. I am here to tell you that your punishment will be more special than that of your so-called friends. In a few minutes, the police will knock on your door and arrest you, just like you thought they would. You'll be questioned, but let me tell you that whatever you say doesn't matter; they have enough to put you away. Even if you tell them about our little exchange here, they will think of it as the ravings of a mad man. Once you have been sentenced and imprisoned, you will meet some of my friends. I want you to remember this when they're fucking with you; you should never mess with a man's business'.

Peter stepped back, pressing into the cabinet and causing several bottles to crash to the floor. Brandon smiled at him, revealing a line of teeth that were shark white.

'I'll let myself out,' he said, standing.

From outside the front of the house, gravel was crunched under wheels. Brandon was already opening the sliding door in the kitchen when Peter spoke.

'He deserved it,' he seethed.

The anger in his was apocalyptic. It wormed beneath his skin like lava underneath the earth.

'He had everything I ever wanted, he had a real life, real friends, people that loved him, admiration, a hot piece of ass. He had what I deserved. My father said that's what you people do, steal, except he was too weak to ever do anything about it. Well, I did. I did something about it; I took it all away from him. After all, it's only fair if I can't have those things, then no one like you should be able to.'

The next words Brandon said were in a voice that could hammer nails.

'There's the monster I was looking for. You enjoy your life now, Peter.'

Then he was gone, and there was a knock at the front door.

12

Jones could not describe his experience of waking. One moment he was in blackness and the next he was in a light, blinding and absolute. As his eyes adjusted, as it dimmed, in its center was a face. Mia.

13

English spied her sitting on the swing seat.
The temperature had risen recently but not enough to
not require a coat. Lucy sat without one. He strolled
over, lighting a cigarette as he did, to the seat beside
her.
'I heard shouting,' said Lucy.
'Aye, Jane decided to take the television,' he replied. 'I
didn't object just reminded her that it was screwed into
the wall, which only seemed to antagonize her.'
The two exchanged a glance.
'You should have seen her pulling at the thing,' said
English. 'I thought she was either going to have a heart
attack or shit herself.'
He continued to smoke while gazing at the dewed lawn.
Eventually, she slid across the bench and twined one
arm through his. She nestled her head against his bony
collarbone, allowing him to breathe the scent of her
hair.
'Tell me everything is going to be alright,' she said.
English could tell she was trying not to look at her
hands. The bandages were monstrously large in
comparison with the rest of Lucy's slender body.
'Everything will be alright,' he lied.
'You're the best friend I've ever had you know that,' she
said and tightened her hold of him.
'Jolly good, to hear it,' he replied, hugging back. 'We
will work something out, the band will find a way.'
'English, I'm not part of the band anymore,' she said,
raising her injured hands.
'You will always be part of the band,' he snapped back.

English rarely expressed anger that Lucy did not answer back.

'As long as you want to be, there will always be a place for you,' he said.

'Thank you,' she said, then looking to the house asked, 'is it really over between you and her.'

'It is for me,' replied English. 'She was a sweet person once, I know you never got to see that side of her, and you might find that hard to believe, but she was. We had some good years together before the band came back into my life. When I look back now I see those years as quiet ones, I suppose Jones would know what I mean by that, he would say he had the same experience with his wife, Rachel. You become each other's worlds, and when something new enters that threatens to change the routine of that life, it can be frightening, especially for someone insecure in the first place. I just have no more patience anymore to deal with her insecurity or trying to coax that sweet part of her out. I suppose that means I have thrown in the towel, which feels pretty shitty, but you can't keep trying to help someone when they don't want to change. And I think that is Jane's ultimate problem; she wants things to be as they were in those quiet years'.

'You'll go mad, eventually trying to change her,' said Lucy.

'Dam, right,' replied English.

His cigarette was finished, so he crushed it upon the swing.

'Come on we better get inside before we both develop pneumonia,' he said, helping Lucy from the seat.

Eli was supposed to be revising.

Instead, his attention was focused on the front page of The Antrim Guardian. The main article concerned the discovery of Patrick Wilson's body by a riverside.

Jones entered the front room on crutches as he read.

'Think you can take time away from your studies to watch a movie?' he asked. 'What is it that you're even studying anyway?'

'Maths,' Eli lied. 'Shouldn't you be sleeping?'

'I've had enough of bed rest after the last three weeks thank you. I've even begun to resent the idea of entering a bed for carnal relations'.

Eli propelled to his feet as Jones threw himself into his favorite chair.

'Sit down,' he said. 'If you and Mia keep jumping up and down like that every time I do something you'll become jack in the boxes.'

'Yeah … well … speaking of Mia, you kept that one a secret.'

'Yeah, came as a shock did it? I guess I enjoyed it ... having a secret.'

'You don't have to explain anything to me,' said Eli.

A look of concern passed across Jones's face.

'Well, shit kid, where did that come from? Come on, even without that comment you're about as readable as a book. You've been skulking around here for days'.

A frown creased Eli's forehead.

'Two of the men that attacked you are in the paper, there dead.'

'And,' said Jones?

Eli's frown deepened. His fingers begun to nervously tap the head of his seat while the muscles around his eyes tightened.

'Aren't you feel pleased that there dead. I mean you haven't even seemed angry throughout any of this. Aren't you angry because I certainly am? I wanted to strangle those men for what they did to you and Lucy. And yet to you its like water off of a ducks back. Aren't you angry'?

His voice broke in pitch on the last word, causing him to cough.

'I am angry,' replied Jones. 'In fact, I'm more angry about what they did to Lucy than what they did to me. They can rot in hell as far as I'm concerned, and that's as much thought as I'm gonna give them. I will not wallow over them or this.'

He struck out his arms, indicating the clutches.

'I've done enough of that in my lifetime. If you want to blame someone for my attitude, then blame yourself. Yes, you. I've lived a hard sixty years kid, yet seeing you putting aside your father leaving and what happened to your mother to give life a chance granted me perspective. Time is precious. I ain't gonna waste it, certainly not on scumbags like those fuckers. You should do the same'.

Eli had clenched the chair head in his hand.

'This is different,' he said weakly.

'How is it different?' challenged Jones. 'The only difference here is the hurt is still fresh, but that will change. I'm healing. I'll be back to my usual self in no time. As for Lucy well, the band is figuring something out. And as for those men … well looks like the two got what's coming to them and the other one, Peter, will get his'.

Eli was speechless. The fury that had eaten at his insides for weeks had become diluted with confusion. He had almost lost his best friend to a bunch of hoodlums and yet it was his friend he had hated for his maturity, his unshakeable correctness.

Exhaustion struck him like a sedative drug.

'Now that we've dealt with your potential origin story as a vigilante when's your play again,' said Jones.

'This is serious,' mumbled Eli.

'So is your play,' stated Jones. 'Everything that we can possibly do about this has been done. It is now in the hands of the police, so you have two choices, rage and sulk, or get on with the life you've been living until this happened. What's it gonna be'?

Eli's jaw worked as he pondered.

'It's on the twentieth of his mouth,' replied Eli.

'Good, book us a ticket, will ya, now how about that movie.'

Later after Eli had left and Mia arrived, she noticed that Jones was distracted. He had promised her a romantic dinner, 'seeing as you've probably cooked for everyone in this town at some point I think you more than owed a meal cooked by someone,' he had said. Though, with his current condition, she had opted to help.

'Jones, why don't we save a cucumber for the bedroom tonight,' said Mia.

'Sounds nice, dear,' he replied.

Mia watched a frown dimple upon her lover's head. His hands, which had been busy, chopping spring onions, slowed to a stop.

'I'm sorry I missed that,' said Jones.

'Ha, and you won't hear it again,' she said, batting him gently with the cucumber. 'Where is your head tonight?'

'Up me arse apparently,' he said. 'I kinda lied to Eli today. Well, I feel like I lied, so I suppose that means I did actually lie to him'.

'What about?'

'Brandon,' replied Jones.

The two exchanged a knowing look.

'It was more that I didn't fully explain everything to him when I had the chance,' Jones said. 'The kid was angry about what happened, naturally, and I kind of put him on a track that would steer him away from uncovering anything Brandon might have any involvement in.'

'So, you do think Brandon was behind what happened to the guys that attacked Lucy and you?' asked Mia.

'Yes.'

'You shouldn't feel bad for lying to, Eli. You were protecting him, which begs the question should you be working for such a man?'

When Jones finally answered her question, it was as they sat for dinner.

'I use Brandon as much as he thinks he uses me,' Jones told her. 'He isn't a danger unless you stand in the way of the Dollar.'

'Don't worry, I'm not going to tell you to quit,' said Mia. 'You don't have to justify yourself with me. This is good by the way, thank you for half cooking for me'.

They smiled at each other over their plates.

'I remember Brandon from the time I kicked around with you,' said Mia, 'and I know him now as a businessman in this town. I know how possessive that man can be. Just be safe.'

'I have nothing to worry about when it comes to Brandon,' replied Jones.

'No, I know you don't. Brandon protects his own, but I feel its something that needed to be said,' said Mia, shrugging. 'Someday, you might not be 'his own' as you put it.'

'So what's this about cucumber and the bedroom,' asked Jones?

He was keen to bring their conversation onto a lighter topic.

'Play your cards right, and you might find out,' Mia replied with a smirk.

14

Eli and Andrew peered at the audience through a gap in the curtains.

They have practiced the play from start to finish several times. The problem was that the hall had always been empty.

'Justin, I need you to come out of the bathroom.'

This was Logue through a very closed and very locked door in a voice that said I-am-barely-controlling-my-temper-and-you-don't-want-to-see-me-when-I'm-not-controlling-it.

Eli spotted Jones, Mia and his godparents in the fifth row. Mia engaged energetically in conversation with Kate while Ryan and Jones exchanged a shrug.

'There's quite a lot out there,' whispered Eli.

'Full house,' stated Andrew. 'I don't remember you telling me that I'd be crapping myself so hard when you bullied me into this.'

'I never bullied,' cried Eli.

'Yes … you … did' snorted Andrew. 'You know dam well I can't resist your puppy eyes. The disappointment, it's like a rod of guilt smacking over my head'.

'I do not have puppy eyes.'

'Justin, this is your last chance,' proclaimed Logue.

'Listen, it's going to be great,' said Andrew, placing a hand on his shoulder. 'So long as nobody breaks a leg walking onto the stage we'll be fine.'

'I'm warning you.'

'Not inspiring much confidence.'

Andrew laughed a single bark that seemed both terrified and exhilarated.

'You turned Logue's ten-pound mangy hooker of a story into a high-class escort. It's going to be *fine*'.

Eli tried to swallow those words. He may as well have tried to eat rocks.

'Are your parents here,' he asked?

'Mums working but dad came. I think he felt sorry for me,' said Andrew.

The nonchalant way in, which he said this caused Eli to regard his friend. Andrew rarely ever referenced his parent's lack of interest in him.

'For Godsake, Mark, what the hell are you doing,' gasped Logue.

'I'm sorry, sir, but someone's stolen my clothes, and I can't find my costume,' said a teenager who was naked except for his underwear.

A regal of giggles erupted from the surrounding bodies that were hurrying about.

'I think I'll get some air,' said Eli.

The gusting wind was sweet release from the enclosed heat inside. Eli wandered away from the building and stared into the dark.

'Is it getting too much in there?' asked a voice.

Embarrassment raced up his spine to his face in the form of heat.

Eli whirled to find Heather standing by the school building, smoking, and staring at him from a cloud of blue/grey smoke. Her willowy figure was clad in her costume; a version of the school's own uniform.

'Is creeping up on me your thing now,' he asked?

Their previous conversation replayed through his head. As the wind brushed against him, it no longer provided easement against his rising temperature.

'It is enjoyable,' she replied.

'What about you? Nervous?'

She pushed from the wall, strolling to his side while releasing more smoke.

'Not really, it's just a bit of fun for me. I'm no actress, but my parents are proud'.

'What about your boyfriend?' Eli asked.

'He chose not to come,' said Heather. 'For petty reasons like he wanted me to ditch and chose him.' She laughed at this, but it was a hollow sound.

'He has pieces of plastic that prove he's an adult, but he still acts like a child.'

Her coffee brown eyes locked with his. Her hair, he used to think of it as spun gold, whipped in the wind.

'You know, I was going to apologize to you the last time we talked for the way I treated you when we were younger.'

'Why didn't you?' asked Eli.

'Because you were such a dick,' she said and laughed.

'What,' he managed.

'Look I'm sorry okay,' she said. 'I even knew it was the wrong thing to do at the time. I chose you over friends that turned out to be backstabbing bitches, and I kinda knew they were like that back then. And well seeing this place as I do now, it's bugged me that I was like them and I've always wanted to say, you know, and I did try last time, but you were a dick'.

She held a hand to her head and chuckled.

'What am I talking about?'

'That I'm a dick,' deadpanned Eli.

'Right.'

Eli let out a sigh from his nostrils and looked at her. He wanted to be mad at her but found he couldn't. After everything that happened with Jones and Lucy, Eli found he was too exhausted to carry his five-year-old resentment for Heather's actions. He was passed feeling that way, especially with Jones's rant about time being precious.

'It's fine, I accept your apology five years too late,' he said, teasing. 'Kids make mistakes.'

Heather paused, her head cocking to the side, seeming to take him in.

'Cool, so can we be friends,' she said, holding out her hand. 'I mean you're a big play writer now I have to get in with you.'

He laughed and took her hand, giving it a firm pump. In doing so, he knew, he was not accepting that they would pick up where they left off. The feelings that he had for her felt like they belonged to a different person. Plus, they made him cringe when he remembered them.

When he shook Heather's hand, he did so thinking that this was a blank stale.

'Sure, friends,' he said.

'Guys, Logue just pried Justin out of the bathroom,' interrupted Jamie McCray.

She was Heather's closest friend, and she had her head poked round the fire door Eli had used to get outside. The puzzled expression she gave them was one he was used too.

'He seems to have calmed,' Jamie added.

'You ready to do this?' asked Heather, flickering her cigarette away.

Eli watched the embers spiral into the dark.

'Nope.'

He knew something was wrong after five minutes. And it was the tiniest of things. A simple shuffle from the darkened hall where the first few rows of faces could only be vaguely discerned.

Yet, his alarm bells started ringing.

It was beyond the actors to notice as their attentions were on their performances. But, both Logue and himself did. And it made Eli afraid and in that fear came a revelation. He had forgotten who his audience was meant to be. Consumed with the high school setting and a secret desire to impress his peers, he had written a play for them.

As the show wound on, it became more apparent that the audience was not interested in this. They were adults that worked nine to five (or more) and had sacrificed their time to indulge their children. They did not actually want to know what their children endured. They wanted something fun, something light and easily digestible.

Whisperings soon joined the shuffling. Eventually, Logue disappeared from the stage wings, leaving Eli alone. He soon returned with his script twisted in his hand.

Despite, the play's seriousness, the cast saved it from total disaster. Each sentence, Andrew launched into the void beyond the stage received laughter. Above everyone else, Justin shone brightest. He was unrecognizable. On stage, he was a creature of depth and emotion that captivated. Long gone was the clownish dickhead.

As the story climaxed, they gained applause but no standing ovation. A few families stood to cheer for their own scions, but Eli suspected their enthusiasm was mostly relief that the play was done and they could depart to whatever adult interests they had.

Their applause was apologetic at best.

Andrew and Justin pulled him, his feet slipping on the boards, on stage. He took a bow with the rest of the grinning, breathless cast who still had no clue.

Only he noticed Logue took no bow.

The most significant blow came at the after-party.

The hall was deserted, and cast floated about the stage armed with a cup of soft drink: a gift from the teachers. They did so jubilantly and in relief from nerves.

Eli managed to break from the festivities, his mind wallowing. Within hearing range, he caught the voice of Mr. Black speaking to Logue.

'Very good, well-done, though perhaps next year I think we will try something a little less heavy.'

'Less heavy,' Logue repeated.

'Yes, a little lighter,' explained Mr. Black. 'More jokes, you know, not that your play wasn't funny that big lad got some good laughs. I think next year I'll take a more proactive approach with it. You can't say you haven't been stressed, Norman. Yes, I'll be more than happy to help you share the load'.

That conversation provided foundations and support for his disappointment.

Making it worse was Logue's reaction. The teacher snapped his head, his eyes finding Eli's ablaze. They held for a second, enough for Eli to witness his hurt and fury.

Mr. Black continued speaking, but he doubted Logue was hearing. He was pretty sure the teacher was thinking of all the times Eli had egged him on.

A hand fell on his shoulder, and he jumped. It was Jones's.

Suddenly, Eli was engulfed in hugs (Mia's sweet perfume smelling like some exotic dream), handshakes and praises, which he accepted humbly, blushing. With knowing Kate contributed to his woes.

'Your mother would have been proud,' she said.

Her words caused his mouth gap and his voice to hesitant.

'Do you think it would have made the top shelf of her bookcase?' he asked.

'Hon,' she said, a hand on his arm. 'She would have made a shelf just for it.'

'We are going to go on and let you get on with celebrating,' said Ryan. 'Think you can leave him home.'

Eli turned to see who he was speaking to. Andrew, Justin, Heather, and Jamie were standing behind him.

'I bought my car,' said Justin. 'I can give him a lift.'

When the adults departed, Jamie proclaimed, 'this is the saddest after-party ever.'

'Weren't we supposed to go to the Dollar?'
'That was canceled because of that attack,' stated Heather.
'Looks like I'm never going to get in there,' said Justin, who then held up his car keys.
'Wanna get outta here.'
Eli noted that Logue had vanished from the proceedings.
'Absolutely,' said Eli.

'WAHOOO,' screamed Heather at an ear-shattering level.
The world was a slide, and Eli was one tensed muscle. Justin's no longer white Audi was sailing around a corner, it's back wheels sliding out of sync with the front two.
Mud splattered the windscreen, leaving them blind. The Audi proceeded to do thirty through the imponderable darkness. Their screams, the blaring *Arctic Monkeys* and the revving engine became mixed with the window wipers snapping in a mad effort to regain vision. In the last instant, they succeeded revealing a blend more staggering and sharper than the previous.
Justin yanked the steering wheel hard.
This time the rear wheels lead the way. The four passengers cried out in unison, making hysterical catcalls only made by those with no thought for self-preservation. Only Justin was quiet. His face clenched grimly on the task at hand.
The Audi skidded beneath the fangs of crooked trees, splashing cascades of thick mud. Justin yanked the wheel. The car fishtailed enough for them to taste real terror and then righted its trajectory. Above all the screaming, he spoke loudest.
'That, Eli is what I do on the weekends.'

They built a fire.

Gathering materials let the adrenaline cool in their systems. When Jamie alerted them to the fact that everything was damp, Justin revealed his supplies. He opened the boot to reveal a box of Carlsberg, several woolen blankets and a can of petrol.

They organized themselves around an area of burnt ground encircled by the remains of tree trunks, which they used as seats. They threw the damp wood onto the previous campfire as Justin dosed it in petrol. Heather set the blaze to life with a click from her lighter. They watched the progression of tiny blue flames bloom into great dancing ribbons of orange and red.

'Your oddly quiet, thinking of your next story, a novel this time,' said Heather, after a few minutes.

'That's the last thing on my mind.'

'Why not' asked Justin?

'Forgot it, its nothing,' he said.

'Hey' said Heather, lowly. 'Your play was great.'

'It was real,' yelled Justin.

'It was the most fun I've ever had in school,' said Jamie.

'Me too,' said Andrew, toasting with his beer.

'You wrote about stuff that we ... that I actually think about or have gone through. It wasn't a pretentious TV program or some cheesy movie. Like Justin said it was real'. This was Heather. She held her beer bottle up. Each of them clicked the necks of their bottles together. Eli never really had a taste for beer, but as he drank to that toast, he thought it wasn't that bad.

Even an hour ago, he would have laughed if anyone suggested he would be here. Their attention was unfamiliar and mildly uncomfortable as they broke into individual conversations. Yet, he felt accepted.

'So, who doesn't want a lift home,' asked Justin grinning?

Four hands rose.

'Fuck off ... my driving wasn't that bad'.

Act Three

In So Far

2015

March – July

The white blank page stared at him as resilient as a gravestone.

It was barren but for a winking icon. With it's every disappearance and reappearance a voice whispered in Eli's head, *go on, write something.*

Eli's fingers rested over the keys. They held there and waited and waited as ideas swirled in the toxic soup within his mind. The poison there was insecurity and as it churned it discarded each new idea as useless, pathetic, and uninspired.

As an act of defiance, his lips grew thin. Tears triple his vision.

Eli collapsed into his chair's back, rasping for breath. Without thinking, the way an action has become a habit; his right fist drove into his forehead with a smack. A red stamp grew on his brow.

The pain was supposed to be a relief, but it did nothing to vent his frustration. He liked to think he wasn't crazy, not like that loony Peter Brett, who hung himself years ago in prison, but Eli knew he wasn't entirely sane either.

With the same frustration, he snapped his laptop shut. *I have class anyway,* he thought, standing.

Eli showered and dressed before searching for food. The wash hadn't improved his mood, so he prodded downstairs in a zombie shuffle. As he did his phone chimed, and on reading the message, he grew even more miserable in his mood.

FROM: JUSTIN BLACKTHORN

Hi, pal I got it!!! The part that is!! WOOP! Someday soon I'm going to get the chance to play one of your characters again! Anyway, I hope you are well, Heather and I painted the town red celebrating, so I'm off to bed lol. Have fun with her today. That woman drank me under the table!!! What are you writing lately?

Eli stared at the last sentence.
'Nothing,' he said to his phone.
He was happy (and more than a little jealous) for Justin. After school and the eventual parting of ways, Justin had pursued his passion for acting at university in London. The part was a supporting role, his first after years of auditioning.
Eli's chosen path was much different.
The thought of it led him to be once more self-absorbed. So much so that as he took a seat at the table in his flat's communal kitchen, he paid no attention to its other two occupants'. It was only when he said, 'that smells good' and glanced at them did it hit him. He did not know one of them. She was female, and the reason for the appetizing smell. She was also, and this was the part where his mind went blank, naked from the waist down.
She was also not naked from the waist up. She was in a t-shirt much too big that Eli recognized as belonging to one of his flatmates.
Seeing it, a puzzle piece slotted into place. *This is Louis's latest pull.*
The t-shirt almost reached the tops of her legs. However, it traveled upward when she stretched for the higher cupboards, rewarding Eli with a curved view. This frequently happened through Adrian's guidance, the kitchen's other occupant. Eli witnessed a clear correlation between the further the t-shirt rose, and the wider Adrian's grin grew.
That cheeky, childish grin beamed at Eli.

'You're looking a bit tired there, sleep okay,' asked Adrian?

Eli gave him a serpentine look.

'No, you were watching The Winter Soldier at three am. You know how I know it was The Winter Soldier because it was playing so loud I thought I was in it'.

'I wondered what all that noise was about,' said the semi-naked chef.

'The guys and I were having a Marvel marathon,' said Adrian, shrugging.

'What guys?' said Eli, knowing that Adrian was practically a recluse.

'A few guys online thought it be cool to watch all ten marvel films back to back. The tricky part was making sure everyone hit play at the right moment'.

'You do realize how that sounds,' sighed Eli.

'Yes ... awesome'.

Eli rolled his eyes. An action that drew his attention to the vacant spot where his cereal box should be.

'Does anyone know what happened to my cereal?' he asked, already knowing the answer.

'Oh sorry, I ran out of snacks and didn't want to make anything complicated.'

'Adrian, what the hell man I thought we talked about this,' exclaimed Eli.

Again his flatmate shrugged, causing his jellied bulk to ripple.

Before he could say anymore, the semi-naked chef wheeled on him. She banished the spatula in her hand like a sword, flinging grease onto his jeans.

'Whoa,' said the shorthaired peroxide blonde.

'What's your deal, man? Why so, uptight? It's only cereal'.

A spatula-wielding stranger who can enjoy a morning breeze is lecturing me.

Adrian folded his arms beneath his massive breasts, observing the fun.

'I suppose,' continued the blonde, 'that you'll have a go at me for using what was left in the fridge and before you ask no you can not have any, it's for Louis and myself.'

She said the last part jumping to a higher, joyous octave.

'As it should be,' said Louis on entering the scene. Whereas Adrian was tall and morbidly obese, Louis was tall and anorexic.

He wrapped a thin arm around the blonde's waist, nuzzling her neck. She giggled in a way that should be kept private and made Eli queasy to hear.

'What's with all the shouting?'

'Your friend here is being an ass over cereal,' informed his latest conquest.

Eli could feel the beginning pressure of a migraine in his temples. Like a marble ball circling the rim of a glass and creating an awful grating noise.

'Cereal? Again? Really?' asked Louis. 'When did you become so uptight?'

'Yeah, you used to be fun,' said Adrian, glumly.

He gazed at them his sense of self drowning under their stares.

Two years ago the three of them had known nothing of each other. But the joint wish to experience university, this new age in their lives, in every manner possible had sealed a bond in them. Somewhere in that time that friendship had become lost.

Eli was highly aware of his own troubles. Troubles that he kept secret and as he sat before this jury he suspected for the first time he was not the only one hiding something. While Adrian had become more reclusive with his online life, Louis had become more outgoing on the nightclub scene. Neither bothered to attend their classes anymore.

'Whatever,' he said. 'I'm going to class, I'll get something on the way.'

Throwing his satchel bag over his shoulder, he exited the now burnt smelling kitchen.

'It's the last day before the Easter holidays,' called Louis. 'Why are you going in? Nobody will be there'.

'Cause I'm no fun,' Eli replied.

'Wait, are you a student?' he heard the woman ask Louis.

'He would be if he actually went to class,' Eli answered for him.

As the front door closed, he could hear the fire alarm begin to wail.

He descended steps feeling the migraine gain a footing in his brain's soft tissue. The marble ball was now screeching over the curvature of the glasses rim.

It wasn't his entire fault he knew. Adrian and Louis had their part to play in their current strained living conditions. Though for some reason they still managed to agree on most things, especially in regards to him. More and more, he was the one in the wrong and being ganged up on. *As if life wasn't doing it enough.* Eli plowed on, his head haunted by such musings, as the grey light filtered down past the Edinburgh skyline.

The first thing he learned about the city was it would keep him fit.

As a student whose first transport was his own legs, he learned this fast. In his early days of exploration, he gained an insight into Edinburgh's geography.

The insight was it was bonkers, and for that reason, he loved it.

For a while, he believed the footpaths were sentient and ever-changing. This was because they could suddenly develop gradients that could rival Everest. As well as this, it seemed impossible to keep his sense of direction. Often he would think *I know where J.K got the idea for the moving staircase.* And that was easy to see. Something was spellbinding about the city. However, Eli was hard-pressed to notice it this morning. He collected a sandwich from a corner shop and missed his bus.

Being late didn't stop him from wasting more time before the notice boards in the university corridors. The flyer, the one he always paused at was sky blue and read in bold, wacky captions, 'SUBMIT YOUR SHORT STORY.' Its zany coloring was eerily similar to those that advertised his play from years ago. Below the flyer was a black letterbox.

His throat constricted as he gazed at it.

He hadn't written a single word in six months. There were no words good enough. Time spent writing had become time like this morning's session.

With a lingering, desperate glance, he moved on to his chosen subject. Business.

The other class members referred to it as, 'the last option.' This couldn't have been clearer for Eli as he stepped into the empty room.

'Dam,' he said, his shoulders sagging.

He supposed it said something about the class when the teacher doesn't even appear.

'Oh no,' said a similarly disheartened voice.

Cara Holden mimicked his disposition from the doorway.

'Don't tell me that I am that sad nerd that comes to class when everyone else doesn't bother, for fuck sake the teacher's not even here.'

Eli could only feel pity for her.

'Hey, your not the only sad nerd,' he said.

Though Eli wallowed in his own misfortune, he felt better in the company of others far worse than him. Cara was one such person. The scars on her arms, which she kept hidden, said this. He was not that bad, yet.

However, there was more to it than that. Cara naturally exuded vulnerable hopelessness. People could feel it in the way children can feel those they can bully. She was pretty, slightly too pale with a mousy bob framed and highlighted her face. She wasn't fat nor skinny but proportionally plump in the way Mia was. Yet, it didn't matter.

All her classmates saw was a timid, frightened child-woman.

'Thanks, Eli,' she mumbled.

He was used to her barely audible speech. He was also aware that she loved him.

The other classmates teased him severely about this.

'Well, I guess coming in here today was a waste.'

'Hey,' he said. 'That's not the attitude to have how much would you have killed for a day off in school. I have to meet a friend later coming up from London, but we could hang out. I didn't get much of a breakfast this morning, fancy joining me'?

There was a smirk on her lips, it was closest Cara came to a smile.

He knew it was despicable using Cara to feel better. But he didn't care.

Breakfast with Cara allowed him to forget his worries. In fact, it made him forget the time until he realized he was going to be late again. 'Shit, I'm supposed to be at the Clubhouse in twenty minutes,' he said.

'It's okay, we were having fun,' said Cara as if asking a question. 'Maybe we could hang out later on … if your not busy with your friend that is'.

'Maybe,' replied Eli.

Not quiet jogging five minutes later he realized he hadn't paid for his half of the bill.

I am an awful friend, he thought, reaching his destination.

The Clubhouse was a café Heather had discovered on a previous visit. It was her favorite 'hideaway' in Edinburgh and often when calling from where ever in the world she was currently exploring she asked how was it doing and when was his last visit.

Heather was already inside and had ordered.

She greeted him with a tight hug. It was like being enveloped in flowery spices.

Holding him aloft, she said, 'you look like shit.'

'Well, at least I don't smell like it,' he replied.

Her eyes lingered on his face in a way that made him uncomfortable. It was like she could see straight through the façade that everything was okay.

The surrounding onlookers returned to their coffees and teas. In the conversation that followed, Eli caught several observing them. He understood and would have done the same if he saw a woman like Heather talking to a sweaty, half-creature like him.

Whereas he could be confused with a heroin addict, Heather could be considered divine.

I pray she doesn't notice my thinning fringe.

'You're lucky I had the time to wait,' she said. 'I'm aiming to be on Skye tonight.'

'Wow, why?'

'Well, I've already toured the Highlands on my last visit, but I missed out Skye. A few days should be enough time, and then I'm off to Spain to begin my European tour'.

'European tour … you make me feel like I'm underachieving in life'.

His remark was of a type that was occurring more frequently. It was honesty disguised as sarcasm. It was as close to telling the truth that he ever came. The grounding pressure of admitting he was a failure was too much. There were too many people, too many faces in the cycling gallery within his mind that would be let down by that admittance.

He kept quiet and listened to Heather's tales from her globe-trotting. Some of them were funny, and some were heartfelt and tainted by teaching sadness. He nodded in the parts where he should and spoke when necessary, displaying joy, awe, but inside, in the red muscle, he was envious and more shameful with each story Heather told.

She had done the unthinkable on their graduation. When everyone else took the school's advice to seek further education, she got a job. Two years later, when those same people, Eli included, discovered that the economy was no better and higher education was a redundant loop with no progression in sight, she quit her job to travel.

She was despairingly still more adjusted than him.

'Why don't you come with me,' she said, breaking his internal self-deprecation?

'You look like you need some time off.'

'What to Spain … ha … I'd love to, but I'm going home tomorrow,' he said.

She gave him that lingering gaze again.

'Its brilliant about Justin isn't it, getting that part. You know I've never understood why you choose to study business, enlighten me. You're a writer, why chose that'?

There it was: his chance to divulge.

'Come on,' sighed Eli. 'I've already explained this to you. I need a backup job, something I can work at that pays while I write. You're looking at a writer whose career consists of a few short stories'.

'You've written novels,' stated Heather.

'Unpublished novels,' corrected Eli.

'Unfairly criticized novels ... they were brilliant, Eli,' she soothed.

'You're sweet to say that,' he said, believing none of her words.

'I just want you to be happy. I get the feeling your not. Justin and I were discussing it last night before I jumped on the train. We both feel the same. Are you happy?'

Eli did his best not to give himself away.

'Of course, I'm happy never better,' he lied. His tongue tasted of rot.

Coward, he thought.

Though they talked on for some time, their conversation had concluded at that. What followed was more discussion on banal topics until Heather had to leave. She hugged him once more, and that smell cocooned him once more.

'Just ... do what makes you happy okay, kid,' she whispered in his ear.

After she left, Eli ordered water to cleanse his palette. It did not work, but he drank it anyway. He watched the passing cars and pedestrians from his seat in the café. The onlookers that had observed their conversation gazed at him with deepened speculation. He ignored them, focusing on the street.

Heather's words were playing like a skipping record in his mind. They did so quietly, leaving plenty of space for dissatisfaction to bunker down.

He was due to fly home tomorrow for the Easter holidays. Something he had booked not out of desire but Kate and Ryan's expectation of having him back.

For the first time, he felt like it might be a good thing. His godparents did not know about his writing, about the toxic relationship with his flatmates, about his suffocating studies. To tell them would mean insufferable embarrassment. He found it embarrassing even to think of telling Jones if he was honest frightening too.

Eli's hand tightened on his now empty glass.

If he was candid Jones and him weren't as close as they used to be. Time and space, those twin fiends had seen to that.

There had been a time when he would have told Jones anything. Maybe he could have that again if he went ...

'Are you okay, sir? Your girlfriends left?'

It was the waitress that had served them. Her pretty face looked concerned.

Eli smiled at her, feigning perfect happiness.

'She's just a friend,' he informed. 'But yes, I am.'

As he said this, he produced his phone, placing it on the table. He sent Cara a text asking if she liked to meet him for dinner at a place that served cocktails.

By the time she arrived, Eli was nursing his second drink. He spotted her before she spotted him and noted that she had changed her clothes from earlier. She was dressed in the navy blue number she wore on nights out.

Seeing it, made him recall the drunken kiss they'd shared one night. The one they never talked about.

'Hi, there,' she said breathlessly. 'How did it go with your friend?'

'It went well,' Eli lied and added, 'you're looking pretty.' This was the truth.

By Cara's standards, she had dressed provocatively in her dress and black tights that showcased her bodies' curves. She more minimal makeup, giving her a glossy, fresh face. She had even styled her bob. She looked more than pretty.

Hearing his compliment, Cara half shrugged, half flinched.

'Take a seat. I know I said about having dinner together but my therapist and by that I mean our waiter recommended some of these,' he raised his glass. 'So I was thinking of trying them all. Have you ever wanted to do that? Just try every cocktail in a place?'

Cara's usual smirk was mixed with bewilderment.

'Meeting your friend must have *very* gone well, what's gotten into you?'

'Ever meet with someone and feel woefully pathetic?'

Cara didn't answer. She didn't need to.

'I'm in a self-destructive mood. You know we went into college today, the last day before the Easter holidays and we went in. That's sad. I need some adventure to get over it'.

His second drink was finished, an overly sweet, heavily alcoholic concoction.

Cara gazed at him from the cute frame of her brunette hair.

'I have always wanted to drink an entire cocktail list,' she said. 'Anyway, it beats sitting at home, playing the third wheel to my flatmate and her boyfriend.'

This sentence was a typical Cara remark. It was said with such throwaway despair that it tugged at Eli's heart.

'Great,' cheered Eli more than he felt. 'You've got some catching up to do.'

They ordered a meal and drinks. The latter appeared first.

From their booth, they could view the entire restaurant. Eli made Cara laugh by making up stories about the other customers. These he whispered to her, leaning close.

The meals arrived. They ordered more drinks.

Soon Cara began to lean back into him. As his head was ablaze with alcoholic mud, he nuzzled at her shoulder.

Cara's giggles lessened. By the reproach in her eyes, he understood he had crossed some boundary. Even aided by alcohol Cara still peeked adorably from beneath the frames of her hair. As if it could shield her from harm.

They didn't speak. There was a feeling of standing on an edge.

Cara lunged. Her hands clasped his cheeks, bring his lips to hers.

The restaurant, the chaotic din of servers and customers, faded from their attention. They were lost in an expectancy, a volcanic build-up that was finally erupting.

On breaking apart, he suggested a taxi.

He couldn't remember the ride home.

They were in his bedroom. That's all that seemed to matter.

Eli dragged his dresser and barracked his door.

'What the hell are you doing?' asked Cara.

'Adrian has no sense of personal boundaries,' he explained.

'Okay, as long as I get to leave and you're not some Irish murderer.'

She tried impersonating his accent. It was painful to hear.

'You're not going to want to leave,' he said.

To his drunken mind, this sentence sounded like the sexiest thing in the world to say. Cara laughed but didn't resist as he pressed against her.

'I've known guys have nude posters on their walls,' she said. 'My flatmates says her boyfriend has one of David Beckham in his underwear but not this.'

Cara was referring to the wall above his bed.

'Its kind of a motivational thing,' he said.

They swayed; pulled close as if moving to a tune only they could hear. Cara's eyes fled his yet her lips were frozen in their trademark smirk.

Eventually, she grew bold enough to meet his gaze. They kissed until his face was hot.

'Would you mind?' she asked

With her head bowed, she turned around and lifted her hair. Her dresses zipper rested on the nape of her neck.

There was the feeling of being on edge again as he stared at it.

Slowly, and with a dry throat, he grasped it and pulled. The cloth parted to reveal skin that was as white as corral beneath the sea.

Cara shrugged her shoulders, causing the dress to fall to her waist. She turned to face him while obscuring her body behind her arms as if she were cold.

Her eyes were struggling to hold his. Eli solved that problem with a kiss.

2

Cara had left him with a message.
She had used the nearest material to hand to write on:
a rejection letter. One of fifty-four that Eli kept pinned
to the wall at the head of his bed. It read in a sprawling
script.

Eli

I'm sorry I have to go I'm sorry.

He crumpled the paper in his fist and pushed the ball
against his brow.
'Fuck … fuck … fuck … fuck fuck fuck,' he muttered.
At some point, he managed to stand. His hangover
pulsated vigorously.
He was due to go home today. How could he fix this
when in a few hours he is supposed to be boarding a
plane? He cast his eyes around his room for an
answer.
They found the laptop on his desk before the window.
It wasn't fully closed.
He edged toward it and pulled the screen up. The
black picture eclipsed into an unblemished and eldritch
white. It was his blank document.
He slammed the screen down.
There was finality in Cara's message. As his eyes
traced over her words, his stomach grew bloated with
guilt.
He hadn't been thinking straight. He had needed
something, and that led to him using a sweet girl who
loved him. *Fuck, I'm disgusting,* he thought.

Determined to salvage something Eli began packing urgently. In his haste, he dislodged a drawer at his desk. Something white peeked through the opening. Pages. Confused, he retrieved them and read the first line. He read the next one and the next one until the end.

Eli chewed on his lower lip contemplatively. He placed the short story in his suitcase.

Wanting to avoid another kitchen scene, he skipped breakfast. He took a taxi aimed for Cara's flat and got as far as her door.

'Where could she be?' he asked into the speakerphone

'I don't know,' replied Cara's flatmate, Morag. Her tone was spiked death.

'All I know is she didn't come home last night.'

'Listen, just tell her I'm sorry,' he said. 'And tell her I'll call her.'

'I think you better not, I think your better leaving it for a while,' was her reply.

Disheartened he made one more stop before racing to the airport.

The black letterbox swallowed his short story. He heard it thud inside and fought the urge to pry it out with fingers.

3

Maria Hunter was feeling the complete opposite of Eli
Donoghue.
If asked to describe how she felt she would have said,
'like I'm winning.' In her hand were eight delicately
crafted envelopes containing letters she thought of as
instruments to her further success. As she posted
them her certainty in herself and her plans swelled.
She was no idea that one of her letters would not reach
its intended destination.

Cara was his headache for the duration of his flight.
She had been at the flat he was sure. Listening to him
plead as Morag rebuffed him.
It had been cruel to use her feelings for him for his own
comfort. He had known that last night, but he hadn't
cared. The drink was partly to blame for that but not all.
He had wanted to take advantage. Why?
The question echoed in his skull shrinking into silence.
Because I could, he thought. *Because I was sick of
feeling pathetic, and it felt good manipulating her love.
I controlled the situation, and it felt good.*
Eli tasted bile.
This was not how he was raised to be. At least not by
Kate and Ryan. But it was something his father, Sean
Allen, would do.
Perhaps underneath, he was nothing more than him.
The despair at such thinking dragged him to a greater
depth than he had ever fallen to. It left him hollow.
It was the first time in years since he had thought about
his father.
As the plane's wheels touched the earth, Eli tried to
reorganize his head.

The last time he was home was Christmas when his issues were beginning. He could not have anyone suspect he wasn't as happy as he had been then. Looking back now, however, he thought of that Christmas period as a happy lie. He had taken a departure from everything that had troubled him in Edinburgh to focus on his family. The expectation Eli had was to sort himself out when he returned. Instead, the time at home had only reinforced his frustrations and the city's loneliness.

What diffused his panic was finding his uncle unaccompanied in arrivals. In all the years Eli had spent studying when coming home, he had always been met by both his godparents. Seeing, Ryan, by himself, was an oddity.

This did not stop them from hugging fiercely. It felt more than good to be embraced strongly.

'Where's Kate?' he asked

'She's at home. How was the flight'?

'Okay, its good to see those H&W cranes flying in,' he said, surprised even by his own honest. 'Reminds me that I'm coming home.'

Their conversation continued as they exited, stepping out into the day.

Kate was waiting in the kitchen.

Ryan had lagged behind him, letting him enter the house first. Eli knew where she was even no; there was no sound to indicate it. His knowledge derived from the experience of the house.

She was at the kitchen table, her cheeks puffy and red. That was a surprise.

'I'll leave you to it,' said Ryan, backstepping.

He didn't slam the front door. It would have been better if he did.

'What's going on?' asked Eli

'Its nothing,' she soothed and coughed. Her voice was a rasp.

'Don't worry about it. It's good to see you. You look good'.

Two lies beside each other, he thought.

'According to Heather, I look like shit. Have you and Ryan been fighting?'

He stood there glaring at her, fists clenched defiantly at his sides. Kate's eyes were just as unwavering as his except the blue of them was drowning in sorrow. Her left hand moved to the black object on the table, hovering over it protectively.

She noticed his eyes follow her action and looked down at how her hand rested over her phone.

'We fought over this ... can you believe it? This little thing ... though it seems, we can pick an argument over anything silly these days'.

Eli knew he wasn't going to have long. She would stop talking as soon as she looked up and met his eyes. Ryan was the same. They hide trouble from him.

He guessed that proved whom he got that trait from. His own father liked to make a display of his problems.

He took the chair nearest to her.

'Tell me.'

'It's nothing,' she said, smiling weakly.

He wanted to grab her phone and throw it at the wall. The moment of confession was gone. Kate smiled, a hurt, sweet twitch of the lips and held his gaze with her drowned blues. Her forehead was ceased by wear.

'And you look like shit,' she said. 'Why is that'?

Eli shook his head.

'You're not helping me until I can help you,' he said.

'Stalemate then,' she sang and chuckled.

They starred at each other. Eventually, she broke out in a smile as radiate and energizing as the sun.

'It's good to have you home,' she said, hugging him firmly.

He asked if she planned on having anyone over tonight.
'Oh, I don't do that anymore,' she said, sadly. 'I'm just too tired nowadays to cook for all those people.' Her face crinkled, readying for his disappointing.
Eli didn't let it show.
'But you should go to see them. They'll be waiting for you. Plus it would give Ryan, and I time to talk'.
There was a tinge of pain in her voice at her vulnerability.
'Go,' she urged again, shoeing him from his seat.
Her hands jabbed at him using two pointed fingers to prod at his shoulder blades. Eli skidded over the kitchen tile, laughing despite himself, recalling a similar time when he had just been taller than the kitchen table, and Kate had banished him in the same manner.
'All right, all right,' he said
'And here take your phone,' she said in the hallway.
She held it out to him, her fingers digging into the frame of the slick object.

The interior cool slipped from him as he stepped outside.
What the hell was that about, he thought, shivering.
He had fled Edinburgh to get away from this shit. It had never occurred to him that the people back home might have their own problems to deal with.
And why is that challenged a voice inside his head?
Briefly, the answered was within his minds' grasp, but it was like trying to catch smoke.
All it left him with was a strange notion of similarity.
Eli found himself thinking of his mother and father's relationship.
Kate and Ryan would never be as bad as they had been. Yet, recalling Kate's puffy face struck him with a terrifying thought. Divorce.

The fear that surrounded that single word stemmed from his parents. Though, in that case, a proper description of events would be abandonment.

No way, he thought. Kate and Ryan were such a fixed point in his head that the idea of them apart was unthinkable. But niggling alongside his fright was the worrying certainty that he had never seen them like this before.

His feet pumped beneath him.

He didn't need to think about where he was going.

They knew the way.

He fell back into a rhythm that had been established over the last ten years. It was a pace that cleansed the mind until all thought was an undercurrent of vague feeling.

To his right, the sky was bleached golden by the sinking sun. The rest was a pale blue that seemed too vivid to be real. The day was warm, but the air that caressed his face and hair was crisp and cool. The streets were deserted.

As a teenager, he would have made his journey listening to music.

He had loved those walks. His empty skull becoming a chamber where music swirled fertilizing ideas for stories he would later write.

Now it was different.

He was different.

The confidence that he had back then was gone. Maybe it had been foolish confidence, but he would have preferred it to how he felt now. Like a breeze could blow him away.

They've been pretending they're happy just like you.

All communication between Kate, Ryan, and himself was via phone. Eli was a master at hiding the truth over it.

The question now is how long have they been lying to you.

The epiphany popped into his head like those story ideas had before. It came out of nowhere and caught him unawares. His gait slowed to a stop.

The return from his mind to the world was like removing a blindfold. There was a familiar crunch under his feet. He had arrived at Jones's.

The woods were just as wild and gnarled as ever, their leaves trapped the sun's heat beneath a ceiling of green. Music drifted to him from the end of the drive. A smirk pried at Eli's lips.

What's that old fool listening to nowadays.

As he drew closer, a frown joined his smirk. The music that throbbed from the one-story was characteristic of trance and could be felt by his feet through his shoes.

'Jones,' he called.

He had to shout, and no voice called back.

Eli mounted the porch steps, whisking through the front door. Everything was the same except for the half-naked woman dancing in the kitchen.

She had her back to him as she proceeded to sway to the playing song's beat. His first thought was, *why am I suddenly meeting people like this?*

'NNNNNOOOO ... I DON'T,' she sang.

Eli froze and in freezing was able to drink in the scene properly.

She wasn't half-naked she was wearing shorts, incredible short shorts, and a loose purple top. Her skin was the color of dark honey. Eli's eyes ran over it, over her supple legs and the bubble of her butt. She danced on with a paint roller in her hand. There were open paint cans on the kitchen table, and dirty sheets spread everywhere.

She wheeled on him in a leap.

'KKNNNNNNOOOOOOWWWW ....'

Her voice cut to a gurgle.

'WHO THE HELL ARE YOU?' Eli yelled.

The mysterious woman screamed spectacularly.

He was still frozen when she launched a paint can at him. A wave of brilliant indigo drenched him before the can itself buried into his groin.

'*WHO THE HELL ARE YOU?*' she screamed back at him.

He was on the floor now having dropped like a stone. She loomed above him with another paint can in her hand raised as if to strike again.

Eli tried to answer her, but all he could make was straw sucking inhales. He tasted the metallic flavor of the paint.

'*TELL ME … OR I'LL HIT YOU AGAIN,*' she said.

'WAHHH…WAHHH,' he gasped.

'*WHAT?*'

'WHERE'S JONES?'

The hand that held the can fell low.

'How do you know, Jones,' still shouting but not as loud.

'I'M ELI,' he managed to shriek from his puddle of pain and paint.

While the pain was specifically located, the paint coated him entirely. He could still see and thus was able to witness horror find the threatening woman's face.

It was then that he heard footfalls from the porch steps.

'NINA … emergency … just talked to Ryan … Eli's on his way'.

Jones's voice didn't gurgle as his granddaughters did. It went silent. His head swung from him, curled in the fetal position, to Nina, who was rooted to the spot.

Then his face seemed to crack and wrinkle. Eli realized Jones was grinning at him.

4

'How are the golden nuggets'?

Eli replied with a dead look. He was sat unflatteringly in the birthing position in Jones's chair with his feet on his coffee table. He held a melting bag of peas between his legs.

Jones's dazzlingly mischievous grin never wavered. The shower was running in the bathroom, which he was thankful for. It was enough punishment having Jones see him like this. He didn't need the girl that had made his teenagers year's hell witnessing it as well, even if she was responsible.

'Beginning to get feeling back? Enjoying the peas?' pressed Jones.

'I'm gonna smack that grin off your face.'

'It's hard to feel petrified of a talking purple blob.'

Eli snorted violently. The paint had dried inside his nostrils.

'How come Nina's here?' asked Eli.

His old friend's grin tightened.

'She lives here now,' said Jones.

So Kate and Ryan aren't the only ones that have been keeping things from me. The thought preceded an ache in his chest.

'Her parents were giving her a hard time,' explained Jones. 'She came here to get away from them. This place isn't exactly massive, and Mia and I were already talking about it, so I moved in with her. Still, keep some stuff here as Mia's loft isn't the biggest'.

'I see that,' mused Eli. 'New guitars, you've been busy. How come you didn't say anything about it?'

Jones's chest expanded with air, which he released in a hard vent.

'I dunno,' he said. 'I didn't want to annoy you.'

'Annoy me?'

'Yeah with you being all the way over there … working away … I just thought it would have upset you'.

Eli could feel his cheeks burning.

'It wouldn't have upset me,' he said, and it sounded like a lie even to himself.

'I'm sorry,' said Jones. 'At the time, you were busy with exams, and I didn't want to add more to your plate. After … well, I guess that's my fault, I wimped out'.

Each word stabbed at the already tender organ in his chest. What hurt most was the apparent gulf that existed between them.

The fact that Eli knew he had helped create that was even more damning.

Living apart required effort to maintain any relationship. As the rejection letters had piled up, Eli had cut back on communication with Jones.

He could lie to Kate and Ryan, but Jones could always read him like a book. Eli employed his breeziest tone and said, 'anyway, what have you been doing besides moving in with Mia, congratulations by the way? What's your latest obsession'?

It was well known that since he had left for Edinburgh, Jones had made a hobby out of undertaking hobbies only to abandon them. Eli still recalled the ship bottle phase.

Jones hummed, digging into his jeans and producing a bent envelope.

'I'm I supposed to guess what this is,' said Eli.

'This is an invitation from Maria Hunter,' stated Jones.

'Maria, as in your neighbor the nut job, Maria,' said Eli and then added. 'The one that hates you, she's sending you invites.'

'Not exactly, Shane knows someone at the post office.'

'You stole her letter,' said Eli.

'The letter,' said Jones, ignoring his comment. 'Is about a dinner party she is throwing in two weeks and we, and by we, I mean the band are going to ruin it.'
Eli stared at the crinkled envelope in Jones's hand.
'And why are you doing that?'
'Cos, the bitch, ran over Maisy,' said Jones in a voice as hard as diamond.
Eli jolted upright in his seat. Maisy was Jones's neighbours dog.
'It happened a few weeks before Nina moved in,' Jones told him. 'Harold was throwing the ball for her in the front garden. He threw it a bit too hard, and Maisy ran out into the road. He tried to call her back, but it was no good. Maria was in that tank of a car she drives. She didn't brake, what she did do, what Harold heard her do was rev her engine. I heard the screams from the house. I thought whoever was behind them must be dying. Fuck, they didn't even sound human. He had Maisy in his lap, at least, what was left of her. Harold was red with blood. Jesus, I thought he was gonna have a heart attack. I was with him when Pat past as you know, Harold didn't say or emote anything. On the day that Maisy died, he let loose. Then there was Maria. She looked embarrassed. She was embarrassed because Harold was bawling his eyes out'.
Jones palmed the tears off his cheeks. Eli mimicked him.
'You really think she did it on purpose?' he asked
'I trust Harold, and you know she hated Maisy. She actually said to Harold as she stood there, 'for god's sake it's only a dog.'
Eli winched.

It didn't need to be said how much Maisy meant to Harold. Jones's neighbor had had a fear of dogs since childhood. Yet, as his wife, Pat's, condition grew worse, he did anything to provide distraction and pleasure to her. They got a dog, a miniature sheltie, and named her Maisy. When Pat passed, Harold found himself alone in a big house frightened of a dog that looked like walking tumbleweed. And it followed him everywhere. He would wake to find it panting in his face. On using the bathroom, he would find the dog waiting inside. It didn't take long for his fears to subside though.

Maisy was apart of Pat, but a part that was new and alive, unlike the memories he wallowed in. Eli knew all this from Harold himself.

'What are we doing about it,' Eli found himself saying. Jones told him the plan. Eli nodded his head and said, 'that could work.'

'So he's enlisted you then,' said Nina, entering the room.

She sat on the seat opposite Jones while toweling her hair. The tips of which he noticed were dyed pink. Eli spotted that she was still wearing her incredible short shorts. And despite the shower, there were still flecks of purple paint on her bare legs.

Their lethal length and apparent smoothness were distracting.

'I can't understand why she would intentionally run over a neighbor's dog,' she said.

'It wouldn't have been about Maisy,' said Eli. The bizarreness of speaking to his teenage nemesis in such a stern tone thrilled him.

'It would have been about Harold, which …'

'Would have been about me,' finished Jones.

'Why does ever drama have you at its center?' sighed Nina

A sacrilegious notion crossed Eli's mind. He agreed with her.

'Maria never forgave Harold and Pat after the time she tried to rally the neighbors into submitting a complaint about me,' said Jones.

'This was the time she said you were lowering the property value of everyone's house by being here according to Maria,' Nina said

'Correct.'

'Still, do you actually believe she's cruel enough, evil enough to do such a thing?' Nina asked

Both Eli and Jones responded with a united, 'yes.'

'I think Maria has a way of justifying things, a way of detaching herself and viewing her actions without feeling or regard for others. That is what allows her to do genuinely evil things,' said Jones. 'The man that attacked me, Peter Brett, they diagnosed him with severe mental health issues. He had a reason for what he did. Maria's reason for Maisy was cold-blooded and selfish but sane. To me, she's a much more dangerous villain'.

Nina paused, pondering over Jones's words.

'Then I guess I'm in as well,' she said, slowly.

Eli stood under the shower while his clothes spun in Jones's washer.

In the living room, Nina seated herself beside her grandfather.

'So that's the legendary Eli,' she said Nina after a moment.

'It is the famous hero you've heard so much about,' replied Jones. 'How did he seem to you after all these years?'

'As angry as ever,' she laughed falsely. 'And a little sad if I'm honest.'

'He's always angry,' remarked Jones. 'Would you do me a favor? I'm gonna be busy the next days would you mind keeping him company?'

He sounded utterly innocent, which, made him somehow look downright perverse.

'Whoa … wait' spluttered Nina.

'You said you wanted to apologize to him for the way you acted when you were kids,' stated Jones before she could argue. 'Look at it like this you've got a new thing to apologize for, throwing a paint can at his dick.'

Nina scowled at her grandfather bitterly.

5

Dinner in the Wilson house turned out to be a subtle sort of torture.

The kitchen air was hostile with the unresolved argument. Other than horrid questions about his university, they ate in silence. Eli lied as best he could. Happily, he retreated to his old bed, which was cool and welcoming.

Eli lay facing the ceiling in the blue/black dark. Cara had not responded to his messages or calls. He sighed, trying to relax and thinking of Kate earlier, instead.

Her eyes had been as blue as sapphires and weeping in their stare.

He understood a curtain had been pulled back in seeing her like that. The person that he viewed in childhood haloed by dignity and sureness was a work of fiction.

A fiction portrayed by the best of actors, a parent.

He could feel the effect of this knowledge. He could sense his mind reasserting, of putting away childish thoughts and notions as if the conversation in the kitchen had been the last straw, and those naïve beliefs no longer had merit in the adult world.

Absurd, I'm a man of twenty-two. I'm past thinking like a child.

Yet he could feel the last remnants of his childhood self being bottled away.

Childhood is locked in a treasure box, heart-shaped and crimson he imagined, like Jones's guitar. All that vast imagination, that divine simplicity, that unwavering belief gets buried to be found in private moments. He had seen stern, workaholics scream and weep and cheer at their videogames. He had seen crones whose hair is as white as snow squeak at movie stars, and he knew now that he had seen their childhood selves.

This is strange.

He couldn't understand 'putting' something aside like personality.

But I have done it before.

There had been an angry, young boy once, mad with the father that caused everything and at the mother who'd given in. The thought of being a child, of seeing the world in their bright Technicolor had been unthinkable to him until Jones. And Jones still had that magic today; he remained an enigma, part child, part shaman forever.

Eli held onto that, to the idea of him. To be a lifeless worker drone, a zombie but for a few moments of levity altered his previous thoughts on hell.

He had come home to get away from being that.

Instead, he had found it here.

Definitely, he clenched his hands into fists beneath the covers.

Tears rolled down his cheeks silently. More than ever, he felt like his intentions were drifting from him. That he was being forced to chose between the aspirations he had for years and the oppressive reality that they may not happen.

He stayed motionless and thinking such thoughts until morning light crept in.

6

Eli moved to the front door, urged by the wailing bell. His immediate thinking was either Ryan or Andrew or both had decided to finish work early. On swinging the door wide, he saw it was neither. Nina stood in their potential place, hands sheepishly clasped at her front.
'Hi, there,' she said. Her tone was suspiciously bright.
'Ahhh ... hi'.
His eyes flickered up and down the street in search of cameras, his immediate reaction to suspect this was a prank.
'Granddad was saying you'd be doing nothing but pining for when Andrew finishes work and I was heading to Mia's for lunch. I was wondering if you wanted to join me'.
'Wouldn't say I was pining so much as ...' mumbled Eli.
'I thought I owned you something after destroying your bollocks ...'
His face fell.
'As an apology,' she finished, smirking.
She was disarming with such a facial expression in her arsenal.
In the mayhem of yesterday, he missed fully contemplating this now adult Nina. She had dyed the tips of her hair midnight blue. It had been pink yesterday. He noticed she chose only the longer strands that hung below her chin. Her hairstyle, long at the front, short at the back, highlighted the features of her face.
The overall impression was that of vulnerability. That was until she gave you that smirk. It had all the sass of her grandfather's.
'So are you coming or not?' she asked

Eli felt the weight of the house, of its emptiness behind him.

'If it makes you feel any better, you can think of yourself as my last resort for a companion; everyone else is busy.'

This was followed by another smirk like a full stop.

With nothing better to do and with no excuses, he agreed.

Her car was a black Ford Fiesta that was neatly kept. As Nina started the engine, *Frank Ocean* crooned from the CD player about *Forrest Gump.*

'Your musical taste has improved,' he commented.

This received a measured sigh.

'So is this how it's gonna be,' she said, reserving the car out of the driving way. 'Us, biting at each other like old times.'

'I was only … ' he stammered.

'Hey, let's do this and get the awkward stuff out of the way,' she announced sounding jovial, exhausted and angry at once. 'Personally, I'm all for the old approach to relationships like ignorance and superficial conversation, but you seem to carve the millennial alternative of being a whining bitch, so let's do this.'

'Ahh, I'd be fine with … '

'I'm sorry for the paint can thing,' shouted Nina, her hands tight on the wheel. 'And I'm sorry for everything else, okay, including calling you a bitch just now. If you need an explanation to help you out, I was jealous, right. You were the white kid whose lovely godparents weren't enough for him and had decided to intrude into my family. I suppose my mother didn't help matters, but that's another story. There I apologized is that good enough for you? I realize it's an angry apology, but …
I'm angry, okay. You want more, or are you happy?'

He stared at her, pressing against the passenger door.

'Actually, no,' he said. 'I'm a little frightened.'

Nina gave him a sharp glance. What she saw in his face caused her own to soften.

'Don't make fun,' she said, shaking her head. 'As I said I didn't want it to go down like this, but now you've got me started I've got years of guilt to vent. I'm trying to turn a leaf and befriend you here'.

'Why would you want to do that?' asked Eli.

'Jones seems to think there's something worthwhile about you. If you want to prove that theory, I suggest you stop being yourself and ruining this; it can be fun if you let it'.

After a moment's pause, she added, 'and sure, it beats anything you or Andrew would be doing.'

'Andrew and I used to do this all the time,' Eli informed her.

'He said,' she replied. 'We were taking Rosalie to the cinema the other week, and he mentioned it. It's where I stole the idea from'.

Oh, so you're with Andrew, of course.

Eli had no idea where such a thought came from or why. But it stunned him, and his face showed it in the way his jaw adjusted itself.

'Be careful. Andrew still has a thing for Jamie,' he warned.

'He's a sweetie and so is Rosalie. But he's sad like you'.

Emotion spiked within Eli at a severity; it was beyond defining. The casual remark like the rest of Nina's words cut straight to a point with no bullshit. Disarming.

'Like me,' he said incredulously.

'Yeah, it's like your both weighed done with something. Is yours a girl?'

He didn't answer, his gaze steady on the passing scenery.

'Yeah, yeah, you stay secretive and resilient to this process. Its gonna happen, before you know it we'll be painting each other's toenails and watching Mamma Mia'.

'You're not serious,' he snorted.

'Completely … except for the Mamma Mia part'.

Despite himself, he chuckled genuinely.

'Here,' she signaled.

The oppressive heat outside caused his armpits to prickle with perspiration.

They had parked in a lot that had once housed Brett's Repairs. The only reference to this fact could be seen hanging from the dilapidated fence bordering the site. He was reading the sign and remembering when Nina spoke next.

'You were there that night.'

She was watching him from the driver's side. Chin resting on her crossed forearms as she leaned on the roof of the car. Her eyes were narrow and unreadable in the sun's glare.

'What was it like?'

Her wild sass had vacated. In its place was a voice that was both hard and soft. He heard for the first time respect for him and rage for what happened.

'Horrible,' he stated. He could think of no better description.

'My parents wouldn't take me to the hospital or even let me call,' she said. 'I ran to the bus station to try and see him myself. My first attempt at running away but Mom came for me. She dragged me out, screaming. I don't think she even noticed'.

'She sounds like a bitch,' said Eli and immediately regretted it.

He tensed for more yelling. However, Nina didn't respond but continued to observe him intensely. He preferred the yelling.

We're breaking all types of barriers today.

'Stop, trying to talk about this sensitive shit,' she moaned, rolling her eyes. 'We're here to have fun, not mope. Now I need a drink'.

She strutted around the car and forcefully knotted her arm around his.

'Me to,' he said.

'The best thing you've said yet.'

They took seats at the bar.

'Andrew and I used to eat right here all the time,' he informed Nina with fond nostalgia. 'We hoped that Mia would serve us, which was silly because he didn't have to hope, she always did.'

As he finished speaking, it dawned on him that he had made an error in imparting this information to Nina.

Time elongated as he waited for her to utter a snide remark as if she was the old Nina, not this new adult version.

'Ah, the hopes of young boys,' she said. 'Though, if I were a boy or that way inclined I'd probably have hoped for the same thing.'

Time snapped back. And he found himself holding eye contact with Nina as he tried to decide what possessed him to omit such a recollection. She held his gaze.

A bartender chose that precise moment to offer his services. Frazzled, Eli fumbled with his words until Nina saved him.

'I'll have a mojito, and this lady over here will have the same.'

The bartender nodded his head and left them.

'Is this what you find yourself doing when you come home, reliving old times?' she asked

Her eyes were on him once more. They were hazel in color and unflinching in their gaze. Jones had said she was having problems with her family.

It was challenging to think of a problem those eyes couldn't handle.

'Normally, its all I have time for,' he explained. 'I plan it, so I get around everyone, kinda reassure relationships by doing the stuff we used to do.'

'Shouldn't everyone plan around you since you've got so little time off?'

Before he could reply, their bartender returned with their drinks. As soon as Eli tasted his, a zesty blend of mint and lemon, he recalled the last alcoholic drink he had. His body went cold.

'Wow,' gasped Nina. 'That's pretty dam good.'

'Only pretty good,' said - according-to-his-nametag - Phil, the bartender.

He leaned on the counter; giving them a disturbing view of his staggeringly whitened teeth and bleached sunbed tan. His eyes disregarded Eli completely.

'You haven't had one of mine yet,' Nina told him.

Phil chuckled, shaking his head and reclining backward. He left to serve someone else, shooting him a scrutinizing glance as he did.

Andrew's got his hands full with this one.

'Okay now we're at the bar,' said Nina. 'Pretend I'm Andrew, what would you order?'

'Ice-cream sundae,' he answered.

Nina's mouth gaped slightly.

'You do know the tradition is to have something before desert.'

'Not here, not on a day like this,' he said. 'Here it's ice cream first. That's what we would get after school on hot days'.

'And hope that Mia served you,' pointed Nina, giggling. She requested the dessert menu while he sipped gingerly at his drink. Her warmth was enveloping. To feel cold beside her was like trying to feel cold on a summer day.

Happily, he let himself sink into the moment.

'Right, now that we've covered that what would you and Andrew talk about? You've mentioned previous infatuation's, what about current ones? That's what guys talk about right, girls. Kate told me about someone called Cara at your university'.

At her words, there was the sensation that the sun had drifted behind a cloud.

'We're just friends,' Eli coughed, quickly. 'Cara is someone Kate has been deluding herself about ever since she started stalking my Facebook. It's a serious obsession with her; she spends all day talking to these groups of mothers she was friends with in school whose kids have left home, discussing potential girlfriends and financial capabilities'.

His words invoked a pang of recognition. But he was too distracted trying to prevent conversation sliding into a guilty slump only he would feel. That wouldn't be fair to Nina, she was trying and succeeding in being friendly. He couldn't ruin this.

'At least she cares,' offered Nina, sincerely.

'I know, I know,' he said, raising his hands.

Phil presented their sundaes and retreated with a scowl when Nina paid more attention to the two towering glasses than him.

They dug in.

'I think you were right about eating the ice cream first,' she said. 'See, your proving Jones's theory about your self worth already.'

'Do I pass the trial or whatever this is?' he asked.

'This … is lunch and I need more time to give an accurate answer'.

Silence befell them as they ate their sugary indulgences. What communication passed between them was purely non-verbal, and Eli found a big, goofy grin had perched itself on his face. He liked it, liked how it sat. It had been too long since he acted carefreely.

He thought of asking her about her parents. But thought better of it.

Not for the first time did he think, *this is Nina, this is weird.*

Once they had finished their desserts, they were too full for more. Nina said it was probably a good thing, as she had to get back to work.

'English has commissioned me to create eight paintings for The Gallery,' she said.

'That's cool,' he told her. 'I remember now. You were always doodling in a notepad, is that what you do now? Painting'.

She blushed at his question. Her shoulders developing a slight awkward shrug he recognized because his own did the same when explaining his writing.

The word that her pose evoked in him was cute. She looked adorable only because he had been a victim to her ruthless will. She had used it to drag him here and out of his brooding mood at the prospect of lunch with her.

Now he was glimpsing what she held in her heart.

He knew this with the same sureness that he knew only he could have deduced this, holding something similar in his. He knew the protective shyness that comes with trying to employ a creative talent as a viable income.

'Yes,' she replied. 'English asked me a week ago after seeing some of my stuff. You wouldn't have seen it at Jones's, it's all outback. I've converted his old bedroom into a studio'.

Her short, clipped sentences confirmed his deduction in contrast with her early rambling conversation.

'You must show me your stuff sometime,' he said.

Her cheeks blushed an even deeper red.

'Sure,' she said.

'It's funny, but even though you've moved in, you still referred to the house as Jones's,' commented Eli.

'What can I say,' she shrugged. 'The man casts a long shadow.'

It was clear that Nina's awkwardness had fed into a lull in the conversation. The pair looked and act sheepishly toward each other as they moved outside the restaurant.

Eventually, Nina broke it.

'This was actually fun,' she said slowly. 'If you're interested and not too busy reliving old memories I could do something like this again tomorrow.'

He could not believe the next words that came from his mouth.

'Yeah, that would be nice.'

He was still smiling that big, goofy grin when she dropped him off.

He waved goodbye from the drive, his brain feeling like wet cotton. Nina tooted her horn in acknowledgment before peeling away.

They hadn't talked about his hateful studies. Nina hadn't asked about his writing, and throughout the whole ordeal, he had not wallowed over either.

He floated inside on distant legs.

'Where were you today?' asked Kate as he retrieved a drink from the kitchen.

'Out for lunch,' he said. 'Nina took me to Mia's. We got sundaes'.

'Nina took you out for lunch, will miracles never cease,' said Kate. 'I hope you were pleasant to that, girl, you know, she's grown up a great deal.'

'Yes, I was,' said Eli.

To avoid further probing, he retreated to his room. Gazing from his window, he absently traced the smiling lines on his face.

He had had fun ... with *Nina.* Even thinking about it was deliciously strange.

Eli slumped onto his bed to listen to *Frank Ocean*. As he did whenever in proximity to his iPhone, he checked his messages. There was nothing from Cara.

The passage of time became marked by the ending of each song as he lay unthinking.

'All you need to complete this picture is a little smoking joint in your hand.'

Eli opened his eyes, craned his neck, and kept craning. The giant that stood in his doorway spread out his arms. A six-pack of beer dangled from one huge paw.

'Afraid I'm not on the best of terms with Logue these days,' said Eli.

'Well, you look like someone who would know a drug dealer,' said Andrew. 'You've got that too thin, too pale look and what's this you're going bald too.'

'Hey least I've stayed consistent,' said Eli. 'Don't you hate seeing those high school rugby guys who've turned to fat after school ends?'

He patted Andrew's protruding belly for emphasis.

The two contemplated each other with ever-widening grins. Spontaneously, they embraced, laughing as they did.

'It's good to see you; I getting worried there,' said Andrew.

Eli's head rocked backward, his eyes narrowing. 'Why'?

'Nothing, just something Heather said to me in a text,' said Andrew. 'She made me expect a corpse.'

He flopped onto the bed. It made a wail like it had been bombed.

'You're looking good though, got a bit of color in your cheeks. Drink?'

Eli followed him, dangling his feet over the bed's edge. Andrew's tree truck equivalents reach the floor with ease as he scratched open a beer.

'I suppose I have your girlfriend to thank for that,' said Eli. 'She took me out for lunch. What is it with everyone keeping secrets these days? When were you gonna tell me your sleeping with the enemy?'

'I have no idea what you're talking about,' Andrew said.

'Nina, your girlfriend, took me out for lunch,' said Eli.

Andrew's eyebrows collided.

'No, don't think so,' he said. 'Embracing the single life at the mo. Nina and I hang out as friends, usually whenever I have Rosalie. The two of them get on like a house on fire'.

He crumbled his already empty can, tossing it into the nearby bin. A second was immediately popped open with a spurt of fizz.

'Tough day?' asked Eli.

Briefly, his friend's eyes meet his before flickering away to stare at the wall opposite them.

'How is Rosalie these days?' asked Eli.

Again, his friend's eyes flickered from the wall. This time they peered at him over the lid of his beer can.

'She's good,' said Andrew. 'I have her this weekend, looking forward to it. Jamie's got a new boyfriend, not sure how I feel about that. Though, I'm sure her parents are ecstatic that she's dating someone who doesn't work in the local computer repair shop and hasn't knocked up their precious daughter, or anyone else for that matter. His name's Derek'.

'Sounds like a knob,' said Eli.

'Rosalie doesn't like him,' said Andrew. He had begun to chew his tongue. 'She hasn't seen him much, just whenever he's come to take Jamie out.'

'How long have they been seeing each other?' asked Eli.

'Three months,' said Andrew.

He threw his second dead soldier in the bin. It danced over the rim.

'Shit,' he said. Already, a third can was at his lips.

'Jamie's parents,' said Andrew with a burp. Eli's stomach turned at the sudden gust of hot yeasty stink. 'Paul and Sinead, remember what they said to me that I had destroyed their daughter's life as if the decision to have sex was only mine. Assholes. It's funny, with me, Jamie's all serious and adult, play dates, pick up times, school work. With this guy, it's all sunbeams and rainbows. At least that's what her *Facebook* shows. You know what I think; I think she's trying to be the twenty-two year old she would have been without a kid when she's with him. Anyway, that's my ranting over. What about you, how's university?'

'It's fine,' he said.

'How do you mean fine? I still can't believe, Eli Donoghue, studying Business Management 101. Aren't you bored out of your mind?'

'It's okay, really,' said Eli.

The can that had been on the way to Andrew's lips froze.

'Don't do that,' he said. 'Don't do that thing you do where you pretend everything's great.'

'I'm not doing anything.'

Hostility worked through Andrew's jaw.

'Fine,' he said. 'If you don't want to tell me shit, its cool but I've had a long day, and I'm not interested in skirting around anything and pretending everything is hunky-dory. Just so you know everyone knows it's not. Everyone knows you're in trouble'.

Andrew heaved himself from the bed, staggering slightly.

'I'm not hanging around trying to help someone who won't help themselves. I've got real shit to be getting on with. Fuck you, Eli'.

Andrew marched out of his room without looking back. Eli's vocal cords were paralyzed by his friend's aggression. He sat on the bed as Andrew thundered down the stairs, his mouth opening and closing, opening, and closing.

7

'How come your head's up your ass?' asked Nina.
They were in her car with Jones's fishing gear rolling
around the boot. He supposed she had learned from
grandfather about their frequent fishing trips and had
been inspired by their previous conversation on how he
relived old events. Except this was a new experience
due to Nina's presence. Or it would be if he could get
out of his head.
Eli licked his lips and answered honestly. It surprised
even him, but then again, Nina was not someone he
was hiding from. Nor, he found, did he want to.
'I think Andrew and I had a falling out yesterday,' he
said.
'I know, he called me last night,' she said.
He stared at her from the passenger seat. Outside the
greenery continued to zip by as if on an overactive
conveyor belt.
'Well, any thoughts?' he asked.
'It's between you and him,' said Nina. 'I am not getting
involved. Though, I will say we both had a right laugh
at you thinking Andrew and I were dating'.
Eli's face burned.
'Ah ... it's just the way you spoke about him ... was,' he
said.
'Friendly,' offered Nina, laughing. 'Listen, Eli when I
talk about a person I'm spending time in bed with, you'll
know I'm spending time in bed with them.'
'Sorry,' he said.
'It's cool,' she said and then added, 'there's something
else isn't there.'
'I think Kate and Ryan are having problems.'
Saying it out loud caused a wedge to dam his throat.

'How do you know?'

'They've been weird around each other ever since I've been back,' he said. 'Take last night, for example. We watched a film, usually, Ryan, and I would dissect it like the nerds we are with Kate objecting, saying it was rubbish and that we were idiots. Instead, she was on her phone all night, and Ryan sat glaring at the TV. Neither of them spoke'.

'What were you watching?'

'Lord of the Rings.'

'Shit, I'd be on my phone too if I was subjected to that,' said Nina.

Her cackling laughter hit him like a slap in the face.

'Look, Kate and Ryan are adults,' she said. 'They've been together longer than you've been alive. Let them handle it'.

Eli wanted to describe to Nina what his biological parents' relationship had been like, that because of them, he couldn't leave it be. But he couldn't. He liked this new Nina and suspected that she might even like him. To let her know would have been like standing before her naked. She would undoubtedly run away screaming.

Instead, he said, 'it's weird being back. You think things would stay the same, but they don't. You expect someone to tell you 'hey, guess what, we aren't getting along so well anymore' or 'Nina's living at my house and I've moved out".

'Do you tell everyone everything that's going on in your life?' asked Nina.

 Eli didn't reply. He couldn't.

'No, didn't think so,' said Nina. 'I think you're spending a little too much time in your head personally, Eli.'

'I am a twenty-two-year-old student,' he said.

'Yes, you're only supposed to think of yourself. Not everyone else. Maybe what would be best for you is to focus on the here and now. Did no one tell you constant moping is very unattractive? Well, yours truly will sort that out with a day at the old watering hole'. Eli shook his head. There seemed to be nothing that could dispirit Nina from achieving her goal. It was impossible not to be infected by her charming optimism. It was then that he thought of her, not as the grown-up version of the Nina he had known but an entirely different person. A person he wanted to know more about.

'I'm sorry,' he said. 'I will endeavor to be less of a mope.'

'Thank you,' she said and then quickly added. 'But don't do it for me, do it for yourself.'

'Do you really hate Lord Of The Rings?' he asked.

'I've actually never seen it,' she said.

'No fucking way,' was his reply.

The river turned out to be as dark as Guinness. A luminous drizzle so fine it was fog swallowed the opposite bank and surroundings. Branches belonging to trees unseen protruded faintly through it, slick with moist emerald fungi. There was bird song, but it was lazy and sporadic as if the birds themselves knew that finding shelter was more critical that mating calls.

'I thought you'd like this,' said Nina. 'Jones said it was one of the few places where you'd shut up.'

'It's calming, don't you think,' he said.

Eli inhaled deeply at the edge of the water. The air was crisp and cold and seemed to fill him until he thought he would float away.

After a few embarrassing moments of fumbling, they cast their lines into the water. These floated downstream until they were pulled taut by the pressure they put on their reels.

The effort of keeping their lines from being dragged was constant that the pair fell into a concentrated silence. Eventually, a kind of mechanical hand/eye automation set in, which required little thought at all. For Eli, this allowed his head to become a hollow place filled only with the sound of the running river. For Nina, it encouraged her to replay their previous conversations, which in turn, lead to an uncommon unease.

'Oh, fuck you, Eli,' she said.

Startled, he turned and saw the stranglehold she had on her rod was causing it to wave comically.

'What,' he said.

'I'm going soft because you've been such a big girl's blouse,' she said. 'Thank you for yesterday, okay. You had the opportunity to make me really uncomfortable and get some payback for all those years where I was a dick to you, so thank you'.

'For what,' he said, chuckling.

'For not asking about my parents,' she snapped. 'I know you've probably been told things already, and I'm thankful that you didn't try to pry.'

'Oh,' said Eli.

'Right,' said Eli.

'Well, I figured I would never want anyone to ask me about mine, so I wasn't going to ask you about yours,' said Eli.

Her expression was hard and questioning from within the circle frame of her hood.

'This is all your fault,' she said after some time.

'What?' he repeated.

'Us bonding like this.'

'I thought you wanted to bond.'

'Yes … but … oh, I fucking hate you,' she screamed.

Eli laughed heartily at her while recasting his line.

'I thought you didn't do soppy talks,' he said. 'You're a bigger sop than me.'

She screamed again, and he laughed again.

'Here, do you want to hear about your grandfather's amazing fishing ability?' asked Eli. 'I mean it's like a superpower, but he actually can't catch a single fish. But I tell you something; there isn't a man on this earth better at getting a hook into a tree'.

Then he was laughing again, laughing because it was funny, for the pure exhilaration of it and it felt good. It had been too long since he had laughed this hard. What made it even more enjoyable was that Nina was laughing too.

When they had calmed down, he found his diaphragm ached pleasantly.

'I read your stuff by the way,' said Nina.

Her words squeezed every last giggle from his body.

'Hey, that shut you up from slabberin' about my granddaddy,' said Nina. She was grinning from ear to ear. Her teeth were wolfishly white in the dark hole of her hood.

'Jones left a lot of stuff behind when he moved to Mia's. Like he says the woman's loft isn't the biggest in the world. I thought your stories were going to be all about guns and women with huge tits'.

'Sorry, to disappoint you,' said Eli.

'They were brilliant,' she told him. 'When I came to Hazel, I found it so strange that you weren't suddenly bursting into Jones's house every day like when we were kids. I knew you were at university, but I still found it messed up. It made me think of all the times I was mean to you. I decided that when I did see you, I'd apologize. Then I found your stories in the bookshelf. I read the play first because I remembered being told about it and I thought how did that little asshole come up with this'.

Eli was floating again, but this time, it was on Nina's words. They were balloons that had roped around him, lifting him to the heavens. It was his own self-deprecation; a developed reflex for protection that kept him grounded.

'Thanks,' said Eli. 'Well, you're the only one that liked it.'

'Don't be so stupid,' she said. 'Everyone I talked to about it liked it.'

'Everyone means everyone that I know, and they have to say nice things, it's like the law.'

'Maybe that's true, but then I don't fit into that category, at least not yet,' she said. 'It's good, Eli and I could explain to you why but I don't think you'd believe me. The novel you wrote, The Child's Place was even better. I think it might be one of the best things I've ever read. Jones told me you wrote that one angry, angry that the play you had written wasn't as successful as you liked and you wanted to prove yourself. What I am having trouble with is recognizing the person that wrote those stories and the person in front of me, because they don't match up very well'.

'If you'd spent as much time as I have being rejected you'd soon learn how grating it becomes,' he said. There it was. The truth. Eli had finally spoken it out loud. There was no anger in him or despair in his omission. Instead, there was a sensation of looseness. Eli stalked across the pebbled shore to the picnic basket Nina had bought. He collapsed onto the tartan blanket they'd laid out earlier.

'So we both run away from things,' Nina said as she joined him. 'You run away and study a subject you have no interest in, that's what Andrew says.'

'There is no course that suddenly gives you a publishing contract,' said Eli. 'I needed something to fall back on. Can't pay bills with rejection letters'.

Nina nodded and said, 'and I run to my grandfather. You know out of the majority of my life it only places I've ever been really happy is here'.

'Me too,' said Eli.

I couldn't have had this conversation with Kate or any of them, he thought. *But I could have it with her.*

'Two fuck-ups, hanging by a river,' sighed Nina. She was observing the passing torrent with faraway eyes, her chin resting on her knees.

'It wasn't that the play was unsuccessful,' said Eli. 'It was ridiculed, yeah my classmates liked it, in the same way, anyone like's a novelty item. I was the novelty to them, but to their parents, I was some freaky kid struggling with past trauma. You have to remember everyone in Hazel believes they know everything about everyone else. Logue won't speak to me, ignored me in classes and in the halls. The rest all gave me those pitying looks I had spent years trying to avoid. So, yeah, I was angry. I took that anger and tried to write a book that was worth publishing. I put my heart and soul into it and used everything I had learned about writing stories into it. It would be my masterpiece, my fuck you to all the pitying looks. All that came out of it was wasted paper and a dozen letters saying, 'no thank you, not for us''.

'You started to doubt yourself,' said Nina.

Eli looked at her. She had taken the words right out of his mouth.

'That's right,' he said. 'So I picked a couple of courses that I thought would least guarantee me a job when I finished with them. I still tried to get stuff published, but it wasn't happening. When I work on a story, I used to write without thinking about who would be reading it. But after a dozen more, 'no thank you's,' I changed. I started to write for specific markets and specific publishers. The comments I got back were even worse. I began to see them before I even typed a word on my screen. I'm at a point now where I haven't written a word in six months. I'm too afraid to. I see the fault in all of them'.

'So you've been judging the quality of your work on whether it gets published or not,' said Nina.

'Well, how else do you know if it's good or not,' said Eli.

'Don't you have someone you trust that would be honest with you?'

He met her gaze again.

'As I've already said, the people I have don't count,' he said.

'Okay, your godparents would probably sugar coat some stuff, but I don't think my granddad would.'

'You can be my first reader,' he said and laughed. It was a single bark. 'You've already helped. All this, it's been nice, getting out of head for a while'.

'Trust the process, my friend,' said Nina.

'Oh, are we friends now?' asked Eli.

'I think we have to be,' she said. 'We've broken some barriers today.'

She smiled at him, and he smiled at her. Thin, weak smiles but smiles nonetheless.

'Did you really enjoy my book?' he asked.

'I loved it,' she said. 'Tell me this, the character Claire, was she based on that friend of yours, Heather? She was, wasn't she?'

'Maybe,' he said. 'If we are going to continue hanging out, there is something you need to do.'

Nina's eyebrows arched with a curiosity that he found sexy.
'You need to watch Lord Of The Rings'
She began to laugh.

They drove back without having caught anything.
The atmosphere in the car was that of a relaxing depression after a euphoric high. Boundaries had been broken between them, and as a result, their relationship lacked definition or a label. It was new, something to be explored.
'Does your mum know you're here?' asked Eli.
They were in the driveway now, the red-bricked façade of the house in front of them.
'She does,' said Nina. 'Sometimes it brings me the greatest joy knowing how pissed off she will be about it, other times it makes me sad. Come on inside I want to show you something'.
Together, they carried the basket, which they had refilled at the Try 'N' Save with glutinous goodies. They placed this on the kitchen table.
'Come on,' she said again.
Nina led him to the spare bedroom. If he was honest following her into it did more than raise his heartbeat.
'It seemed wrong sleeping in Jones's old bedroom,' she said. 'When I used to come here as a kid, I always stayed in this one. My parents never did, as you know, always preferred to stay at a hotel. Every night I prayed for them to leave cause granddad, and I always had more fun without them. His bedroom's now my studio'.
'Huh,' said Eli. He was forcing himself not to look at the bed too hard.
Nina had her back to it and was surveying the shelves of a bookcase. 'Here,' she said, removing a bound book from the rest.

Eli recognized it instantly as one of a dozen that he had paid to be made. Inscribed on the cover at the top was his name. At the bottom was the title: The Child's Place. She offered it to him with her right hand and a pen with her left.

'Can I have your autograph before we watch this stupid film?' she asked.

The stupid film silenced her after fifteen minutes. She kept the eye-rolling up for a little longer. By then, the wraiths were on the screen, and Nina's mouth was slightly agape. He whispered in her ear, 'what do you think?'

'You bastard,' was her replied.

Empty plates smeared by residing curry sauce lay scattered on the table.

Nina had nestled into his bony shoulder. Her arm was slid through his while her feet curled beneath her. They lay like that until the first film ended. Initially, the touch of Nina's skin caused alarms to blare in his brain and his muscles to tense. He was sure that if the sofa, on which he sat, were removed, his body would have hung steady in its seated position. Nina seemed not to notice, and eventually, he relaxed, enjoying her scent, a faint earthy musk and the warm smoothness of her skin.

When The Fellowship of the Ring had ended, Nina announced that it was her turn to chose, 'and for revenge.' She decided on a Pixar film called UP that he had never heard of.

'What type of kids film is this,' he said after the first devastating twenty minutes.

She threw her head back and cackled at him.

They were halfway through, Eli engrossed, when white light slashed across the living room. His pulse spiked. Through the picture window at their backs, they could see Jones and Mia stepping out of Jones's car.

They detached instantly. The sofas leather crinkling as they swept apart, putting a safe distance between them, a friendship distance. Nina shot him a knowing, sly look, cheeks flushed in a way that he wanted to question, but it was too late.

The front door crashed open.

'Here they are,' cried Jones enthusiastically.

Eli was no Justin Blackthorn in terms of acting, but he tried to portray innocence.

'We wanted to run something by you ... '

Jones's voice jumped from zealous enthusiasm to barely hidden awkwardness without pause as he noticed them on the sofa. As his voice altered, his facial features did acrobatic feats.

' ... about organizing a BBQ for everyone here ... ' he carried on.

Both Nina and Eli tried to exude innocence, which unintentionally caused them to radiate a despicable level of guilt. They'd been caught watching TV. Jones's stare made Eli believe that if they'd been caught having sex, it would have been an improvement.

Mia saved them, her voice a dizzying, calm breeze.

'We wanted to run it by you, love, seeing as your living here now. Didn't we?'

'Ahh ... yes … em we did,' stammered Jones.

'Of course, you can,' said Nina. 'It's your house.'

The next few seconds passed as the second most horrendous of Eli's life. The first came next when Mia, not so innocently, asked, 'what have you two been up to then?'

Before either of them could reply the power went out.

'Well, that's interesting,' said Mia.

Eli stretched to his full height, leaving Nina on the sofa.

'Must be the fuse box outside,' said Jones somewhere to his left. 'Eli could you come with me, my eyesight's not what it used to be.'

Oh great the perfect chance for him to have me alone.
Any other objecting thoughts were prevented by a crystallized crack that came from the kitchen.

'What was that?' asked Nina.

There was another crack, and a crash as a kitchen window shattered. Whatever had punched a hole in it skidded across the kitchen table.

Jones and Mia approached the object.

As Eli watched them, he caught movement out of the corner of his eye. The figure, a solid shadow in the night's darkness, was on the lawn. Before he could react, the living room window smashed inward, and something heavy smacked into his right temple.

The force of the unseen object propelled him off his feet.

'Jesus,' shouted a voice.

There was a noisy clatter belonging to the dirtied dishes. Eli had fallen on the coffee table. A fire had erupted across his brow, stabbing into his skull. Hands grabbed at him. Voices that were speaking through water were shouting at him. Eli sank into darkness.

There was blood in his right eye.

It was like seeing through a red lens. Eli pressed the cold cloth against his gnashed forehead and winched. Above him, giants bickered.

'We should phone the police,' hissed Mia.

'I don't think that's wise,' said Jones.

'Why the hell not, she's fucking hit him,' yelled Mia.

'As vile as Maria is we can't prove it was her that did this,' he said. 'If we did call the police, it would only alert them to us when we get payback.'

'Guys, do you think we should take him to the hospital.' That voice belonged to Nina, who was palming his cloth deeper onto his wound. She was also holding his hand. Her voice sounded tiny, and he wasn't surprised she was ignored.

I can taste metal, thought Eli as his tongue wormed against his cheek.

'Look, look at this,' said Mia.

She held a nasty looking piece of broken brick, the culprit.

'If she had hit him with the jagged side, it could have killed him. Forget about your back and forth with her and think about Eli. This has to stop'.

'Guys,' whined Nina.

They didn't listen. Eli decided to make them.

'SHUT UP,' he yelled.

Jones and Mia's gaze tore from each other to him, wide-eyed and terrified.

'We are not phoning the police ... that's it done, Mia. But you are going to take me to the hospital, so stop arguing and get the car ready,' he demanded.

'You're not taking his side ... ' said Mia.

He shot her a look. It was easy to do with the lights back on.

'I am not taking anyone's side, thank you,' he lied.

Nina and Jones helped him to his feet while Mia waited in the running car. As they stepped down the porch steps, Jones whispered to him, 'we'll get her for this.'

'I know,' he replied.

Eli gained insight into head injuries.

They were wondrous for cutting down the wait time in A&E. Such an injury was referred to as a priority, which is why they only had to wait an hour to be seen. Not the standard NHS twelve. He didn't mind, his heads no longer felt like a bowl of soup that had been sloshed about and he was enjoying the bizarre family drama enfolding in the corner of the waiting room.

'That ill teach you not to play on the fucking landing now won't it,' proclaimed the suspected father of the troop. The recipient of this abuse had his head low.

'Shhh … Tom … you want the whole world to hear,'
hissed the suspected mother.
'Mia's away to the car,' whispered Nina.
She was also observing the unfolding scene,
mesmerized.
'I guess she didn't agree with lying to the receptionist.'
Eli nodded in response, distracted by the show. The
entire waiting room was secretly watching it to the
extent that when the nurse called them, they left
disappointed.
Eli joined those luckily few on the next call.
Forty-five minutes later he returned to Nina with his
head bandaged. The family was still stationed in the
corner and looked as if they been there for some time.
'Next time … leave flying to Superman,' said the father.
'Shhh, Tom,' said his wife.
'All, clear, no stitches, no concussion,' Eli proclaimed.
'Brilliant,' said Nina. 'Jones just texted to say he's
boarded all the windows up. I'll have to endure the
draft for tonight, but tomorrow he'll get someone round'.
'There's a spare room at ours,' he said before he could
think.
A speechless limbo swelled between them, in which
they stared into each other's eyes.
'Though, Kate might kill me when she sees this,' Eli
heard himself say. 'So there might be two spare
rooms.'

Kate and Ryan were as expected fine with Nina
staying.
What they weren't okay with was Eli's neatly bandaged
head. 'What the hell happened to you,' yelled Kate as
he entered the kitchen. She was on her feet and
examining his head while Ryan appeared trapped in his
seat at the table by the sight of it.
Eli quickly narrated the lie he told at the hospital.

/

'We didn't call because it was barely anything,' he said. 'I just tripped on the leg of Jones's coffee table when the fuses broke. Nina drove me to A&E'.

'Well, she has some sense,' said Kate. 'Thank you, Nina, for looking after a twenty-two-year-old toddler.'

'It's okay,' replied Nina. 'I now fully understand the stress you must have dealt with in raising such an idiot.'

Ryan let out a laugh. 'You don't know the half of it.'

'Thanks, all, thanks a lot,' said Eli. 'I'll show Nina her room now.'

'They seem okay,' whispered Nina on the staircase. Eli agreed. The energy in the house was different, less hostile and cold. Kate and Ryan had looked deep in conversation but not one that sent his alarm bells ringing.

The spare bedroom was down the hall from his. A cozy space not unlike her room at Jones's. They stood on either side of the bed, silent, the space between them filled with things unsaid but achingly felt. They said goodnight to each other as he slid silently from the room. He held onto the doorknob long after shutting the door, his hand white.

Alone, beneath his covers, he still felt that palpable, uncertain energy trying to seduce him. He recalled her warmth nestled against him. How easy and free it had been.

Before. Before. Before.

She is Jones's granddaughter.

He gritted his teeth, and his hand traveled to his temple. He fell asleep, feeling the rough fabric of his bandage and dreamt of dragons.

Eli wasn't the first to wake.

Years of domestic living acted as internal alarm clocks for Kate and Ryan. By the time he descended the stairs, freshly showered and dressed, Ryan was at work, and Kate was in her usual seat at the kitchen table, taking a break from morning chores via her phone.

'I'm just going out for a walk,' he said.

He didn't wait for a response.

Outside, the clouds suffocated the sky, their color grey/white. He walked beneath them, fingers tight and jaw set. The surrounding geography churned by from that of a rural townscape to woodland. Soon, he was climbing a rutted track that had once been a driveway. Only dared teenagers climbed it now.

The trees on either side were dead, their bark as white as sharks teeth. As if they had died with the evil that had lived on the hill above.

The house that had once sheltered on the summit was a wreck. Its windows were boarded and infected with thorns. The buildings left side looked sunken, a ruined crown upon a decaying hill. People had spray-painted its outsides in angry proclamations. One read 'RACISTS BURN IN HELL.' Those words echoed icily inside Eli's head.

There was noise behind him like a bone snapping.

'Is this one of the things on your to-do list?' asked Nina, grimly.

He felt the skin around his left eye twitch. He didn't turn.

'I've been living in Hazel for some time now, and I've never thought to come here.'

'I had a nightmare,' he told her. 'It reminded me of the man who lived here. It made me wonder what if someone had caught him before he did the things he did'.

'This is a Hitler question.'

Nina had worked her way to his side. He shoved his hands into his pockets. Both stared at the house without a word for some time.

'Come on,' he said. 'Let's go prank a dragon.'

'We could go inside,' whispered Nina. 'See what's there.'

'There's nothing,' he told her.

8

Maria Hunter sauntered down the hall, sipping her morning coffee.

In her mind, she moved with sensual erotic grace that showcased her curves. In reality, she invoked the image of a duck waddling thanks to her schoolboy figure.

She collected the post puddled beneath her letterbox. Her manicured fingers reached for the handle of the front door and paused. She rearranged her nightgown, plucking at the pink satin to reveal a considerable bit of her ivory neck and chest. Once satisfied enough of her cleavage was on show, the small apples of flesh she had been already amped up by the support of a lace bra (also pink), she ripped open the door.

Already, the postman was halfway down her drive and moving fast. She called to him in a loud sunbeam of a voice reserved for jolly matrons in old TV shows.

'YOOWOOO ... MR FLETCHER'.

Several birds shot into flight from the treetops in response to that voice.

Mr. Fletcher, a twenty-something uniformed postman, flinched. To an onlooker, he appeared as if someone had shoved a gun into his back.

Slowly, he circled around, his arms pointed skyward. Maria waved her fingertips at him.

'Hi, Misses Hunter,' he said, lowering his arms.

She sniggered.

'Its Miss Hunter dear, any chance I can convince you today to come inside for some breakfast, even some toast. I'm sure you must be hungry being up so early'.

'I've already eaten but thanks,' he said, patting his stomach. 'I really must get on, I have a schedule to keep.'

Mr. Fletcher was tiptoeing backward as he spoke.

'You're sure,' she said and pouted at him.

'Very,' he replied, grabbing his cart and shoving.

If he was moving before he was now high tailing it. Maria watched him go, a fingernail circling the rim of her coffee cup.

Maria had no intention of seducing her postman. Her flirtations were simply a flamboyant ruse to vent the giddy drunken happiness she felt. This was the result of last week's maneuver in the ongoing war effort. The smashing of Jones's windows had been retaliation for his previous assault: the cementing of her flowerbeds. And back and froth it had been since she had run over his friend's mutt. But even before that their tennis ball dance had existed ever since she had met him.

She knew she hated him, but she could not remember why. That their dance was similar to Northern Ireland's parliamentary conduct was lost on her.

Her grey eyes drifted from her drive to the foliage that separated her plot from his. Her lips parted to form an ever-widening grin.

She slammed the door closed, referring to the postman as a 'cock tease,' as she did.

I can't say I'm not getting any, she thought, *Bruce saw to that.*

It had been Bruce Dalton that had suggested the idea for her latest prank.

'You know what we did in college if we wanted to scare someone,' he had said in his Texan drawl.

Bruce talked as if everyone should already know what he was going to say. Maria associated this trait as being horribly American, cocky to the point of stupidity.

She had met Bruce through her work at Coyle & O'Connor's Insurance. And he had employed a smoother style of seduction at the time to obtain her. Bruce had no clue, of course, how much of their courtship had been down to her orchestration. Maria's grin became a tight, twisted smirk at such knowledge.

Over the last several months she had weeded Bruce into something presentable, and she usually would have corrected his language, but she was drunk. She had felt the need to after seeing her ruined flowerbeds. In the present, the power of memory pulled her into the living room.

They were lying before the fireplace (a romantic cliché she allowed but would never advertise that she indulged in it to others, especially those at work).

'We would wait until it was dark,' said Bruce. 'Then we would stone their house; usually a frat house this was. We weren't doing anything bad, you understand. This was college boys' misbehaving. It was a game, score points for any windows that you could smash'.

Her eyes grew huge over her wine glass.

'Could we do that,' she said.

There had been humor in Bruce's voice as he had told his story. There was none as he stared at her and said, 'we could.'

'And you'd do it with me,' she whispered.

'Of course,' he replied.

The idea that what they were discussing was wrong never occurred to them.

She wanted to win. She always wanted to win, which was why the conflict between Jones and herself frustrated her.

The day she arrived home to find the stems of her prized roses poking through hardened concrete, her anger had been directed at Jones's lack of submission. It didn't matter what prank he played. What infuriated her was that he would not give in.

Victory through his surrender was her objective. But it was more than that she wanted to dose that carefree jubilance that he strutted around with. It had insulted her more than anything he had ever said or did. Life was so easy for him.

What did he know of struggle and sacrifice?

Bruce's motivations were so akin to hers that if she had known them, she would have been reassured about the man she had chosen to be with. They were of domination and self-worth. For the first time in his life, he had met someone unimpressed by his good looks, his perfect physic, and his charm. She made him feel maddeningly inferior to the point that if she suggested jumping out of an airplane, he would with a smile.

The night had cloaked them as they crept through the partition of trees that separated her property from Jones's. The air had been icy cold that tantalized her hot skin.

At the sudden recall, Maria tousled her coppery and coughed as heat filled her face. She remembered its icy fingers caressing her spine, her hips, and breasts as she straddled Bruce on the hallway floor, the front door wide open and forgotten. In its rectangle frame, the land had been black while stars twinkled in the blue velvet of the sky.

This was after they had smashed Jones's windows. The pair's desire for each, their sheer hornyness at having overstepped a judicial line was ferocious. Maria stared at the floorboards were the act occurred.

If they could speak, what would they say? They'd tell you we know how to celebrate and there's going to be a different celebration tonight.

After they had untangled themselves from the floor, they had waited for Jones and his ilk to seek retribution. They hadn't. A week had passed, and there had been nothing but workmen placing new windows in the panes of her neighbor's house.

She had won. Finally.

As if devised by fate she was hosting a party tonight for the other members of her company's board. That she despised all of them didn't matter.

Her original intention for the party was to announce her engagement to Bruce. However, it would now serve two purposes though, in her head, it was victory she most thought of.

Coyle & O'Connor's Insurance was a cesspool of conquest.

These either fell into two categories. The sexual conquests made by senior staff members upon their underlings and the ladder-climbing of said underlings. Sometimes these went hand in hand. An example of this was Mark Lawson and Amelia Brown.

Amelia quickly bounced from a junior accountant to a senior in the space of a few months. It was widened discussed (always behind her back) that it was due to her 'special relationship' with board member Mark. What was surprising was when Mark, a man in his sixties, decided rather than continuing his semi-secret affair, he made it public and left his wife. Though, being unfaithful was the norm in the company being honest about it was not. To add further surprise to the frenzied channels of office gossip, Amelia later left him once his divorce, and her position as Head of Accounts was finalized.

That Maria had kept her own conquest a secret caused that the tight, twist of a smirk to reappear on her face. With her cheeks glowing, she wandered absently into the kitchen.

It was mid-morning, and she had little to do in terms of preparation for the party. She threw the post down on the table and sipped at her coffee.

She had never trolled the office for sex before. She found the whole practice disgusting, but she made sure to listen out for any information about her fellow colleagues.

Her secretary, Linda Hall, was such a source though one she had never exploited. The workplace was for work not to encourage a perverted hunting ground. It was this professional integrity that had allowed her to become the only woman on the company's board she believed. As such, they maintained a strict but effective relationship. However, when Bruce had started with the company less than a year ago, Linda had let it slip. Maria had heard her gossiping to Mark Lawson's secretary, Judith Larkin. As the two women chatted, she had left her office chair and stood listening from her doorway.

'I heard that too,' Judith cooed. 'I wonder what department he's working in.'

'I heard it was marketing,' replied Linda. 'He used to work for an advertisement company in the states, lord knows what he's doing here.'

'Probably, a woman,' said Judith.

'Nope, he's single.'

A sound of crazed glee had erupted from Judith. Her shoes tapped danced on the carpeted floor as she rocked in her chair, shoulders hunched. She looked like she had an epileptic fit. The pair giggled manically together.

'What's all this crackling about?' Maria had asked

A hood of cold indifference had swallowed Judith's schoolgirl hysteria instantly. Linda had turned to Maria; her eyes were bright. Her smile had held only good cheer.

'The new guy, Lawson, just hired,' she explained. 'He's an American and apparently very fit.'

Linda had inclined her head while her hands tidied at her desk. Maria had barely noticed the two men Linda had gestured at wandering nearer. She had been jarred by her secretary's words.

The new guy, Lawson, just hired.' Not Mr. Lawson but Lawson. As if he was some chum from her secondary school days she still hung around with.

What was worse was the line that existed between them that said, 'I am the boss, and you are my secretary' had been crossed. They were just women now, equals.

Maria's face had been a mask, concealing her shock and offense.

'Really, well we have to see about that,' she had replied.

She hadn't decided right there, but that's were the germ for the idea had come from. It bubbled with her outrage as the frenzied piranhas chittered away about this American God. She had noted the competitive edge to these conversations, and an idea had sprung upon her fully evolved.

Maria Hunter, the cold fish, the office cunt, would go on the hunt.

She cupped her mug in two hands and drank deeply. *And I got Bruce,* she thought. It had helped that Bruce was built like a God. He was young too. Twenty-eight. How would they chitter about that after tonight? What would they say about the new start that had been bagged by the thirty-nine-year-old board member; especially after every single one of them had practically thrown their knickers at him for a year? And they would say it had been her that got him, not the other way round.

Dimness had entered her kitchen as the sun ran behind a cloud. She switched on the overhead lights, which flickered to life and continued to flash.

She gasped as some coffee spilled upon her right wrist. 'Fuck,' she grunted.

Fear settled in her stomach as a steel bearing. She could feel the icy air from that night again as she stared upward at the flickering lights. It stroked her spine, causing her skin to goosebump and quiver. Her nipples grew painfully hard against the fabric of her bra.

She clapped the mug down, speeding for the back door.

The fuse box was situated above her rubbish bins. It appeared intact and untouched. Maria's eyes panned inside to see the lights had ceased there flickering. They narrowed on the surrounding environment as if attempting to crush it into giving up its secrets.

A faint wind sieved through the trees. Birds sang from somewhere close by.

She retracted inside, closing the door. Once the sounds of her grew harder to hear, the bin lid lifted open to reveal a dirtied and foul-smelling English.

By the time she climbed the stairs, she had forgotten about the lights.

She undressed as the water ran before a mirror larger than most TV's. With her light garments puddled at her bare feet, she pivoted left, right on her heels; doing the bathroom shuffle. Her hands moved over her softening belly to her hips. She craned forward, balancing on her toes while sucking in her cheeks. Those same hands moved again to press her cheekbones then stretch the skin around her eyes.

Not bad for thirty-nine, she concluded.

She entered into the shower and commenced screaming like a banshee. The water was ice cold.

'I think … we got her,' whispered Jones on hearing screams.

They were faint from their position hidden in the sweltering jungle before Maria's house. He exchanged sniggers and smiles with his co-conspirators camped out beside him.

'What do you mean it's impossible,' she yelled into the receiver.

The plastic casing released a crinkling sound as her fingers choked upon it.

'I need this done, and I need this done today. I have a significant engagement tonight, and I need my boiler working. This will not do. There is no such thing as last-minute, your plumbers; all you do all day is drive around in vans and then spend hours wasting time with your asses out on a job that would take five minutes. So tell one of your boys that if he drives my way and fixes this quick, I'll pay whatever his scheming mind comes up with'.

Maria stormed the graveled driveway in hiking boots. Her bathrobe swished against her bare legs. Other than those two articles, she was as naked as she had been in the bathroom. She didn't care. She had won. They would not take that from her, and they would most certainly not ruin today.

She started yelling as soon as she reached her neighbor's porch steps.

'Is that it … that the best you and your fucking hermit friends can do?'

She expected the man himself to greet her bellows. Instead, his skinny-legged granddaughter with the plump ass stepped out from the house's insides, fists clenched.

Maria inhaled, ready to tear her to shreds. However, Nina reacted quicker.

'Get the fuck off my porch, bitch or I'm calling the police on your old ass.'

The girl, just a kid, produced a ferocious noise.

Maria recoiled, and her heel slipped on the porch's damp wood. *Fuck me, no.* Yet her arms were already cartwheeling, clawing at the air in the hopes of finding purchase. They didn't find any, and she flopped hard on to the pathway. The gravel bit into her ass. She shut her eyes and hissed profanities through her teeth. When she opened them, she saw the girl above her was caught between helping and staying at her defensive post.

Maria looked at her with perplexity that darkened into a rage.

'No, don't you worry about me,' she yelled. 'Stay right where you are, I'll help myself.'

She ungracefully recovered. Her robe had dislodged from her shoulder. She corrected it without haste, more shamed at the fall than her revealed flesh.

She stabbed a finger at Nina saying, 'this isn't over.' Stomping off, thinking of nothing crueler to say, she shouted over her shoulder, 'I hope you're enjoying your new windows.'

Seeing, Ryan behind the shop's counter before him was not surprising.

Andrew had given up trying to beat him to work.

Strolling in, he began his role in the light-hearted exchanged that had developed between them over the years.

'Don't you ever leave here?' he asked.

He expected Ryan to snort and say, 'if I wasn't the only one that did any work, I could.' Instead, he looked at him, and his eyebrows jerked upward.

Andrew's arm, which had been swinging his lunch bag, stopped.

'What?'

'Your not supposed to be here, today,' said Ryan. Before Andrew could speak, his employer nodded at the entrance. He was turning as Eli stepped into the store.

'We've got things to do,' said Eli.

He spoke brightly, yet his hands had dug into his jeans, giving him a hunched look.

'I have mercifully allowed you to have a personal day,' said Ryan, bowing. 'Now get going before I change my mind or before Mark finds out I can be merciful, he's covering your shift today and as usual, is late in.'

'Yes, sir, boss,' replied Andrew.

'Okay, okay, okay,' muttered, Maria.

Her hands were frightened birds. She tried to clasp them, palms together, in front of her lips but randomly they'd escape to sweep through her unwashed hair or tug at her bathrobe.

'It's fine, just ignore them; all they want is a reaction. They want, they want, they want … just breathe, you've just gotta breathe,' Maria said.

She inhaled severely, her hands snapping apart, her eyes squeezing shut.

'You've won already. Don't let those bastards get under your skin,' Maria said before releasing her breath. It didn't calm her but allowed her to grapple her panic and fury.

She needed to find out what else they had done and fix it. They had surprised her; she would give them that, nonetheless she would be the winner of this game by the end.

Andrew examined the novel balanced on the dashboard.

'It's Nina's,' said Eli, getting into the driver's seat. 'She lent it to me, like the car.'

He nodded vaguely, tossing the book back to its perilous position.

'Yeah, she lent it to me to a few weeks ago as well,' said Andrew. '*Joe Hill* has a fantastic imagination. I've read all his books now'.

Nina's Ford croaked into life. The novel jittered slightly where it was.

'Are you going to tell me where we are going?' asked Andrew.

Eli ignored him until he had edged the car smoothly into traffic.

'We are going to Antrim, to the cinema,' he said.

'And why are we going there?'

'The new Avengers film is out,' Eli replied. His overly bright tone grated on Andrew's ears.

'Can't afford it, I'm afraid,' he told him. 'My cinema money is only for when Rosalie wants to go, sorry.'

'And your money shall stay that way,' said Eli. 'I have a student account that is far too full and in need of some abusing. This is on me'.

Air jetted from Andrew's nostrils.

They were speeding beyond Hazel, heading for the dual carriageway between Antrim and Ballymena. The novel seemed to flatten against the dashboards cheap leather.

'Is this your attempt to make up for the last time we spoke?' asked Andrew. 'Getting Ryan to give me the day off and paying for a movie.'

'I'm buying the popcorn and coke too,' said Eli.

'Oh well all is forgiven then,' proclaimed Andrew. 'Really?'

'No, of course, it fucking isn't,' Andrew snapped. 'What happened to your head?'

Andrew watched his friend touch the thick bandage above his eyebrows.

'Maria's latest salvo,' Eli explained. 'Don't worry, I'm perfectly fine.'

'I wasn't worrying,' said Andrew.

Eli sighed, his eyes boring out onto the road. They were on the carriageway now, speeding. The novel was now flat on the dash.

'Actually, I'm only fine in terms of this thing,' he said. 'In other matters, I'm a complete mess. I completely ruined a friendship I had with a woman named Cara Holden last week, and now she won't even talk to me. My flatmates hate me. I hate the course I'm doing as it prepares me for a job I will equally dislike. And to top it all off the one means of escape, I used to have I haven't been able to do for months'.

'You're not writing,' remarked Andrew, 'the guy that had to write at least two hours a day no matter what when were teenagers.'

'No, I can't,' said Eli. 'I just can't. I overthink everything I go to put on paper. It's exhausting and frustrating and to make matters worse, I hid it from everyone.'

Andrew brooded briefly on this information before replying.

'Well, you didn't exactly hide it that well.'

Eli shot him a tight smile.

'You don't look too upset by all this,' said Andrew.

'I was for a long time, but it didn't make anything better,' said Eli. 'I'm home now, and I'm kinda focused on that. I think being focused on the here and now will help me'.

'That sounds like a Nina thing to say.'

'It is … she's helped,' said Eli.

He considered this as they slowed down before a roundabout. The book slide from the middle to Andrew's side as Eli maneuvered the car to the correct lane.

'So your idea of living in the here and now is to go see a film?' asked Andrew.

'Hey, I have socializing problems,' replied Eli. 'This is a huge step for me, plus this is male bonding at its core element.'
'Sitting in the dark together, staring at a screen,' said Andrew, grinning.
'What better way than to put this shit behind us than to spend some quality time not talking at all in each other's company?' said Eli.
'That is the core of male bonding.'
They were almost at the cinema now. The book finally flew off the dash past them and into the back seat as Eli braked into a car space.
As they clapped the doors shut and made their way to the entrance, Andrew asked in a mocking, suggestive tone, 'so … Nina, huh'.

Gerry Taylor trundled up his next customer's drive. Ena, the firm's receptionist, had phoned him about the job. The way she had spoken told him the customer had not been friendly.
The decision to waste the woman's time didn't just become easy but a joy then. However, on meeting 'Misses Hunter' to the greeting remark, 'about time,' he wanted to be done as quickly as possible. She was dressed in a soiled bathrobe (there was a dusty print on her buttocks) and she smelled slightly ripe. She fluttered about behind him as he accessed the boiler, pacing back and forth over the floorboards.
Gerry spotted the problem instantly but remained stoic. He hummed regretfully. People didn't realize how much of a plumber's job is acting talent.
'What? What is it?' asked Maria
He could feel her particular case of neediness on his shoulders and clenched.
'Looks to be a mess in here but I might be able to … '
He didn't finish the sentence. He had never finished it on any job.

Gerry tinkled with the boiler aimlessly. He knew what the problem was, and its only cause would have been if someone switched it off. But he dare not tell her, as it would spoil his charade.

When the boiler did spark into life, the frantic woman appalled.

At the door, he had every intention of ripping her off. This was unnecessary as Hunter dropped a wad of notes into his hand and shut the door without another word.

The pleasure of counting was his, and he discovered he had over two week's wages in his hands. He thought about the small amount he had managed to save with Ross, his boyfriend. They intended to go on holiday, their first together, and his first with any partner.

Gerry discovered that their exasperation over the length of time it would take to save the funds had been pointless. He phoned Ross to tell him the good news.

They sniggered for some time while the plumber was inside.

The partitions that divided the properties on Belmont Road were what reminded of woodland that had initially colonized the land. They acted as the perfect barrier to view Maria's home unseen while providing a space for them to set deckchairs and a cooler.

'Think this has gotten her on edge?' asked Shane.

'I have no doubt she's shitting chickens,' said Lucy.

Jones, whose eyes had slid from the front door to English's position, gasped. Suddenly, the humorous atmosphere vanished as each person tried to see what he was staring at.

'What? What the fuck is it?' asked Shane.

Wisps of smoke were rising intermittently from Maria Hunter's bin.

'He's mad,' said Karl.

'He did volunteer to hang out in a bin all day,' stated Harold.

'No, he didn't,' said Lucy. 'He was only one out of you all that was skinny enough to do.'

'Didn't we find out that you were small enough to do it,' said Shane.

'Yes, but I have fucking sense,' replied Lucy.

The day's heat was suffocating in the open. They had contemplated English's agony to be confined in a plastic sweatbox. He hadn't even taken in water with him, but from appearances, he looked to have taken his favorite vice.

Jones raised his walkie-talkie to his lips.

'English, don't you know smoking is bad for your health,' he said.

It squeaked a reply.

'I've already had one nagging wife. I don't need another if you don't mind old boy'.

Maria's front door opened and out stepped the plumber. The smoke seeping from the bin's lid progressed into a steady, snaking trail. The bin itself was positioned against the house's side.

From their comfortable position sat in a row of deck chairs, they had a view of both. All it would take to spoil their current plot was for Maria or the plumber to notice the smell of smoke. Jones and Harold were posed on the edges of their seats while Lucy, giggling at the entire scene, reclined further into hers, sipping from a beer can.

Maria seemed to have finished paying the man. She had slammed the door in his face.

He didn't seem to mind from the notable briskness of his gait to his van. Smoke was now piping from the bin as if it were coming from the funnel of a train.

'What's the plumber doing?' asked Jones.

His head bobbed up and down to see the stationary van.

'I think he's counting the money Maria gave him,' said Lucy, giggling.

There came a squeak from the walkie, from which they all heard English's strained voice.

'Shit … guys, I think I'm in trouble here'.

The walkie re-laid the sounds of English fumbling. Five pairs of eyes shot to see the bin being jostled from inside. Smoke streamed from the lining of its closed lid.

'He's set himself on fire,' said Harold.

He moved forward, but Jones stopped him.

'That bloody guy is still there.'

He nodded in the direction of the van.

The five froze watching as the bin jostled more forcefully from side to side. It was the two-wheeled type where the wheels located at the rear. English had managed to scrape its blunt front forward before delivering the final blow that sent it spilling onto the grass.

The van's engine had started, but it had yet to pull away. In the time before it departed, they watched a pair of sinewy hands claw at the grass and pull an equally sinewy sixty-two-year-old man out of the smoking bin. His right trouser leg was on fire.

As the van rolled off the five stumbled from the trees. They immediately fell upon him, rolling him on the grass to put out the small fire licking at his ankle.

'What the fuck,' he blubbered as they rolled him. 'It's out, it's out, the fucking fire was out an hour ago will you leave me alone.'

They did, but none of them could stop their sniggers or tears. English glared from them to his burnt trouser leg, a bent cigarette clung to his lips.

The only damaged appeared to be his mood.

'Some bloody firemen you'd all make,' he said.

They looked at the bin. Whatever it had contained must have been extremely flammable as its insides were a torrent of flame. The plastic body bubbled against the heat, producing a plume of black smoke and a nauseating stink.

'We have to put this out,' said Jones.

He was thinking of Eli and their intentions not to cross a line like Maria had.

Before they could act, they recognized the sound of an engine. Though they couldn't see around the corner of the house, they knew that the engine noise belonged to Maria's boyfriend's Jag.

'Fuck it, run,' he said, grabbing English by the armpit. With Harold grabbing the other and the rest following, they ran.

Maria had many opinions about Bruce.

On hearing his yells from the bathroom (on the precipice of showering) she assumed he was overdramatic again. She based this opinion not from experience but from the fact that he was an American and that his Texan drawl reminded her of a cowboy. With this mind, she reluctantly went to him. It was on seeing her front door ajar did her pace quicken. She found him by the trailing the hose line around the house.

He stood jetting water into a black cloud originating from her lawn. At its base amongst the scorched grass appeared to be the melted remains of two wheels.

'They did this, didn't they?'

She moved at him with her eyes, fixated on the burning pyre. Her hands tightened her robe at the neck.

'I'll kick their skulls in for this. I'll … '

'You'll do no such thing,' she commanded.

Her needy hands latched onto his arm. They clung with a strength that caused Bruce to glance at them before finding her hard eyes. Their grip didn't lessen.

'We won, Bruce,' she told him. 'We won. This is nothing but a stunt of desperation, and we are going to take the high road and ignore it.'

'But ... '

'We have a party to hold,' she yelled.

Words, which usually spilled with ease from him, fled. The severity of Maria's tone was of such ferocity that for a brief period, words didn't seem to exist to Bruce.

'The chef will be here at two with his crew. The house needs a once over, and we need to get dressed. Priorities, understand? So wash that up and meet me in the shower'.

He watched her strut off, his eyes naturally traveling downward to her behind. The fury with which it wagged told him it had been wise to be mute.

She held her face into the spray, so she didn't feel her tears.

The water was hot and intense, cleansing the grime from her body. She swayed beneath it for a timeless period until two hands gripped her shoulders.

Maria began aware of him as his nude form pressed against hers. She grabbed his hands in her own.

'Maybe we should cancel tonight, do it some other time,' said Bruce.

'No, we've put too much effort into it,' she replied, turning into his chest.

The diamond on her finger jabbed him.

'Hey,' he gasped then remarked, 'you're wearing it.'

She looked to her finger where the ring sat.

'Yeah, well, its today isn't it.'

Maria convinced him that the party had to happen tonight, as its purpose was to announce their engagement. In her persuasion, she did not tell him she loved him. Love did not feature in their reasoning for marriage. To Maria, love was merely a word. Her reasons for marriage stemmed no further than from the image perceived by others of herself at her current age. She was thirty-nine. It was time. Bruce's reasons were the same, only with the added novelty of having moved aboard and marrying a local.

Their scheme was sourced from the shallowest of waters: self-worth.

Within this joint venture, Maria had her own plans. If she waited, any longer rumors would soon spout at her inability to keep a man. That perhaps she was becoming an old crone. To marry after a successful career within the company as a single woman would galvanize her image as such. Once more Bruce would appear even more dependable and resourceful as being the one that tamed Maria Hunter, especially considering she would be quitting to raise the children after quietly ensuring that Bruce will advance to position higher than all her co-workers. She will not tell him this. *A man should feel like a man afterward.* From then onward, she will focus on child-rearing, keeping her contacts at work if ever she needed to intervene.

They had designed their entire lives like this. Not based on feeling but on the image.

When he agreed to continue their plans, she took his penis (now pressing on the softness of her thighs) in her hands. The sex that followed was as functionally cleansing as the water that fell on them.

9

Rosalie slide across the backseat of Nina's car.
She greeted him with a frown that was both confused
and angry.
'Hello, sweetie, expecting Nina were you?'
Eli tried not to sound out of his depth and failed. His
voice jumped octaves, and he seemed patronizing even
to himself. If Andrew noticed he showed no sign,
crashing into the passenger seat and causing the car to
bounce. His attention was on a sheet of A4 with a
painted picture of a sunflower on it.
'I thought you and Daddy weren't friends anymore,'
Rosalie said.
'No, we're friends again, sweetheart,' corrected Andrew
without looking away from the picture. 'Your drawing is
excellent, do you think you'll be an artist?'
Her frown vanished replaced with a tooth gaped smiled.
She giggled, tiny, light and entirely awing giggles while
her little legs swung.
'No,' she shouted.
She looked nothing like either of her parents. For one
she was blessed with a head of coppery auburn hair.
Whereas the faces of other children seemed to become
an amalgamation of their parents, Rosalie looked
nothing like Jamie or Andrew.
'Is that what you did today, wow, that's amazing,' said
Eli, referring to the picture.
It wasn't really, but lying was what you did to the
children, especially those of your friends. At least that
was Eli's experience of them.
'Well, guess what we did today, we went to the cinema.'
Eli watched as Rosalie's nose wrinkled in the back
mirror.
'Daddy,' she shrieked. 'You went to the cinema, and
you didn't take me.'

He wanted to shrink into the car after hearing that shriek.

'It was to see something you wouldn't have liked something boring.'

'Oh … oh okay,' she said.

The tempest of a tantrum appeared avoided as quick as it would have started.

'Hey, you ready to stay at my house this weekend?' asked Andrew.

Her reply was another giggle and more swinging feet.

To Eli's amazement, he watched Rosalie plug in headphones and begin to listen to whatever music she had.

'When did you get her an iPhone?' he asked.

He drove into a gap in the queue of cars, leaving Rosalie's primary school.

'It was a gift from Ryan. Some customers never came back for it at the store. They all have them these days, mate'.

Eli shook his head, wondering, when exactly had they gotten old.

'You're not coming tonight?' asked Eli.

'Nah, I have a date with this little chick, but I wish you luck though.'

'Thanks, I'll going to need it for what they've got me doing,' said Eli. Speaking in a quieter voice, he added, 'you know if you ever want to talk about Jamie.'

'Thanks, man,' said Andrew. 'Though I've been listening to the wisdom of Nina Jones and no offense, I think she's better at advice.'

Eli agreed with Andrew's words. Once more, the oddness stuck Eli that he could think so highly of a woman who had tortured him as a teenager. However, as it did this time a secondary thought followed it, which was; because the person she used to be doesn't exist anymore. And as soon as he thought it, he knew it to be true.

The needle dropped into the spinning groove.

There was a sound like a scratched crackle. Then like the sun peeking over the horizon, the horns blasted out the first few notes of *Glen Millar's In The Mood.*

Karl cheered, raising his glass in response. Lucy and Nina begin to dance a fifties-style swing on croaking floorboards. Lucy twirled her and Nina's hair fanned in the air, the new lime green dye catching everyone's attention. There was a cloud of smoke in the living room counter with a smirking English in its center. By the kitchen table, Shane's friendly but loud voice could be heard saying, 'we should have kept at her.'

'That's what I said,' said Harold. His tone was that of a sledgehammer knocking on stone despite the jovial mood in the house.

Jones raised his hands to them, palm out.

'Look, guys, we drew a line in the sand that we said we wouldn't cross' he said, pragmatically. 'We will not stoop to her level. Plus what do you think was more harmful doing more and risking her canceling her little party or letting her strew and allowing us to really piss her off'.

Eli was slouched against the wall, observing them all with a mild expression of contentment on his face. At one point, he took out his phone and took photos. This was not something he would regularly do, but he felt compelled to capture not just the image of his friends but the atmosphere they generated. Even Harold, who still grieved for Maisy, appeared slightly less dour as he viewed the dancing pair. Eli sent the photos to Andrew, Heather, and Justin with the caption, 'IT'S GOOD TO BE HOME.'

Then Nina grabbed him by the arm.

'Come on, you. Show me what you can do'.

Before he could protest, Nina had pulled him onto the small space between the kitchen and the living room.

'Always a schemer this one,' Harold said, nudging Jones.

'Yeah, well if he's so smart what do you make of them?' Karl asked.

He nodded at the dancing Nina and Eli. The two men observed Jones's face slackened, the lines their sagging, the skin around his eyes growing more open. If they had to guess each of them would have said he looked fulfilled. Both men experienced the same emotions; surprise followed by understanding. The surprise was a gut reaction similar to when a father learns his daughter is dating. The agreement came as they viewed the dancing couple, seeing how happy they appeared.

'I think,' said Jones. 'I'm going to show them how it is done.'

Jones exited from their company and offered his hand to Lucy. She looked at it and then placed her hand, the scars on which gleamed silvery in the light, in his. He spun her, doing so carefully so as not to hurt, and slide his other hand to her back.

The music swelled as Karl turned the dial. The four dance. Eli and Jones lead their partners and in sync, twirled them to the hilarity of the onlookers.

At the same Maria Hunter welcomed Clive Arnold and his plus one, none other than her secretary, Linda Hall, to her home. Clive had shoved a bottle of wine into her hands before she could finish speaking while Linda stood wide-eyed at his side.

Maria smiled a smile that was mostly teeth at them.

'Sounds like they're having one hell of a party over there,' said Clive.

He somehow managed to hiccup and burp at the same time, and then stood as if he hadn't done so right in her face. Maria guessed from his ruddy complexion and his poisonous breath that he had had a sip or two already.

'Oh, yes,' she replied coolly. 'But don't worry, we will have much more fun than them.'

A look of perplexed doubt flashed across Clive's face that Maria wanted to claw off.

She stepped aside, letting them enter, while her face smiled rigidly. Bruce, who was waiting to bounce close by, strode forward to shake Clive's hand. It was a firm shake, in which, the two men laughed heartily at something her fiancé had said.

Suddenly, Maria experienced the greatest pleasure in her life. It was watching how much more full Linda's eyes flew on seeing Bruce and in seeing twin rosy dots glow in her cheeks.

She observed Linda's eyes dart. They were a blur of movement, but Maria had been paying attention. Linda Hall had just noticed her engagement ring.

Back at Jones's, the dancing was over but not the music. *Miss You* by *The Rolling Stones* was playing loudly from Jones's speakers, selected by English.

Eli, Nina, and Lucy were on the sofa. Nina had asked Lucy about her hands.

'They aren't sore, are they?' she asked. 'I wouldn't have made you dance if I'd have known it would have hurt.'

'No, no, it's fine,' said Lucy. 'They don't really hurt anymore, except in the cold weather. It's just my dexterity that's the main bother. In saying that they're much better than what they were. I can't play, but I'm fine doing the day-to-day tasks, mostly. Sometimes I don't even think there my hands but someone else's'.

Nina winched. Her eyes shot to the numerous paintings dotted around the room that she created with her own hands.

'It's okay,' said Lucy, shrugging. 'I don't let them slow me down. You know its funny I never wanted to sing for a crowd. Oh, I enjoyed singing to myself but putting a feeling across to other people well I did that with the piano. When I couldn't anymore, I suddenly discovered I did have something to sing about'.

'It worked out then,' said Eli.

'Sort of,' said Lucy. 'I still miss playing, though.'

Jones saved him from saying anything more damning by saying, 'it's time.' He stood cradling the 'package' in his hands.

The music was turned off, and the others were shuffling outside.

'Okay, then,' said Eli, standing.

The house emptied, and the group split into two. Jones and Eli walk around the side of the house as the others headed through the trees.

'No cheating now,' Eli said. 'You carry the light stuff, and I'll carry this.'

He jogged past him to ladder resting against the house. With a grunt, he heaved it into his hands.

'Sure, sure, just like we agreed.'

'And ... ' Eli stabbed a finger at him, 'it's me that's doing this.'

'Totally, totally,' said Jones.

Without another word, they ventured into the trees. They did this at the back of the property while the others stumbled about at the front.

'You know what would have been great?' said Harold.

'If someone had bothered to bring a fucking flashlight,' said Lucy.

'What's the problem,' said Shane. 'You've been here all day; you shouldn't need a light to find your way. Hey, there's something weird ... '

'That's my heel,' snapped English.

The beginnings of Karl's deep-throated chuckles ceased in a meaty flop.

'What the hell was that?' gasped Nina.

Her answer came via a series of bushes being violently dislodged.

'Nothing,' said Karl, having risen from his fall in the undergrowth.

Eli and Jones crept low and slow across the back lawn, doing so to prevent the ladder from rattling. Their breath huffed. Their eyes were fixed on the house's lit windows.

The night had pressed against the building but for the squares of glass, which beamed their elongated shapes onto the lawn. They crushed themselves against it, huffing toward recovery. From inside, they could hear the chatter of voices.

'Sounds like a belter of a party,' murmured Jones.

Side by side, close to his warm, natural smile, Eli joined him in laughter.

Jones scratched a match alight on his thumbnail, its head flared yellowy amber in the darkness. He used it to light a cigarette, from which he dragged deeply.

Even after all these years, Jones was still unbelievable cool.

'It's been nice having you here, kid,' he said in his usual graveled drawl. 'You know you're the best friend I've ever had.'

Their purpose was irrevocably lost to Eli. The world shrunk to the rough brick against his back, the layering night, and Jones's eyes in, which, the glowing tip of his cigarette was reflected. 'Your mine,' he said, distantly.

For the first time, Eli noticed how tired his friend's face looked even as it wrinkled with joy.

Jones clapped him on the shoulder and said, 'let's get this done.'

He moved for the ladder. Eli beat him to it.

'No, no, now, you know the rules,' he said.

Carefully and quietly, they worked so that the ladder latched with the roof's lip.

'Make sure it's fully on there,' said Jones.

Still reeling from Jones's previous remark, Eli stepped underneath the ladder. He squinted upwards as the apparatus began jerking drastically, its metal jangling. Jones was scaling the ladder rungs.

'Get back here,' cried Eli.

His hands caught Jones by the ankle, but it was a loose hold. Jones kicked him off and continued to climb, leaving Eli with nothing to do but brace the legs of the ladder.

'Jones', Eli hissed as quietly as possible.

He had already reached the roof, turning to give him a two-fingered salute before disappearing from his view. Eli stumbled backward, captivated by the tall, gaunt figure clambering over roof tiles with a backpack slung over his shoulders.

Jones is like Santa Claus, delivering a present.

When he reached the roof's peak, he boldly stood upright.

Seeing him, Eli stole a lungful of air and held it. The others seated in the trees at the front of the house fell silent as he loomed above amongst a starless background.

'What the hell is he doing? It's supposed to be Eli up there' spat Nina.

'Mia's going to kill him,' said English.

'Mia ... I'll kill him.'

Jones unzipped the backpack. Its contents, a long, cylinder object held together by plastic wrapping, required both hands to carry. He laid it upon the chimney and roughly yanked its bird protector off. Soot dirtied his hand, a grainy feeling.

The fumes reared at him. Already his eyes were watering. Grasping the chimneystack with one hand, he began to force the cylinder into its pipe, all the while coughing. The instant effect of this was that the smoke rising within could no longer escape.

Coincidentally, he did this at the most opportune moment.

Clive was currently toasting Maria for playing host, his back to the fireplace. Her guests either sat or stood in a circle, their champagne glasses upheld to her. She beamed benevolently at them like a Queen that could quickly sign someone's death warrant.

Smoky fingers began to snake from the fireplace. Maria's face, high cheekbones, sharp jaws, and glossy magazine quality skin fell. So did her outstretched arm. Clive was continuing to prattle on but doing so with a frown, his speech disjointed.

'Jesus,' yelled Bruce.

'Oh my...Linda quick, open a window,' ordered Clive. Linda simply looked agog at the plume of smoke rising to the ceiling.

Maria edged past a backward stepping Clive. As she did, the smoke bloomed into a cloud that dosed her cream carpet before rising. Shrieks originated from around her. She sensed the others pushing themselves into her leather sofas or jumping to their feet.

Jones grunted, coughing. The cylinder object had jammed halfway.

Maria bent forward, peering into the black willowing orifice.

'Little fucker ... move,' said Jones.

Huffing, he drew back and with a surge of strength shoved the cylinder. It slipped through the pipe, leaving him thrown against the chimney.

The package speared down the chimney's insides, hit the crackling logs and burst, enveloping the living room below in an explosion of white. White that thrust from the fireplace, striking Maria first and continuing onward, engulfing them all.

People were screaming all around her.

She could hear and sense them all scrambling about, wailing and cursing. To her, eyes clamped shut beneath whatever had struck her, her living room seemed to contain a stampede. She did not join them. Her body was a prison of locked muscle, frozen in its bent position. She forced her arms to move, for her hands to scarp at her eyes.

When she opened them, she still saw white. For a brief moment, she had the horrid thought that she'd been blinded, but that wasn't the case. The white was in the air, hanging like a thick mist and fat droplets. It coated everything, including her. She could taste it on her lips: flour.

The stampede seemed to have gained some level of direction. Instead of individuals throwing themselves randomly about the room, they were all leaving via the front door.

Maria followed them, and so did the flour.

It extended from the house like a thin mist. It sieved off the bodies of her guests as some ran for the cars while others ran aimlessly. She could feel it turning to crust as her tears fell. A serving girl was sneezing puffs of white over her empty flowerbeds.

Mark Lawson scampered back and forth, screaming, 'I'm blind, I'm blind.'

She turned away from this to find Bruce walking toward her; his powdered face that of a shell-shocked victim. They all had similar expressions, but their noise was the worst. Everyone seemed to be screaming or wailing or screeching about themselves, even from her trees, she could hear catcalls. There seemed nothing left to do. Maria fell to her knees and unleashed the loudest cry of them all. Amongst, the furious din she produced two words.

'You win.'

'That was a prank,' said Eli.

Jones agreed with a gasp, resting upon the ladder. His arms clung to it limply.

'The night is young,' he said. 'And I've got a shift to do.' The tired breaths that escaped him made Eli think otherwise. But then he thought Jones has never missed a show before and he never would. The two carried the ladder back through the trees. Eli in front, Jones at the rear.

10

The Dollar never changed, not in the time Eli had known it.

He thought this in the very same booth he had sat in on his first visit. He was in the very same seat looking out on what appeared to be the very same crowd. There was one difference tonight, and that was his current company. Nina and Harold had replaced Kate and Ryan.

'Maisy would have been pleased,' boomed Harold.

They cracked drinks together above the table's middle.

'And Pat too,' he added and they cracked drinks again. The constant toasting had resulted in their drinks being emptied pre-maturely. Eli's head was a swimming pool balancing on a spinning top. Even drinking with Cara hadn't been this bad.

Harold, much to Nina's delight, held up his glass and peered at the bottom.

'Well, this is no good; would you mind getting me another if I give you the money. I've quite found my home here'.

They agreed they didn't mind and that Harold need not give them any. There was no questioning this, in the same way; there was no questioning that they would head to the bar together.

It was almost showed time, and Jones was alone.

He could hear the audience (a dull murmuring roar) and the band (tweaking their instruments), and he wished Mia were here. She had refused to be involved in the prank after Eli was injured.

Still, he wished she were here.

He was in the dark, in a narrow corridor behind the stage. He was doing nothing but thinking of Mia, thinking of her lips, the curve of her thighs, the way her eyes always held his and way she laughed. When he made Mia laugh, she sounded as if it was a forbidden thing that she couldn't help doing when it came to him. He was thinking this because it helped regulate his breathing. Pain radiated from his heart in a fiery clamp down his left arm and along his jawline.

One last show, he thought, *one last time with my friends.*

Eli trailed behind Nina in the push and squeeze of bodies.

He loved this, the hot encapsulating sensation of being an audience member. What bettered this experience was Nina casting glances over her shoulder at him.

In his life had never been looked at with such ferocious interest. The effect was many things, frightening, intimating, joyful, but mostly humbling. He felt he should do something, anything to deserve that interest. As the throng grew even tighter, he reached and grasped her straying hand, feeling the softness of her palm, so neither would become lost from the other.

The action caused a delightful shock to transmit from her face.

She led him finally to the bar as the Dollar lights winked out. They let go of each other's hand to join the rallying applause.

The band had Eli's attention that he didn't see the guy pushing past. Without warning, he was shoved into the closest barstool, which was not unoccupied.

'Sorry,' said the culprit before slipping through a gap in the crowd.

Eli paid him no mind as he recognized the face scowling at him from the stool. He was somehow smaller, his face more craggy and his hair had receded to a few lonely wisps' clinging to his egg-shaped scalp, but it was undoubtedly Logue, his former English teacher.

They didn't speak; there was no point with the blaring music. They stared into one another's eyes, steely grey against pale jade. Eli saw hate, unconditional, immeasurable hate in them.

'Eli,' said Nina beside him.

She had grasped his arm. This jogged him from Logue's accusing gaze to take in his surroundings and realize the music had stopped. Concern rippled through the audience.

His eyes found the stage to see Jones collapsing over his guitar.

Kate wondered, what would someone think of the house now.

If they saw her phone as it lay having been crushed on the living room floor. Would they call the police when they saw the out of place furniture? Certainly, they would if they saw the staircase where the photo frames had skidded down the wall after Ryan had carried her upstairs, they would phone. She hummed at the thought.

Kate felt free for the first time in a long time. Her shame and panic would return, but she couldn't care less as the sensation of her orgasm lingered. It was her first in months.

Kate rolled over, her naked body coiling the duvet tighter as she did. Ryan was in the en suite doing whatever it is that men do after sex. She gazed at the door, her legs playfully kicking the air as his phone buzzed on the nightstand.

It had been her own that had caused such ill-feeling between them in the last couple of weeks. Or more the group chat she had joined. Some old friends from secondary school that she hadn't seen in decades had created it for mothers whose children had recently moved away. It was a place to express their fears and hopes for them. Then it had turned nasty. Her site for advice and comfort had changed into a position to bitch, specifically about the men who seemed unperturbed by their children's absence. And Kate had even indulged in it at first, not recognizing the danger. It was dangerous, which is why she hesitated now to even touch Ryan's phone. All their arguments and squabbles stemmed from that little chat of nastiness. She had found herself angry with him for things he might do.

'In this new pact of ours,' she called to Ryan. 'Does this mean we both give up our phones.'

'Yes, I suppose it does,' Ryan replied. He stood naked in the bathroom door.

It was a sight she hadn't seen for some time, and it surprised her to feel even more desire for him. The phone buzzed again, it's screen-beaming light.

'Go on,' he said. 'See what it is.'

As she reached for it, she thought it hadn't been the sex that saved them. It had been talking for the first time in weeks about how they felt.

They had cried, and that had led them to laugh, and that had led them to their bed.

Kate read the missed message on Ryan's phone. Before she had even finished she was yelling, 'its Eli, we have to go to the hospital.'

11

They were back in the same hospital corridor.

After five years it had not changed from the night Jones and Lucy had been attacked. The walls were just as oppressive, and everything reeked of piss topped with bleach. The only difference this time was the sound of two women weeping from the ward.

Jones is saying his goodbyes, thought Eli, his inner voice lifeless. *This can't be happening.*

Nina and Mia exited the ward clinging to each other for support, their eyes red-rimmed; their faces glistened with tears.

The nurse that was herding them changed direction toward him.

'He would like to see you,' she said.

Roy Jones, Hazel's last mayor, contemplated him with uncertainty and disbelieve. They were all looking at him, Mia, The Renegades, Brandon, and his godparents.

Eli kept his face stoic and stood to find his legs worked without feeling.

On passing, Nina broke from Mia and hugged him. Her arms were like steel. Her wet cheek pressed against his dry one.

She was back in Mia's arms before he could think of anything to say.

The nurse led him into a ward that was silent of human noise. Jones was in the middle bay on the right, propped up by pillows. An oxygen mask had been placed over his mouth. It fogged with each slight rise and fall of his chest. Wires trailed from him.

Someone had pulled the curtains of his bay to give the impression of privacy. They didn't.

Tears welled in Eli's eyes, distorting Jones's image into a bleeding color. Seeing, him caused his chest to constrict, making him feel like he was being strangled. His heart had become a piston that thundered in his temples.

He made no effort to disturb him. He stood and cried, his tears like pearls in the wards blue/black gloom.

'Hey, their kid,' said Jones in a frog's croak. His eyes were now open, staring over the oxygen mask.

Thoughtlessly, Eli dashed for the jug of water and poured a drink.

'Sweet Jesus, I must look bad if that's your reaction,' Jones muttered.

'Drink,' Eli demanded, not quite keeping the quiver from his voice.

He accepted the glass, his fingers enclosing Eli's wrist to do so. Their old strength, that firm, relentless power was absent from them.

'If your going to start blubbering remember Nina will never sleep with a pussy.'

The remarked speared through Eli.

He clenched to the degree that he believed his ass could have crushed walnuts and yet he felt the need to laugh on seeing Jones's grinning face, like some poor goblin. He chuckled. It sounded like a blunt saw sieving through old wood.

'It's okay, can't fool an old dog like me, not when it comes to affairs of the heart.'

The old man reached out and gripped Eli's forearm. There was strength in this grip but of a fading kind. From the look in his eyes, eyes that had not so long ago held fire, he assessed he had received Jones's blessing. His tears began to run again, and he found he couldn't cope seeing Jones or the bed or how the mask rested awkwardly against his neck or any of it. He struggled to shrink back, but Jones' grip hindered him.

'This isn't a bad thing,' said Jones. 'Sit down, go on, sit ... there. You're a good kid, you know that. Your not that angry little rut that I saw when we first met'.
Jones regarded him thoughtful with eyes as dark as caverns. They held him.
'Aye, well your still the asshole you were back then,' said Eli.
They laughed together as would have on the porch.
'I'm sorry, I haven't been around much since you've been home,' said Jones. 'I've kinda been enjoying living with Mia a little bit too much. It's been years since I lived with a woman, I'd forgotten how much I missed it'.
'It's okay,' said Eli. 'I've been preoccupied myself lately.'
Jones seemed to understand what this meant. In that second, he seemed to understand everything that Eli had experienced in the last few months.
'I've been struggling, with my course, with everything. I didn't say, sometimes you just get in so far with something you feel like you can't pull out. And to say to someone, to admit your struggling, would be like admitting you've made a mistake'.
'Nothing wrong with that,' said Jones. 'Making a mistake is how we learn.'
His breathing had taken on a cruel wheezed quality that hurt Eli's ears.
'Any big plans this summer?' asked Jones. 'I thought of taking up surfing.'
Eli shook his head and said, 'I think I'm gonna stay home for a while.'
'That's good,' croaked Jones.
He reached out a hand for him. Eli grasped it and squeezed. Nearby, a patient was snoring.
'I shouldn't have let you get on that ladder,' he said.

'Like you could have fucking stopped me,' replied Jones, crackling euphorically. 'This isn't your fault, kid. I'm here because of myself, too many years being the life of the party, too many years taking my body for granted, that's why I'm here'.

Jones's eyebrows drew together.

'Now, I have to tell you something important ... the gold is buried under the house'.

Eli shook his head slowly. The tears were falling, but his laughter was also escaping to join Jones's own hacking bark. Later, he would suppose it was Jones's way, to laugh even in death, after all, it was how he lived finding humor in the most inappropriate of places, but Eli would also think it was how he wanted to be remembered.

Jones spoke with them all, one by one.

He spoke with English about Nina's paintings. He told Kate and Ryan he was fortunate to have known them. What discussed with his brother led Roy to stroll from the ward and the hospital without speaking a word. He held Shane as he wept like a child. He even told a disgruntled patient (the snorer) in the next bay to, 'fuck off' when he shouted about being quiet. The charge nurse intervened and forbid further visiting, which led to Lucy being escorted from the hospital after arguing with her. In the end, Mia was the only one allowed to stay. Jones died around midnight holding her hand.

12

Jones was buried on a Tuesday under a sky as blue as a robin egg.

It was pristine, but for the sun, which was the bright orange of a child's lollipop. The progression marched slowly through its muggy gaze, all dressed in black finery. From afar they looked like blackbirds forced from the heavens by the day's heat.

Later, grey clouds would strut across the sky filled with thunder and lightning of biblical wrath that agreed with Eli's own. For Jones was dead, and he felt robbed.

The minister said kind words to deaf ears. The only phrase that would be remembered was a quote of *Lou Reed's*, the minster being aware of Jones's personal sensibilities. This caused a stir from the attending and a hoot to issue from Shane. There were even a few that laughed, Eli and Nina included. It would have been the way Jones wanted it.

Among the attending was a surprising few. Maria Hunter and Bruce Dalton stayed for the service and did so in respectful silence. They left quickly and without event.

This could not be said for Hanna and Martin Jones. They spent the day folded around Nina like the wings of a playful predator. Their tongues held until the somber feast at Mia's restaurant after the burial.

Of her own mourning, Mia did in private. She disappeared upstairs to the loft she had shared with the man that she had loved all her adult life.

The argument sparked when Kate had innocently offered Nina a place to stay.

'If you don't want to be alone,' she had added.

Whatever Nina had intended to say was never heard as Hanna Jones answered for her.

'That's perfectly fine, thank you, but Nina will be coming home with us.'

Her tone was polite and courteous but cold. Somehow that coldness coupled with her own lifeless expression implied an indignant attitude.

'No, I won't,' said Nina softly.

'Its time you came home, don't you think?' asked Hanna.

Nina discarded her empty plate on a nearby table before thrusting to her feet.

'I don't think so,' she yelled. 'And if you think your appearance here will achieve that you're going home disappointed.'

There was a clatter of plates. There's always a clatter of plates when a family dispute is aired at an inappropriate time as everyone suddenly wishes they were somewhere else.

'Your mother didn't mean … ' mumbled Martin but Nina continued to speak.

'Nothing has changed, only my grandfather is gone, and all you can think about is getting your way,' she yelled at them.

'Please, this is embarrassing' whispered her mother.

'Get out of here. Get the fuck out of here right now'.

Hanna's eyes scanned the many staring faces. Harold, who had been worryingly feasting on alcohol alone, growled, 'you better listen to your daughter.'

They fled swiftly and fearfully from the angry eyes of their daughter's protectors. In the years to come, Hanna especially would remember those eyes and the mad dash she made through the lashing torrent. How the sky crackled above as she, on reaching their car, looked back. She could barely see the restaurant through the rain, but as she paused, she grew aware of a vague hurt beneath the overwhelming fury within her. The wrath would always become her focus, whereas pondering on that disturbing hurt lead her to think unwanted, peculiar thinking.

Jones left his land, the house and its contents to Nina. Eli received his guitar, it's body still scratched below the strings from the fall he had on the stage. He stroked the strings at night, feeling no desire to have it fixed. By this time Eli had returned to Edinburgh to retrieve his things. To do this, Ryan and him took Ryan's car across on the ferry and filled it before the happily unhelpful Adrian and Louis. He bid them goodbye with little feeling and received less. Truthfully, it was Cara he wished to see most, but she refused to reply to his texts or answer his phone calls. She had also unfriended him on *Facebook*. He guessed some bridges stay burned.

Being home and jobless, earning an income became an initial concern. With each passing day, the gage on his student account was getting desperately lower. Despite the foreseeable problems this could create, he did not dwell on it. Worry over such things seemed beyond him due to his grief.

The world was dulled to him. Time became about existing and thinking and remembering. Yet it was pleasant to live this way after the kinetic insanity of student living.

He became stagnant, and the world churned on.

Much was the same for Nina Eli observed except her grief seemed vaster, deeper. She had little visitors and rarely left the house. She threw herself into her painting and spoke little.

Aimless, Eli, on a whim, started to tend to the garden that was now hers. It seemed a shame for its quality to diminish. The thought was not lost on him that Jones had kept it in memory of his wife, and now he intended to keep it in his memory.

After years of watching Jones, he was knowledgeable in the upkeep of the garden. What he hadn't expected was the extent of the work. There was always something new to do.

A routine began to set in. Eli would walk from his godparents home each day and work until lunch, which Nina prepared. They would eat on the porch, as inside was her domain in the way the outside had become his, then they would return to their tasks.

On one occasion she asked him if he could replace a few roofing tiles. Thankfully, *Youtube* provided the how-to-do on this.

His practical ability surprised him and his godparents. Upon, seeing his work they offered to pay him to do the same for their own home. He accepted.

On seeing the quality of his work, the neighbors began to gossip likewise. This lead to inquires, which lead to a reputation, which eventually led to an end to his immediate financial concerns. He had so many jobs he had to buy a notebook to keep track of everything.

If he wanted, he could have made a business of it. But that would have required too much forward-thinking as well as the hiring of others.

That summer was not about forward-thinking but about mourning. Part of that came in thinking about nothing as he roofed homes and trimmed lawns. Another element, afar more essential part, was in remembering Jones.

The work provided him with this opportunity. It was something his body did while his mind did the real job. And his customers didn't seem to mind. Plus thanks to being fed by Nina and Kate and his laboring he quickly lost his scrawny appearance.

No matter how busy his schedule, Eli always put the time in at Nina's place.

Grief was fruitful for Nina also.

The paintings she had sold to English attracted interest. English wouldn't part with any but provided her phone number. It wasn't long before Nina's landline persisted in ringing with potential customers.

That was how May passed for him.

His days were labor and sweat. His evenings were blissfully spent with Kate and Ryan before the TV or listening to them planning a holiday for July or taking Rosalie with Andrew to the cinema. On rare occasions, he stayed overnight with Nina. They never shared a bed; instead, he would sleep on the sofa while she took the spare room. He had yet to write a word. Nor had he seen any of The Renegades since the burial.

It was one of the many things he did not think about that summer.

The change to their routines came as any change does: unexpectedly.

The day was a scorcher even for that summer, and Eli found himself moping at his brow more than usually.

He was doing soon when he heard a footstep behind him.

Nina was on the lawn.

Every day that he had spent in this garden for two months, she had never stepped on the lawn. At least not while he was here. She usually called him from the porch.

'I was thinking of doing something different today,' she said. 'I fancy a ... '

She quietened as something stirred the bushes. What emerged into the garden was a puddle of moving night with a pink tongue. A longer look confirmed it to be a puppy wiggling its rump as it pranced for them, its needle-like tail reciprocating above.

There was a crash behind it, followed by a voice.

'Come back here,' it said.

The noise grew, and the greenery shook to Jurassic Park style proportions. Instead of seeing a Velociraptor a disheveled, red-faced and slightly scratched, Harold stumbled out.

Nina was already descending to her knees. The puppy leaped into her lap and zealously began to lick at her face.

'Hi, there, hi there,' cooed Nina, giggling.

The sound of which made Eli's knees jelly.

'She's a little devil, don't be fooled,' said Harold. He bent forward and spoke to the squirming bundle in Nina's arms, 'what are you doing, running off.'

The puppy ached its head backward. The floppy tongue that had hung from its panting mouth was sucked back in. Eli laughed; the dog's face was nothing if not apologetic. When it turned back to Nina, it's tail begun to wag, and its tongue fell out again.

'Little tease,' muttered Harold.

'Is he yours?' Nina asked.

'She is, I got her last week. The house was getting lonely ... I don't get the visitors like I used to so I thought what the hell ... I could use the company. Her name is Poppy'.

'Ahhh that's cute,' cooed Nina.

She stood cradling Poppy, whose tail became a whip at the delight of being held.

'That's how she gets you, all wiggles and kisses then she's eating the steak off your plate when you're in the kitchen getting a drink.'

Harold stabbed a finger at Poppy. She licked its tip.

'Eli and I were just discussing lunch. I was gonna suggest a trip into town for a chippy would you like to join us?' Nina asked.

His face beamed at the prospect of this with merriment that could rival his dogs.

'I won't want to impose,' he said.

'Not at all, your welcome to. Eli can you drive us down, I wanna play with this one'.

'Sure thing,' he said, flummoxed by the amount of conversation Nina had produced.

Poppy recommended licking Nina's face as they ambled to the car.

Harold, who had fallen into step beside Eli, said, 'you've done a good job here.' Though he was glancing at the house's roof, gardens and garage Eli couldn't help notice his eyes took in Nina ahead of them.

They ate at the kitchen table.

Poppy sat obediently at their feet, tail squishing behind her. Her head bobbled and craned to the movements of their hands.

Eli and Nina fed her scrapes and Harold pretended to scowl them for it. Their voices and laughter ricocheted off the walls. The conversation rolled out naturally.

Eli spoke honestly, unafraid, about his plans for the future, which were none. He told them about stories he had daydreamed about while working. Nina expressed a desire to show her paintings. Harold talked about missing Jones.

Eventually, all three were talking about him.

It was painful and joyous to do so. The three toasted to Jones as sunlight poured like hot oil through the kitchen windows and sparkled off their glasses.

After months of mourning, seeing Nina enraged in conversation, to see her smile made Eli drunk with joy.

'That was fun,' he told her after Harold and Poppy had gone home.

He was on the sofa, nestled tightly between two painted canvases. Nina replied, blithely from the bedroom in agreement. Eli started to say how fun it was to see Harold again and how cute Poppy was when she stepped into the hallway.

She was without clothes and standing on her tiptoes, her eyes were lit with a warm light.

Wordless, Eli went to her. Not once did his eyes leave hers.

Nina's chest heaved as if against a great weight. He felt it too, hooked to his collarbones. They melted against one another.

The bedroom window was ajar, allowing a breeze to gust in.

Her body was coiled to his and his to hers through an entanglement of limbs. She trailed a finger, doing circles on his collarbone. In return, he stroked her spine.

'I want to have them all over tomorrow night,' she said. 'Mia, Kate, Ryan, Harold, English, all of them, it's been too long since we've seen them.'

'We could do it tonight,' said Eli.

She stared into his eyes with that earnest look that transfixed him.

'Tonight's for us,' she said.

Their period of mourning ended that night.

They drifted back into workings of the world, their time now spent on healing. They organized an evening with the others, inviting them to a barbecue. Everyone came, though their moods were at first tentative. Like the lunch, with Harold, it started painfully, even awkwardly, mired by the loss of a friend, but that changed and became a celebration. Embarrassingly, it was because of them. The others could tell by how they spoke and how they looked at one another that they were together.

Ryan and Kate beamed at him from the kitchen table. Mia and Lucy snatched Nina into a corner to be interrogated through rapid whispering. Eli left them to it and sought the safety of the porch, taking a seat beside Harold and Poppy. The rest were there, drinking from Jones's old beer cooler as the sky dimmed from a mosaic sunset to pale twilight.

The conversation was about The Renegades in the wake of Jones's passing.

English surmised this best to Eli. 'Sure we worked without him for years, but that doesn't mean we can work without him now, least in any good way. We had ten years playing with him, more than we had when we were young pups and starting the band. I know what your gonna say, you replaced the singer when he left and got a new pianist to boot, but that isn't the same old boy, the singer's come and go. It's the players that matter; each with their own unique sound that they bring into the fold. When it's lost, even if you fill it with new talent, it's still not the same. The Renegades have retired, and into legendary status, I might add'.

'I take it Brandon isn't to pleased by that fact,' said Eli.

'Actually, I think he understood,' said English.

The news did not sadden nor disappoint Eli. It seemed correct in some way.

'Never mind Brandon, I want to know what's going on with you two,' said Karl.

Eli smiled and glanced over his shoulder to look into the house. Nina, Mia, and Lucy were dancing to *'In the Mood'* once more and laughing loudly.

'When I figure that out I'll let you know,' he said.

This was how the rest of their summer passed.

The days were busy as Eli worked in people's gardens and Nina painted. The nights ranged from intimate moments alone or in the company of others. There were shopping trips to Belfast, romantic weekends at the north coast, dates to the cinema and restaurants and naturally more barbecues. English invited Eli to his poker games, where the stakes were the various pills prescribed to the aged players by their GPs. Nina, Mia, Lucy, and Kate arranged 'girl's nights,' resulting in Eli organizing 'boys nights.' These were more sober affairs than the girl's ones, as they tended to be hanging out with Andrew and Rosalie, which he didn't mind and enjoyed. There was even talk of Heather and Justin returning for a weekend. Regularly, they would invite Harold and Poppy for dinner, and as the sunset, walk the woodland trails.

'How's the novel going?' asked Harold on one such evening.

The sky was a vivid amalgamation of oranges, pinks, and reds. As the colors filtered through the forest canopy, the light turned golden. Poppy was off the lead and rooting about the undergrowth. They watched her and had not spoken for some time.

'It's going well,' replied Eli lightly.

Nina's hand, which he held, squeezed.

'Go on tell him,' she said.

'Tell me what.'

'I got a phone call today from my university. It was the Head of English, ringing to tell me he had read a short story I had submitted into a completion before I left'.

'Holy shit,' said Harold and then added, 'and?'

Eli exchanged a glowing look with Nina.

'He loved it,' he eventually said. 'And was greatly displeased to see I was not one of his students or at the college anymore. He actually told me off a bit'. Harold laughed heartily causing Poppy to glance at them.

'He said business students were usually the most unimaginative bunch. I told him I was working on a novel and he gave me his email in case I wanted a sharp eye to go over it'.

'That's brilliant,' said Harold.

'You actually titled your book today,' said Nina, who was beaming at him.

'It's a working title,' Eli said, quickly. 'I called it Mister Jones.'

Exact from Eli Donoghue's novel, Mr. Jones.

How many roads do we walk down in our journey? This pursuit of fulfillment and meaning guides us with lonely highways across the vast landscape of life. Against its wild teachings, the violent struggle of a tenacious heart against the pouring rain, the calmed soul in the embrace of warm sunshine. It gifts us with crossroads, challenges us with mountains, and tempts us with short cuts.
These shifting lessons teach us the value of the journey. Our flaming passions give us heat, let us dream, allow us to spread our wings and like candles light the way.
There will always be jealous winds attempting to obstruct others from their destinations. In the end, it's us that walk the journey.
We can be thrown down and picked up by others, influenced by their cheers and their protests, but we're the ones that drive. We let in the sunshine or the rain, and we chose to stall in the wind.
It's a pleasant hope, for it's us that step over that home line. Mister Jones taught me that.

THE END

Acknowledgments

This bit is for the readers (if any). Thank you, everyone, who has purchased and read Mr. Jones. I hope that you got as much joy out of reading it as I did out of writing it. Actually, I hope that you got more enjoyment out of reading it than I did out of writing it because some days were hard.

This bit is for family and friends. Thank you to Ross Mackintosh, Joe Sutherland, Lee-James Fairbairn, Neill Sandison, Dylan Harwood, Keith Heggarty, Amy Johnston, Mark, Amanda, Nathanial and Victoria Stewart for allowing me to take up so much of their time blathering on and on about this novel I was writing for years. Thank you to Mark Watson and Aidan Reid for reading Mr. Jones and offering some great advice. If anyone has any issues with this book its because I didn't listen to these guys. Also thank you, Kayleigh Watson, for letting me take so much of your husband's time with constant rereads. A special thank you to my wife, Claire, for putting up with a husband who is always halfway between reality and fantasy.

About The Author

Jamie Stewart lives in Northern Ireland with his wife and their two dogs. He started writing stories at the age of nine after being inspired by R.L Stein's Goosebumps series, old horror movies, and videogames that in hindsight he was far too young for. In 2019 he published his first short story Insular. Mr. Jones is his first novel.

He can be found lurking on Twitter at @JamieStReading.

Insular

'Remember now, the others and I were working people, working on getting by, month to month. They keep their heads down and push through, and when they can, they dream.
Their dreams are an escape. That wasn't possible with Julian stalking the aisles, his ever-grey pallor, his gaunt figure serving as a reality check. That's what was scary. When there were no dreams anymore.'

Julian Kensi is about to start his first day in retail.

What he doesn't know is that to his supervisor, Peter Smith, he is just another pawn to be used in his rise to the top. That is until Julian begins to act strangely.

As Peter attempts to learn, more his ruthless methods cause events to take a macabre turn beyond control.

Insular a short story about one man's life long fear and regret. It's a story about obsession, the power of a person's imagination, and the terrible consequences once it has been unleashed.

Insular is available in eBook format on Amazon worldwide.

Trick Or Treat

The doorbell rang, the chime cutting through the house like an alarm bell, making her jump. It was too early, and even though Halloween was in full swing outside, she had not expected any callers.
They all avoided even looking at her home nowadays. Wiping, her tears away she stepped into the hall, which ran the length of the house. Her front door was as black as tar after its new coat. It stood at the end of the hall, its impersonal freshness like a foreboding omen. Jane drew to it slowly, reaching for the gold handle with caution.

It's Halloween. For the residents of Denison Street that means face paint, costumes and swapping horror stories. Or at least it used to be.

Last year Logan Conway went missing while Trick Or Treating. The police have no clues, no suspects, and no leads.

Some say The Reaper Man did it.

Others say he's an old wife's tale. Logan's mother, Jane, disagrees. So much so that she's invited him back again.

Trick or Treat is perfect for fans of works by Stephen King, Neil Gaiman, Joe Hill, Shirley Jackson, and Mike Mignola.

Trick or Treat is available in eBook format on Amazon worldwide.

Alfie & The Dead Girls

The car continued to keep pace, trailing her.
It was unlike any other car she had ever seen. It was
old and well maintained, its coat a brilliant aquamarine
that gleamed in the sun's rays.
'Do you like my car?' asked Fred, catching her admiring
gaze.
Emma's cheeks burned.
'Most people do,' he said, chuckling, 'it's a great ride.'

Emma Woods, a quiet, bookish, eleven-year-old is about to start her first day at secondary, which means new classes, new teachers and new classmates.

Emma is terrified, and in her terror-stricken state, she reaches out to her new school's social media page to make friends. That's where she meets Alfie.

Alfie is joining Radcliff Secondary School as well. Alfie likes the books she loves, and most importantly, he wants to be Emma's friend. However, now there's a strange car driven by a peculiar man trailing Emma with a promise to take her to Alfie.

What follows next is a story that is every parent's worst nightmare. Alfie & The Dead Girls is perfect for fans of Stephen King, Joe Hill, John Grisham, Shirley Jackson, and Harlan Coben.

Alfie & The Dead Girls is available in eBook format on Amazon worldwide.

Printed in Great Britain
by Amazon